THE RISING SEDITION

I0621688

OTHER WORKS BY RICHARD TREVAE

The Dalton Crusoe Series

The TARASOV SOLUTION

The ISRAELI BETRAYAL

The SECRET TEMPLAR ALLIANCE

Novellas

The ARAL MILL MURDERS

LEELANAU STORIES

Short Stories

RHYTHMS of LEELANAU

The LAST SEASON

For Vicki, Megan, Tyler, and Jacqueline

THE RISING SEDITION

A Dalton Crusoe Novel

By

Richard Trevae

Treline Publishing

CAST OF CHARACTERS

Jameson Dalton Crusoe "JD"
> *NSA Prodigy*

Declan Faden Crusoe
> *Dalton's Half-brother*

Carolyn McCabe
> *Dalton's Fiancée*

Ed Kosko
> *Mentor to Dalton; former NSA Director*

Colonel Brad Ronet
> *Decorated Special Ops Leader*

President Harold Barriman
> *President of the United States*

Brandon "Badge" Demarche
> *Chief of Staff to the President*

Charley Rhodes
> *Political Strategist, Pathroads for America*

Hasid Khamal
> *Premier International Contract Assassin*

Lars Nevin
> *CEO of Adrestia LTD, International Constructors*

General Jack Watts
> *Chairman of the Joint Chiefs*

Lei Zhang
> *Chinese President of the National People's Congress*

Treline Publishing, *a unit of Treline Enterprises, LLC*

PO Box 418

Glen Arbor, Michigan 49636

www.richardtrevae.net

Contact: richard@trevae.com

The RISING SEDITION/Richard Trevae

COPYRIGHT © 2014 Richard Trevae

Paperback ISBN 13: 978-0692334133
                    10: 0692334130

First Edition: December 2014

Published in the United States of America

INTRODUCTION

This book involves tension arising from fabricated issues with significant geo-political impact. Several sub-plots interconnect with the main plot—a deliberate plan, set over years, to drive America to a Chinese *client state*. The action begins in near current time, in America during an election year, as well as Canada and the Caribbean and specific remote settings. As such considerable research was undertaken to present the political processes accurately. Several reference sources, experts, and knowledgeable individuals generously assisted in this effort. Nevertheless, the author takes full and complete responsibility for any inaccuracies and inconsistencies.

Creating fiction from reality has been my journey over the last six years. As an author one can be drawn to a piece of history but not be restrained by all the *historical facts* when conceiving a plausible new story. To take a piece of history, preferably engaging history, and twist it into a credible take-off on reality is what many authors of suspense and thriller novels seek. That is why after several weeks of struggling to come up with an engaging plot for The TARASOV SOLUTION, I researched the Cuban missile crisis and asked...*What if history lied to us?* In the second Dalton Crusoe novel, The ISRAELI BETRAYAL, I examined the world energy issues and created a cheap energy solution tempting nations to murder and also betray allies to gain control of the technology. Likewise, in The SECRET TEMPLAR ALLIANCE, I studied the Swiss banking relationship with Hitler and created a story of corrupt bankers, descended from the Knights Templar and later lured into becoming the financial enablers for the Nazis.

As I explored the implications of today's political and economic concerns, I was drawn to the partisan, and frequently vitriolic, tone in our political discourse. I imagined what Americans would do if our nation's sovereignty was truly threatened—from both our own actions and those of other nations. That broad plotline ignited my imagination to create—The RISING SEDITION.

The result is *reality-inspired-fiction*. I hope you enjoy the novel.

Imagine America as a Chinese Client State

PRELUDE

Near Present Time, United States of America

With seven months remaining in his first term, President Harold Barriman is weathering fierce opposition. Despite a likable personality, the President finds himself in a political firestorm. The liberal agenda he campaigned on, and narrowly won with, is enraging conservatives, libertarians, and independents as the emerging details impact everyday American life. The President and his powerful Chief of Staff, Brandon (Badge) Alan Demarche, are steering America down a very different path for its citizens. Overreaching using executive orders infuriates conservatives. Legal challenges are stalled or dismissed through a corrupt network originating within the White House.

Demarche's deep connections with the Chinese have morphed from a convenient alliance into an increasingly dominant role re-aligning America as a *client state of China*. Thirty-six states have successfully rallied support for a Convention of States as provided by Article V of the Constitution. Under President Harold Barriman, the nation's debt has risen to $26 trillion, the economy is weakening and near collapse. Months before his next election, President Barriman promotes, and *slow-walks* the details of an agreement for a $12.6 trillion financial aid package from China to fund a massive government stimulus program. Many controversial provisions buried in the aid package have Americans divided against each other. Liberals relish the expanding "entitlement" government move towards an eastern European socialist state. Conservatives resist the dangerous path toward fiscal Armageddon and losing our sovereign status. Allegations of treason, impeachable acts, unconstitutional executive orders and selling-out are fueling vitriol among the electorate. Sporadic violent eruptions between rival factions separate cities and states from one another. Legal challenges against the Chinese American Solvency Pact ("CASP") are stalled or denied the courts. In order to get the Chinese financial aid, Congress has approved, by the narrowest of margins, using questionable tactics, an unprecedented intrusion by a foreign power into the nation's sovereignty: a non-aggression treaty limiting any US military action except through United Nations approval; gun ownership limited in style and type to one firearm per family, or individual; ammunition production is taken over by the government and dispensed only through a lottery system; a price freeze is put in place for five years; confiscatory taxation is put on businesses and high income taxpayers; and the President's Economic Council is headed by a Chinese diplomat.

Most disturbing are the financial guarantee terms of the bail-out: title to development and mineral rights on 240 million acres of federal lands for fifty years. Most of the lands are in Alaska, and the western and Great Lakes states bordering Canada. A new "recovery currency", guaranteed by the Chinese government, similar in size and coloration to a twenty-dollar bill, is introduced with a value pegged at 2.5 times the US ten-dollar bill, and which has small Chinese images and words displayed throughout.

Early efforts at impeachment fail to draw enough votes in the House; and citizens gather in town hall nationwide meetings to move the Convention of States process forward. Liberals and conservatives argue over the airwaves on the best direction for a *new* America. A ground swell of change forges a coalition around a political action group; Pathroads for America, un-officially promoting Ed Kosko, Dalton's friend and mentor, now retired from the NSA to become the New Libertarian Party ("NLP") candidate for President. A date was set, July 7th, only months away, in Dallas Texas, for the Convention of States to return the country to sovereign control with a vastly different agenda than that of President Barriman, his Chief of Staff Badge Demarche, and their powerful operatives. Lines are drawn, the tension grows and lethal decisions are made.

♦ ♦ ♦

Northern Afghanistan, outside Asadabad, near the Nawa Pass, two months before the Convention of States

The sergeant's laser ranging scope measured 1,345 meters to the target. The forty-one degree temperature had dropped from fifty-nine degrees over the last two hours. The sundown quickly melted away to darken the clear night sky. The seven-man elite Army Ranger team waited for command approval to proceed with the mission. From their elevated vantage point tucked into a mountain crevasse the team reviewed their attack and capture plan once more. The CIA intel was compelling: a significant Pakistani Al Qaeda leader, Aza Bashir, was spotted near the Nawa Pass—the historical mountain valley crossing point into Pakistan. A local deep-cover asset had learned of a planned meeting by Bashir with regional commanders at a home in a remote region outside of Asadabad. The route to the target meeting site was a concern: steep terrain from over the rocky mountain slope to a pine forested ravine, which opened up over the final four hundred yards to a field with small outcroppings near the home. A mission plan designed to capture Bashir was in place and awaited Presidential approval.

Colonel Brad Ronet focused on several large screens displaying the images arriving from satellite feeds from the loitering MQ-9 drone and the helmet cam on the senior Ranger leader Matson. This was not the first time Ronet had been chosen to manage or lead a highly covert military operation. His reputation in the intel community, successes with NSA assignments, including those with Dalton Crusoe, all made him a favorite with General Watts. Capturing Aza Bashir was a high priority for the CIA and a political godsend for the administration. Ronet was Watt's *"man on the scene"*.

The mission was risky: the dark sky was helpful, yet the final approach was exposed. Touching his headset control Ronet said, "Matson do you copy?"

"Captain Matson here, 5 by 5 sir. Where are you positioned? How is your reception?" Matson looked into the tiny camera secured to his helmet laying a few feet away.

"Reception is good. I'm coordinating mission control from onboard the Aircraft Carrier *Carl Vinson*, cruising fifty miles off Muscat. We have two staggered satellite feeds, the drone and your helmet cams. Do you have confirmation Bashir is in the home?"

"Yes sir, our local contact confirmed the location last night. Bashir and his four man protection team arrived just before 1800 hours. We tracked them from satellite images through the Nawa Pass to this location." Matson paused, then continued, "We have confirmation through facial recognition Bashir is present."

"Can you verify the head count inside?" Ronet had been personally assigned by General Watts, Head of the Joint Chiefs, to provide oversight command on the highly secret, dangerous operation. The primary objective: intercept, capture and extract Bashir. The secondary objective: eliminate all other hostiles. Cell call intercepts had revealed several attacks on western interests and individuals were in the works through Aza Bashir. All mission support operations and Intelligence were directed through the *Vinson* from a sequestered communications center and patched into the secure "war room" beneath the White House.

"We have two women, and five men onsite before Bashir and his four man team arrived. The five men came together four hours earlier. One has been identified as a regional commander under Bashir—thermal imaging shows two guards patrolling the house perimeter. Three vehicles are parked at the site."

"Excellent. Maybe we'll get real lucky tonight and knock out the entire AQ leadership in northern Afghanistan. The extraction chopper is on deck, fueled and on alert awaiting your call that you have Bashir in hand, Captain." Ronet looked down at his confidential copy of the mission plan, crafted by the CIA and managed by a very small team on a *need-to-know* basis. "You and your men ready to proceed, Captain?" Ronet awaited an answer.

"Yes sir. We are less than a mile away—only a handful of lights to avoid in the small mountain village of fewer than a dozen homes and buildings. The sun is down, quite dark now, with little wind, and no bad weather to delay us. At 0230 five of my team will start their advance. Our Hellfire II missile-equipped drone will broadcast the event in thermal mode; and my UAV drone pilot is linked in real time with my communication specialist who along with our long-range sniper will remain at our staging location here. My men are briefed, rested and capable. We intend to neutralize any opposition, seize Bashir, drug him for the ride out and recover any files, computers, phones or maps on site. We're ready Colonel."

Ronet checked the display of clocks and confirmed it was 0211 Asadabad time. "Hold for five Captain." Ronet picked up his satellite phone and called General Watts. "We have a go situation on the ground for Operation SnagLift sir."

General Watts had Secretary of State Renkin, President Barriman, Vice President Garrison, CIA Director Cavanaugh, several aides and Badge Demarche in attendance. President Barriman had arrived in the room only minutes earlier. Watts addressed the group of viewers, including those remotely managing the communications and drone functions, and then offered a brief update as the imagery flowed in and said, "We need your approval Mr. President to proceed with the mission."

Barriman looked away, then to Badge who had earlier convinced the President to proceed if the opportunity to capture Bashir arose. A successful capture of a high level AQ terrorist like Bashir would unquestionably strengthen Barriman's standing with the public. The President glanced at Badge, then addressed Watts and said, "Proceed with Operation SnagLift." General Watts re-connected with Ronet and approved the mission.

Ronet clicked into the Captain's phone and through the headset speaker arm, Matson heard, "We are approved to go as planned. Good luck and Godspeed Captain." The small surveillance room aboard the *Vinson* became abuzz of activity following drone, satellite and troop movement, all captured on the ship's massive computers linked to the NSA, CIA and the Defense Department.

The situation room was quiet, orderly, with lights dimmed and all eyes trained on the large screens at the end of the room. The march of the five-man black ops Ranger team advanced in a staggered formation. The thermal, off-white glowing images revealed the Rangers moving in quickly. The President felt his cell phone vibrate, checked it, and left the room somewhat startled.

Watts looked curiously as the President excused himself, and then to Secretary Renkin, who held his gaze. The drone surveillance was uneventful, as expected, tracking the tight formation of five Rangers advancing on the house. Modest rock outcroppings and sparse vegetation made their final approach detectable. Yet the near cloudless sky and no moon gave a dark backdrop to the team's movements. After twelve minutes had passed, Secretary Renkin, using a tone of disgust, said, "I think the President needs to be in here as all this unfolds." Matson's team had closed he distance to the target to within 200 meters having just left the pine forest cover in the ravine.

Badge stood up and said, "I'll get him—just a minute." Badge found the President down a hallway alone, speaking on his secure satellite phone—he held up his hand to quiet Badge.

"I need to do this...to show some leadership against terrorists...and build support when our financial aid deal becomes public. I'll get back to you when it's done." Badge listened inquisitively as the President spoke.

"Was that Lei Zhang?"

"No. It was his brother Tan. He says Lei doesn't like our plan...fears it will alienate the Pakistanis further. He doesn't want us to use ground troops, and demands we keep it totally out of the press however it turns out...and deny any involvement."

Badge shook his head. "Great! This relationship with China is going to be a tough one to enjoy." Badge ushered the President back to the situation room.

Ronet watched as the five-man Ranger team moved out towards Bashir's location. The drone followed the unit from above angling side-to-side to give perimeter views to the communications specialist monitoring from the mountain crevasse. The drone screen suddenly lit up with multiple muzzle flashes. Satellite coverage provided a broader view, confirming the drone images. Ronet thought... *damn, they're not close enough.* He tried to reach Matson on his head phone gear just as a call came through from Matson... "Colonel we are under attack, heavy incoming fire."

The hostile fire came from three forward positions each between Matson's team and Bashir's location. The sweeping drone path managed to briefly show seven hostiles surrounding the team's position. A dozen rapid rounds streaked toward Matson's team as he checked on his men then radioed Ronet. "Two men down, I'm hit—we are retreating to staging RP1— send rescue chopper. Proceed with missile attack, capture not possible..." The message stopped, as rapid gun fire erupted again. Ronet opened the com link to General Watts who had listened to Matson's pleas for help. "We have a situation, sir."

The drone operator lit the target where Bashir was known to be and armed the two air-to-ground missiles upon Ronet's command. "General are you following the action on the mission? I recommend approving secondary objective and send in the rescue team now." Ronet heard no response to his call.

"General I need the rescue chopper crew in there now to get our men out. We have not captured Bashir...sir do we have extraction approval?" The General played the message over the audio speaker system for the President and others to hear.

General Watts looked to Barriman, "Mr. President, I await your command." The President froze, unable to fathom the surprise attack going on before him on screen. He glanced at Badge.

CIA Director Cavanaugh blurted out, "Give the order now!"

Watts added, "Mr. President, do I have your approval to proceed with the secondary objective?" Barriman studied the fire fight thermal imagery showing Matson and two other Rangers firing as they dragged back two downed men. The Ranger team collapsed to a small depression, seeking cover, as the hostiles advanced with increasing gunfire.

The seconds seemed like minutes until finally Barriman said, "Proceed with the secondary objective."

Watts grabbed the command mic and stated, "Colonel you are approved for missile launch. Repeat—you are a *GO* for missile attack."

Brad Ronet immediately shouted the order to the drone operator who stabilized the craft as its computer established the coordinates for a missile launch. Seconds later the target lock was confirmed and the drone pilot looked to Ronet. "Target locked sir."

Ronet reacted immediately, "Fire Now!" Two missiles flared, a fraction of a second apart, and headed into the house, resulting in a massive explosion. The drone circled and headed back to the staging location only to be hit with gunfire disabling the controls. The camera, still broadcasting, captured the craft's slow plunge to earth. Matson's last words were devastating, "Team lost—sniper and I are holding off incoming forces. Rescue needed now. Respond."

Ronet angrily called Watts asking, "Have the rescue craft and reinforcements been released? Our men are under heavy fire."

Watts looked to the President for a response. Nothing. Badge stared at the President. Barriman felt trapped: abandon a covert Ranger team under attack, or ignore a strong mandate from the Chinese leadership. He weighed the options trying to select the better of two horrible choices. The real-time screen coverage showed Matson's men, pinned down, repelling steady incoming fire.

"Mr. President, can we *please* release the rescue effort?" The sense of panic was palpable.   Again the question, "Mr. President?"

President Barriman, looked aside, stood up and stated, "Shut it down. No rescue, secure all records of the mission under my executive privilege."

Director Cavanaugh, several aides, and Secretary Renkin all uttered spontaneous objections: "...no, they'll die; we can't do this; reconsider; and What?"

CIA Director Cavanaugh erupted slamming his fist into the conference table, stood up and left. Secretary Renkin lowered her head, eyes shut for a moment only to then engage VP Garrison in an intense stare.

Badge ushered the President out of the situation room, shut the door and then approached General Watts and remarked, "You have to understand. Bigger issues are at play here General. I know the President can count on your understanding and cooperation." The General could not believe his ears. He struggled to control his rage as he inched towards Badge's face.

Badge then turned to the remaining officials in the room, stating, "Remember what the President said, this mission is protected under executive privilege. He expects your allegiance."

Watts had left the mic open for Ronet to hear directly. He then watched Badge leave the room before saying to Ronet, "We are shut down Brad. Sorry. Your men are on their own—try to do what you can."

Likewise Ronet could not believe the words coming from the President. The damaged drone continued to show massive muzzle blasts coming in on Matson's retreating team. The final imagery flickered and began to fade away from the action—seconds later it went dark—it was down. Ronet's mind burned with disgust, first toward the enemy, then to the local intelligence asset, and finally to the President's actions. He reflected for a moment on General Watts' last words... "*try to do what you can*". Ronet surveyed the control center: every face grim, every voice silent. He then turned to the young seaman manning the communications, moved close and whispered a few words in his ear.

"Yes sir—I'll see to that immediately." The seaman understood.

CHAPTER ONE

June, Cairo West Military Airport, Egypt

The four Presidential limousines were staged by the Secret Service team to receive the Secretary of State, Andrea Renkin, Vice President Robert Garrison and their top staffers. Air Force II pulled up to the diplomatic gates and the airport team set up a small receiving line with the traditional red carpet. The heat was intense on the tarmac at 3:30 p.m. Cairo time. Garrison stood, looked out the cabin windows and said, "Time to grip and grin Andrea—are you ready to calm down the Egyptians on our China deal?" He pulled on his sport coat and smiled at the veteran Secretary of State. She was nearing the end of her political career, as was Garrison, yet she was nine years younger, and wanted to retire in a few years into a second Barriman term, hopefully at the *top* of her career. The trip to Egypt led off a middle-eastern tour of Arab states to *assure* the new "Agreement" with China would not upset relations. Secretary Renkin had to do the "heavy lifting" while Garrison was there to offer some photo ops for the Egyptian press suggesting he carried a personal assurance from the President. In fact, Garrison could not offer any assurances beyond what Renkin would lay out.

"I think I can reassure them of our ongoing support although it's clear the Chinese will be tweaking our budgets. If the Egyptians don't get control of their people and stabilize all the rebel factions in their government, they will be shut out. Period. That's the bottom line message."

"You obviously can't let them conclude we've lost our sovereign authority over our financial aid." Garrison waited for a response as he watched Renkin button her jacket, obscuring her increasingly robust shape.

"Of course not, but we cannot proceed as in the past— pouring $30 billion a year of good money after bad. It is our new reality, right Robert?" She revealed a cynical look, and then took the lead with Garrison following down the jet ramp staircase.

Four diplomat types stood in the 98-degree heat to greet the Secretary and VP. The brief greetings were cordial and business-like. As expected, cameras clicked throughout the handshakes and smiles, both from the Egyptian and US photographers' corps. The Secret Service quickly moved the two along toward the second limo and closed the doors. The caravan drove off and headed to the Presidential offices near where the young mixed government of Egypt met with the Parliament. Garrison and Renkin were alone together opposite each other in the center compartment of the limo, with two Secret Service men—one in the passenger front seat and the other just behind them. As the four limo caravan gained speed on the divided highway a Marine helicopter followed above and behind the cars.

"Do you think the President can manage the coming blowback from the China aid package once all of the conditions flood the airwaves?" Garrison asked the question of Renkin knowing full well she was a critical, albeit skeptical, part of a tight inner circle surrounding the President that he seldom entered.

"I have my doubts. He had few choices and none were good. The US and China are in the same pickle barrel—fact is they hold *our* debt and we're close to default. They call the shots. The New Libertarian Party is gaining real momentum, and soon they will hold the same power and influence as the Progressives. His domestic policies are now at record low approval levels. The Convention of States, if it really happens, could be his most serious challenge—and perhaps his last. Soon we will be in full damage control." Renkin's face could not hide her true feelings of the President's ability to manage and lead the country.

Garrison listened and thought about the last time he and Renkin were together. "It seems like the President and Badge successfully clamped down on any reporting of the botched Asadabad operation."

Renkin revealed a troubled look as she remarked, "Bob, I can't even express my anger with the President...I'm so disappointed. I still don't understand it. He refuses to explain himself and Badge is blocking all attempts to get answers."

Garrison displayed a sympathetic look signaling he agreed with her frustration.

Two thousand feet above the caravan the Marine helicopter cruised under senior pilot Major Ted Makin's command. The trip to Cairo had been scheduled at the request of the Egyptians after parts of the Chinese financing package became public. The Secret Service felt enhanced security was needed and Badge Demarche ordered a helicopter support for the meeting. The modified and lightly armed Sikorsky S-92 scanned the air space for intruders. The throbbing engine noise echoed off the tarmac as it slowly circled. The clear sky allowed a stunning view of the Cairo city center in the distance. The agents on board were quiet and calm watching the limo unit below begin to move out. In a disguised move Makin reached for his full face gas mask, stowed in his flight bag near his feet. Just as the Secret Service agent in the co-pilot seat remarked, "What are you doing?" Makin threw a small nerve gas container against the floor deck behind him, smashing it and releasing the gas, which would be deadly to the other three agents on the chopper. He shut down radio communications with the ground team for several seconds. Makin ignored the thrashing about and gasping then checked to confirm all the men quickly dying. He re-opened communications and activated a ventilation fan purging the cabin of the gas with fresh air. He began to descend until he was less than one-thousand feet above the highway and eight hundred feet from a bridge overpass. Makin grasped the firing stick for the two Hellfire II air-to-ground missiles he carried. He radar-targeted the first limo and locked on to it. The targeting buzzer blared and the screen showed a steady red bulls-eye over the first limo. A press of his thumb sent the missile flaming downward, hitting the first limo directly, and creating a huge fireball, stopping the remaining cars at the overpass edge. The caravan came to a halt—agents talking frantically over each other on the communication links. Makin took a quick three-sixty turn and came in targeting the stationary second car. Garrison and Renkin were thrown from their seats to the floor as their limo skidded to a stop. The driver yelled, "Stay down! I'll get out and find out what's happened."

The flames were yards away as the two agents jumped out of the vehicle and drew their weapons. Confused, the agents could not determine where the attack had come from. They saw the helicopter circling but could not reach it on their head sets. The rear limo agents screamed orders over the channel as Makin listened in silence to the group chatter below, "Missiles appeared to come from our Marine chopper...can't raise the pilot...non-responsive. Missile may have misfired...don't know. Major Makin, do you copy? Get VP and Sec under the bridge...now!"

The last missile finally locked on the motionless second limo, its rear doors opening as agents set up a protective perimeter. Makin thought of his older brother, and only living family member, working with a NGO humanitarian group, lost a few years earlier during an Egyptian terrorist attack. His mind replayed the video images of his brother being tortured and then beheaded at the hands of terrorists demanding American forces leave the Arab nations. The State Department was no help and tried to side step the event. Letters and calls to the President were ignored, and Badge Demarche muzzled the press. The pain and anger changed Makin from a loyal marine, to a reserved, resentful victim seeking revenge. The current financial aid package to Egypt's radical-loaded government had pushed him over the top. His persuasive handlers had already provided half the $500,000 promised to his sister-in-law Jamie, once Makin had agreed to the mission. The remaining funds, provided through a bogus charity, would surely be sent once Makin completed his assignment.

The second missile-lock signal buzzed and Makin pressed his right thumb down one final time. He then angled the helo to follow the missile into the flames below. The chopper appeared to be out of control and diving to the ground. Secretary Renkin's death was a necessary revenge act for Makin to settle the loss of his brother. A second burst of orange flames erupted near the overpass, just as Makin flew the helo into the fireball.

◆ ◆ ◆

A mile away, stationed on the open eleventh floor of a new building being constructed near the Cairo city center, a man loaded his fifty second encrypted video of the attack onto an email destined to Adrestia, Ltd in Budapest. The "sometime" field asset had never met anyone at Adrestia; still he liked the occasional $10,000 wired payments for simple assignments usually involving data or images. Near Budapest's Ferenc Liszt International airport top Adrestia personnel gathered in a small, private meeting room around an oval conference table to view the video. Eight men, led by Lars Nevin, secured themselves in the locked room and, as the lights dimmed, they watched the start of a short video, and then looked to Lars for instructions. The men surrounding Lars were hardened ex-military, three from Australia, including Lars, four from the US, and one from the UK. Each man was apolitical—indifferent to their client's persuasion and drawn only to the enormous compensation for their services. A ninth man sat in a chair near the wall, typing notes on a tablet as Lars spoke. Lars explained the status of the Egyptian mission to the group, saying, "Major Makin successfully fulfilled his commitment to the 'unit', as you will see here."

The clear, steady time-stamped video zoomed in to the Sikorsky as it circled and then trailed the caravan as it approached the bridge overpass. The visual details of the explosions left no doubt Makin had done his job. After the video played out a question came from the group asking, "Why did he agree to fly his chopper into the limo? We could have extracted him and used him in the Unit."

The group looked to Lars, who responded, "Yes I offered him that option. He turned us down."

The Australian nicknamed Jake remarked, "Really, why take on a big financial gain assignment only to die completing the mission."

Another said, "Sounds nuts."

Lars lit a fresh cigar, then exhaled a circular blue smoke ring as he explained, "Makin wanted his own death in the attack rather than suffering the ravages of advanced pancreatic cancer discovered weeks earlier. It was his request. It made the operation easier to explain as a mechanical accident. I felt he might die with the chopper regardless of what I said. Our timing to complete this contract for our client was tight and this trip by Renkin and Garrison offered a unique window. We had to complete the mission. But you're right—he would have been a valuable asset for us." Only Lars had known before the explanation that cancer was close to taking Makin's life, a fact rationalizing his own death in the attack.

Lars ended the video, looked to the ninth man still tapping at his tablet, and said, "Proceed to transfer the remaining $250,000 payment to Jamie Makin, through the Grand Cayman branch of our banks." The ninth man, an accountant, responded, "Yes sir, I'll tend to that immediately."

Declan Crusoe sat attentive yet shocked at the brazen assault on two prominent US politicians. Declan had been allowed to join in on the *"mission closing report"*, after he recently impressed Lars by successfully disrupting a drug ring trying to coerce Adrestia on a construction project. Lars Nevin had taken notice of Declan's combat skills. The brazen, well-organized attack by Makin raised questions: first in Declan's mind was who had ordered and financed the attack—the second question was how and when he could escape from the Unit.

Lars Nevin ran Adrestia, the exclusive consulting and construction/engineering firm. Since the Iraq war large construction projects had become more competitive and Adrestia LTD fell to a lower tier of contractors favored with work. Still Adrestia handled scores of large financial transactions with suppliers, contractors, vendors and consultants each week—masking their other financial dealings through a tight network of European and US banks. Nevin ran the company much like a military camp. He was in charge...period. He was a fit fifty years old, very intelligent and combat tested, before taking over Adrestia LTD. Nine years earlier, he quietly transformed a subunit of the firm to provide other functions built around their established internal kidnap-and-rescue teams. He expanded the 'unit' into covert operations dealing with political objectives, procurement of armaments, small mercenary forces, untraceable financial transactions, communications and assassinations. The secretive assignments grew rapidly and the coffers of Adrestia soared. The Chinese leadership learned of Lars Nevin and sent intermediaries like Badge Demarche to make a connection. Despite numerous past and present construction projects in China and the far east, the Chinese government denied any knowledge or relationship whatsoever with Adrestia or its rumored "special unit", yet in reality, they became a lucrative client for Adrestia after the Barriman administration took office.

Six Days Later, Funeral for Vice President Robert Garrison

The news coverage for Robert Garrison's funeral was not impressive. The press was largely muffled, at least temporarily, having been told the tragic deaths in Egypt were the result of mechanical failure on the Sikorsky helicopter. The VP had served the Barriman administration in a true standby capacity, failing to gain access to the day-to-day decisions and actions of the President. The helo attack which killed Garrison left the administration in a unique position to strengthen its progressive team. Garrison was a strategic pick in Barriman's first term campaign, yet he was neither charismatic nor progressive enough to be trusted and welcomed inside the close inner circle of the Barriman team. Badge Demarche felt Garrison should be replaced on the ticket for a second term run anyway. He felt a solid progressive from the northeast would counter balance the growing New Libertarian Party. The choice to add Garrison to the ticket in Barriman's first run for the presidency was based solely on his moderate positions, compared to Barriman, although he was a long time Democrat. The choice narrowly secured the key state of Texas with its thirty-eight electoral votes to put Barriman into the Oval office. Garrison's family chose to bury him in his home state of Texas, near Austin, and the President flew in with his small entourage to honor the man.

Marine One came to a stop on the cordoned off parking plaza surrounded by security and press. The President stepped down the staircase after it dropped from the fuselage. He stopped to address a few vocal reporters. "Mr. President, when do you plan to fill the VP slot?"

While not surprised by the crass question in light of the setting, the President responded, "I'm here to pay my respects to a good man who served me and his country with dignity. Later a more appropriate time to deal with the succession issue will be announced. Thank you."

Badge stood a short distance from the burial scene, watching and listening to his President deliver a few well crafted phrases and testimony—all orchestrated by Demarche personally. He felt this was a valuable photo op for Barriman, acting compassionate and Presidential—and it served as *good practice* ahead of Renkin's funeral. The helo attack in Egypt was a double blessing for Badge: Garrison's sudden death removed any speculation that Barriman's plan to replace him as VP was political; and Renkin's death, after signing and authorizing a draft of the "Agreement" with China, eliminated her tendency to spill any remorseful thoughts should an *"ambush"* interview occur. It was serendipitous in Badge Demarche's mind: his Egyptian *"twin-*

win-solution" plan worked perfectly. The way was now cleared to further align America with the *"blue print"* he had crafted and presented to the Chinese leadership. The hint of a smile revealed itself despite Badge's attempt to control his expression.

CHAPTER TWO

Eight Months Earlier, Seven Mile Beach, Grand Cayman Island, Caribbean Sea

The stranger stood just outside the beach bar. His floppy sunhat revealed only the eyes of a lightly bearded face. The sky, thirty minutes after sunset, provided little illumination. Most of the resort's vacationers had strolled along the beach before turning in for the evening. Carolyn and Dalton approached slowly saying nothing. It was the last evening of their much needed vacation for the couple. It came after a five week, grueling assignment Dalton had completed against corrupt Swiss bankers. Dalton surprised Carolyn with his formal proposal of marriage two nights earlier. In both their minds there was no doubt they wanted to get married. Carolyn was careful not to press Dalton too hard when he was in the middle of a dangerous and complex assignment. Dalton used the respite in George Town to present her a classic, white gold 3-carat engagement ring which would interlock with the wedding band. Carolyn wasted no time in delivering her answer of 'Yes', repeated several times as she embraced Dalton with a long hug and kiss. It was the high point of the day for both of them.

The previous day had ended with a menacing note left for Dalton at his room door. Carolyn's excitement and joy of their engagement and their agreeing on a marriage date, after three years of committing herself to Dalton in every respect, had waned after the strange note arrived the last evening. Dalton was both intrigued and perplexed by the note's message.

Carolyn noticed the man first and instinctively grasped Dalton's right arm. The stranger moved out from the shadows, removed his floppy hat and extended a hand saying, "Dalton?" He had many of Dalton's features—older for sure, but a similar build and skin tone. The eyes were more severely tightened, although the color, an intense blue-gray identical to Dalton's was piercing. The accented voice was clearly Irish or Scottish. "I'm Declan Crusoe, your half brother."

It was as if the note delivered to Dalton's room the night before had just been re-read aloud. Originally regarded as preposterous, now the prospect of Dalton having a half brother felt possible.

"Hello Declan." A pause followed as Dalton studied the man. "How is it you believe we are brothers? I've never been told I had a brother." A smile crept across Dalton's mouth, easing the tension created by his question. Carolyn stood motionless, absorbed in the moment.

"Our father is Jonathan David Crusoe, who worked in Europe, mostly Brussels, for six years. My mother who worked in the Brussels office too—became involved with him—her name was Karin."

Dalton continued to study the man trying to sense any hint of a lie. Declan continued, "My father did die suddenly and while in Europe—I never knew he was ill when we spoke weeks before he passed." Carolyn could feel Dalton stirring, hearing this man claiming to have spoken with his father mere days before his demise.

"You said, 'her name *was* Karin'—what does that mean?" Dalton could see more of himself in Declan as he spoke. Carolyn remained fixated on the man.

"She died shortly after I was born from complications during me birth. That was thirty-six years ago. I was adopted by a family in Dublin when I was four. The Crusoe name was kept secret, I was told, because dad arranged the adoption through friends in Ireland." In a friendly pose, Declan addressed Carolyn saying, "You must be Ms. McCabe. I've read a lot about your career Maam. It's a pleasure to meet ya." Carolyn was speechless and smiled approvingly.

Dalton struggled to keep his numerous questions in a sensible order. Assuming the man was genuine, he began down his list. "Your note said something about having information about a plot by the administration against the current Congressional figures— what's that all about?"

"Aye, yes, that's correct. A number of powerful administration folk along with outside groups are planning to stage a Presidential assassination, blaming the New Libertarian Party."

"How do you know this, and when is this supposed to happen?"

Declan grew uncomfortable, took a deep breath, and continued in his Irish brogue "I was paid ta organize and time the attack—then two weeks ago I begin ta have reservations. That's when I realized I couldna go through with it and tried to connect with you." Declan paused. "The schedule is fluid but for sure, ahead o' the election by a few weeks."

"You're an assassin?" Dalton's voice took an edge to it. Carolyn tensed at the question and pulled closer to Dalton.

"Nay, not really. Not so's you'd notice." Declan paused, looked directly at Dalton and began again, "I was a kid when the IRA had their quarrels with the Brits. I learned a lot about politics and how war worked—folks took note. As time went on, I got calls. I've run weapons; armed 'freedom fighters'; shut down extortion groups; discredited foreign politicians and helped manage a Middle Eastern *coup d'état*, but I was not about to participate in something like this mate."

"Because it was against America? Killing a sitting US President or Senator?"

"Nay, that wasn't the deciding factor, but it were important." Declan revealed a trace of shame in his answer.

"Well what *was* the factor which changed your mind?" Dalton's disgust surfaced. Declan became very humble. An unexpected pause from Declan made Carolyn more uncomfortable.

"I learned you were actually *one o'* the possible targets, and the President was not. It will look like the President was targeted but he will survive. He's being *managed* to carry out a hidden agenda fer America. The bogus attack is aimed at eliminating his opposition rivals." Carolyn's face froze in fear at hearing Dalton was a target. She looked at him, speechless, and shaken. Dalton held his hand up, signaling Carolyn should not react, while he focused in on Declan. A moment of silence allowed the words to sink in. Dalton stiffened, forged a stern look and organized his next words.

"The President has many enemies—and many devoted friends these days. You say some are willing to fake a Presidential assassination to kill another—a rival or Presidential contender?" Dalton's mind flooded with many questions.

"Aye, and these blokes can get it done—believe me." Declan nodded his head holding Dalton's stare.

Dalton controlled his expression, softening it a bit, yet he clearly doubted this man was truly his half-brother. Declan took note. "Do you recognize this?" Declan handed it to Dalton.

"What is it JD?' Carolyn strained to see the object. Her face tightened, fighting back tears.

"It's dad's college graduation ring. I remember it." Dalton stood speechless looking at the classic ring.

"Aye, it's inscribed on the inside of the band with his initials...JDC—same as your initials. He gave it to me four days before he died—ya know, when he sensed he was failing. We spoke only a few times a year, but before he died he told me of me real family—and you. He told me to use it ta verify my story when, and if, I *chose* ta connect with you." Dalton began to consider the possibility that this man, Declan Crusoe, was his true half-brother.

"I must have verification of both stories—being my half-brother and the assassination plans, agreed? If your information proves to be true, I'll need you to meet with me at the NSA and with contacts in the FBI, and CIA." Declan did not respond to Dalton's demands—simply staring into the crashing Caribbean waters.

"Dalton, both stories are true—you'll come to believe. Look here at me passport—Irish citizen, Declan Faden Crusoe." The photo and name matched Declan's claims. "But I must contact you, on me own schedule, to avoid being eliminated by some of the same folks you want me to meet. The group I am workin' fer believe I'm still in place. I will find a time ta break free, go silent, and I'll try ta help you stop this madness. But these folks are powerful, ruthless, committed and very dangerous." Declan pondered his next remarks. "There will be deaths, some viewed as accidents, suicides, or natural causes, but trust me they will even sacrifice their own, it seems, ta achieve an enduring result. Beneath the surface America is at war with itself. I want ta be on the surviving side me brother."

"You say I may be a target. How is it I'm connected to this bogus assassination plan?" Carolyn snapped her attention back to Declan waiting for the answer.

"All I know is when the real target was indentified through a photo yer name was also mentioned as a...*secondary target*, if possible."

"Who is the target; did you learn his name? And if I was identified as a secondary target, how is it they didn't connect me with you?" Dalton pressed for details.

Declan smiled, rubbed his jaw and answered, "Nay, the real target list is still being assembled, and they don't invite me in fer those discussions. I'm told ta expect three or four chaps—all critical ta the Convention of States project. But soon it will be fixed and I'll have ta step up or step out, ya know." Declan reached for a cigarette and his lighter, seeking to calm himself down. "And yer right, if they knew my real name when you were recognized, I'd have been killed in a flash, but they know me as

Declan Faden—me mother's last name. I carry a driver's license and other ID using me mum's name, including a second passport from Ireland—safer."

Carolyn saw pain and concern in Declan's face, first for his own safety, the reference to his mother and the danger for Dalton. She clutched Dalton's arm again alerting him that she was persuaded Declan was truly his half-brother. Dalton's mind robotically stored the thought...*my half brother's mother's name is Karin Faden...Karin Faden,* then re-focused on Declan.

"So how much do you get paid for this kind of work?" The question had an unmistakable tone of disgust. Declan took note and met Dalton's eyes—he knew he could not lie.

"I get paid by the assignment basically: $15,000 for a week's reconnaissance and photo work; $25,000 fer a break-in ta plant devices or snatch a computer maybe; and $150,000, or more, ta arrange a death—a bomb, a shooting or staged suicide. I get lotsa vacations between assignments too—like this time in Grand Cayman. Ya might like ta know I never signed up for the $150,000 jobs."

"So you've never killed anyone? That sounds like easy money although the work is dishonest, maybe even illegal...right?" Dalton wondered where the limits of Declan's greed stopped.

"Yeah, I've killed ta avoid being killed—it was war. Trust me I'm not inta killin' regular folks brother. But yer right, the money is good, there's lots of it and it flows in freely—from the Chinese I'm guessing." Dalton returned to the comment about America being at war with itself.

"You mean this rogue group actually *penetrates* the security agencies of the US? You think the Chinese are involved? Who are they? What do they call themselves?" Dalton's eyes narrowed as he projected his disbelief.

"Aye, mate—they do. Mind yerself, brother. I'll reach you soon." Declan nodded to Carolyn, then to Dalton and as he walked away he grinned. "And Dalton...if I told you their name you'd surely not come up with anythin' meaningful. They don't carry business cards, ya know. The name's only a tag ta cover the top dogs and their doings. They're everywhere and hide in plain sight."

"When can I expect to hear from you again, Declan?" Carolyn reacted with surprise at the sense of concern and respect she noticed in Dalton's words and facial expression. Dalton's emotions ran a revolving course between rage and anger—to an odd affection and trust for the man claiming to be his half-brother. His story was compelling and terrifying if true.

"I'll be back ta ya soon brother—but first I must complete my escape plan, so's I can really stop this thing. Trust me I'll be Ok."

Dalton stood in disbelief at what Declan Crusoe had to say. Carolyn also found Declan's story incredible—and she worried about a new list of concerns: the country, Dalton's safety and her marriage hopes. Declan tipped his hat to Carolyn and disappeared around a building. Dalton stood motionless and looked to Carolyn. "He really is my brother—isn't he?"

CHAPTER THREE

Present Time, Quebec Riverfront, Antoine's Bistro

Saul Abboud sat next to a propane heater stationed near the covered outside patio tables and clutched his hot coffee. The plastic sheeting used to halt the cool winds was working and maintained a mild seventeen degrees Celsius. The early June weather often produced night time temperatures near freezing yet the strong sun warmed the day. Still the outdoor patio was almost vacant—ideal for a very private meeting Abboud scheduled earlier at 1:00 p.m., in only three minutes. Being unaccustomed to clandestine meetings with an assassin's surrogate made Abboud nervous. He was ambitious and timid in the same moment—a stalled political operative, nasty at times and fierce in his perseverance, but not a buyer of death. Abboud lacked the camera-friendly appearance and verbal dexterity to be out in front on major political issues. He knew that and over time had accepted the role of proxy for the administration's leaders. Badge Demarche used Abboud like an old plain sweater—reliable, but not suitable for prime time exposure.

The outlook for President Barriman was dire; the Convention of States initiative could de-rail his entire agenda, halt a major stimulus plan, and install a new Congress intent on impeaching the President. Those closest to Barriman knew Abboud could be relied upon for the task. As a long time admirer and supporter of the President, but functioning in the shadows for a key administration member, he was perfect. A man walked past the waitress as she returned to the main dining room from the patio. He approached with a confidence and sophistication that was apparent.

"Might you be Mr. Abboud, sir? Yes?" The distinguished looking man that approached Abboud was adorned with a brimmed hat and a light overcoat. He was fit and appeared to be in his sixties, slim, educated, and serious. He extended his hand in a friendly, non-aggressive manner and smiled.

"Yes I am, and you are Mr. Thomas, correct? Abboud stood to greet his guest.

"Yes, of course." Thank you for being prompt I have a rather tight schedule this afternoon. What can my principal do for you Mr. Abboud?" The question was direct and designed to avoid any chit-chat.

"I represent a group of American patriots who believe this coming Presidential election may be corrupted by a small yet powerful faction of traitors committed to reversing the President's progressive initiatives—even if it harms the country. We intend to stop them. While unorganized for the most part, the planned Convention of States will surely produce a name, a face, and a mission embodied in a strong opponent." Abboud paused to form his next thought. "We would like to have this individual...eliminated, if you will, during or after the Convention and long before the election—if possible."

"I am guessing you are part of an independent contractor group assisting the Barriman administration. Yes?" Thomas never took his eyes off Abboud; testing his authority to seal a deal.

"It's true I am not part of the official Barriman administration, yet I can assure you my patriot group is real and committed to carrying out this assignment." Abboud began to fidget and squirm.

"Who is it *exactly* that will contract with and pay my principal's fee?"

"I'm not at liberty to say...actually I don't know." Abboud's tell appeared: a twitching left eyelid muscle when he lied. Thomas reacted immediately.

"You're connected with the Adrestia group, correct Mr. Abboud?" The bold, unforeseen statement caused Abboud's eyelid to go spastic and he started uttering incoherent denials. Mr. Thomas took notice.

Thomas smiled and said, "Relax Mr. Abboud. My principal has dealt with Adrestia in the past. It's fine. We know they are apolitical, available to the highest bidder, generally speaking." Abboud withdrew his handkerchief and wiped off his sweating brow, saying nothing as he revealed a quivering smile and a nod of his head.

"This could backfire on your group if the target's message is compelling and draws others to come forth." Thomas spoke with a calm, steady voice, without any hint of shock or disgust. Abboud's body language hinted at nervous indecision, or maybe uncertainty, or even paranoia—it then settled into a fear of incompetence.

"We have considered that possibility, and believe absent this *one* man, the movement will collapse." An uncomfortable silence followed. Abboud looked around the patio and seeing no onlookers slid an unmarked photo upside down across the table to Thomas. The silence continued. Abboud began showing stress, his hand trembling.

"You understand that should my principal accept this assignment, he alone will choose the specific timing, location, and methods to carry out his role. He may require field operatives, which he alone will select, perhaps from within the Adrestia Unit. There may be collateral damage as well. You will have no further direct contact with me. If he accepts the assignment I will call you on a cell phone I'll provide you. If payment is made as instructed within forty-eight hours of the call, the assignment is active. Is that clear?" Thomas studied Abboud for any sign of hesitation—none appeared.

"Yes, of course." Abboud wiped his flushed face once more with his handkerchief, nodding to affirm.

Thomas slid the photo to his side of the table and turned it over—studied it—placed it face down again. It was from a recent public event, taken from approximately thirty feet away. He controlled a visceral reaction to the photo.

"Do you recognize the man Mr. Thomas? He's the one near the right side circled in red."

"You've never done anything like this before have you Mr. Abboud?" Thomas was testing the man's resolve and nerve.

"No, I haven't. But do not assume I represent an inept group. They will get this done." A pause ensued. "Your principal came recommended without equals." Abboud forged a stern look and glared at Thomas. "Do you recognize the man, sir?"

"Yes. There is no need to speak his name." A long pause followed during which Thomas put on his brimmed hat, gloves, and sunglasses and retrieved the photo. He stood and reached in his coat pocket. "Here is the phone I spoke of. There is a recorded message for you. Listen carefully to it. I will meet with my principal soon. Good day, Mr. Abboud." Thomas left the bistro directly. Abboud enjoyed another cup of coffee and settled down, having listened to the phone message twice before leaving. He stowed the phone and its ear bud device.

Khamal never, *ever*, presented himself as the principal; rather as a contact working for the principal under an alias. His disguise, as the Mr. Thomas, was extraordinary, complete with colored contacts, a gray goatee, a hairpiece, a prominent facial mole, and a tiny fake scar on the left side of Khamal's chin. If that wasn't enough the voice delivery and Parisian-French-accented English, dispelled any hint of the assassin's true middle-eastern Arab background.

Khamal was the only son of a beautiful French author and librarian and a Moroccan-born economist working for the French International Trade Authority. It allowed Khamal a rich exposure to western education before his brief service in the French military as a combat strategist. Fluent in French, English and Arabic, he was able to transcend cultures and customs throughout the Middle East. When his parents died in a horrific car accident on Khamal's twenty-fourth birthday, he redirected his life, vowing to avenge his parent's death from the drunk driver, a French Assistant Minister of the Interior, who was never brought to justice. The assassination was skillfully done to appear as a mugging gone badly, never solved, and established Khamal as a rising star in the secretive world of killers-for-hire. Arab leaders took note and sought him out through Mr. Thomas.

The photo Abboud provided was provocative: stirring raw memories and emotions on an open contract with the Iranians: eliminate the last conspirator who they believed had led to a bomb attack on their secret nuclear facility—one Jameson Dalton Crusoe. He would call Abboud in two hours and accept the assassination contract. Unknown to Abboud the photo of the man circled in red showed him standing next to Dalton Crusoe.

Khamal quickly devised a plan to fulfill the contract and satisfy another score—*a painful older score*.

Saul Abboud felt like the *burner* phone weighed a ton. He walked back to his car and drove home, constantly starring at the simple flip phone waiting for it to ring. Time dragged on, then a ring. "Mr. Abboud, my principal has confirmed to me the funds have been transferred. You may consider the contract active. Destroy the phone after the contract is fulfilled. Do you understand?"

"Yes, I do. Will I hear from you again?" Abboud timidly asked.

A reply came, "Unlikely."

Abboud closed the burner phone, swirled the earpiece into a coil, stared at it a moment and stowed it in his coat pocket. He then retrieved his personal phone and entered a saved number.

"It's me, Saul, the contract is active."

CHAPTER FOUR

Pathroads for America Headquarters, Washington D.C.

Ed Kosko had still not made a decision to run for office on the New Libertarian ticket. Were it not for the dismal state of affairs the country found it in after decades of expanding socialist programs, which were ramped up under Barriman, he would rather retire and go fishing. Yet the pressure was mounting and the Pathroads organization had raised over $191 million in their war chest to deflect the liberal agenda of President Barriman through the upcoming Convention of States. Pathroads CEO Charley Rhodes sat in his private conference room studying Kosko. "Our polling has you 52%, Barriman 45%, 3% undecided as to whom they prefer for President. The President is upside down for the last year on his approval/disapproval rating: 42% to 58%. These are good numbers against an incumbent President who has fallen twenty points from his high approval numbers months after his election."

"Is that interpreted as a guaranteed win?" Kosko smirked at his own sarcasm. "Besides no one knows me unless they're already in government."

"No, no one can guarantee a win. But you do have name recognition, through your close relationship with former President Jerome Conner—its damn encouraging Ed. We both know the defeat of a first term President is difficult. With this Convention taking shape you will certainly get that group's support in the election."

"Really?"

"Well right. No one else is going to show up. The Republican Party is so fractured it can't even get a viable candidate to step up. Most broke with the old Libertarians to the New Libertarian Party along with independents in hopes of forcing a major reduction in Federal government power and executive branch overreach, all of which I endorse. Yet I've never sought political office and don't much want to now." Kosko rubbed his neck in a somewhat involuntary action to ease his nervous tension.

"Barriman is losing support every day—he's just not going to recover in light of this crazy Chinese financing deal." Charley stood and leaned towards Ed on the conference table. "Ed, listen to me. We have the big banks, major manufacturers, small business, the Chamber of Commerce, and the religious right solidly in our camp. You're the ideal man to carry the message." Kosko looked to the room windows and seemed distracted.

"Exactly what is the message Charley?" Ed Kosko needed to hear once again the platform he'd have to campaign on.

"You know it all. States' rights, reduced executive office powers, smaller Federal government, balanced budgets, line-item veto, term limits, debt reduction, restructure social programs and no transfer of Federal lands in a foreign bailout loan. The rest is easy: strict adherence to the Constitution, the Bill of Rights, solid defense posture, avoid reckless social issues." Charley waited for a response from his friend, and followed up with, "Ed, my sources inside the NLP tell me they would strongly welcome your candidacy. I'd bet you wouldn't even have an announced challenger." Ed remained contemplative, listening and thinking. "Ed, we are talking to no one else, not even Senator Welch, from North Carolina, or General Watts." A pause allowed Ed to reflect on the offer. "Besides I can't believe you'd pass up a chance to rectify the mess Barriman and friends have made of the NSA after asking you to retire."

Ed reacted with curiosity, his head snapping to full alert—eyes staring at Charley. "You've spoken with Jack Watts about running?" The question hid the pain Ed felt over the present administration's misuse of the NSA.

"No, absolutely not. I assure you. We have been merely running private polling of several prospects against Barriman—you and the General lead the crowd. Watts polled 50% to 46% against Barriman, and 4% undecided."

Ed Kosko remained expressionless, looking out the window, clearly struggling to make a commitment to become the New Libertarian Party candidate. He straightened in his high-backed chair, swiveled it to his left, and tapped the mahogany table top twice before raising his hand to point a finger at Rhodes. "I'll let you know tomorrow what I've decided to do. I need to talk to a close friend about all this. Ok?"

"Your wife or family...I assume?"

Ed Kosko smiled, "Close, Charley, you could call him family—I think of him as the son I never had. Irene is ready for whatever—I think."

Disappointed but hopeful, for the moment, Charley Rhodes nodded and remarked, "I'll be here in my office all day Ed. Looking forward to your decision." A pause followed, "Ed, do I know this *close friend*?"

"You might. Dalton Crusoe."

◆ ◆ ◆

The unusually balmy late spring weather meant no burdensome overcoat or gloves for Ed Kosko as he walked to the third floor of the parking ramp serving the Pathroads for America office complex. The air felt warmer than the fifty-five degree high reported by the morning news networks. The sun was strong when not covered by slow moving billowy clouds, which gave a sense summer was close at hand. The remote key clicked and the Audi sedan flashed its lights and unlocked the driver's door. As Ed reached for the door handle, he paused, something was wrong—out of place. His eyes shifted over the windshield to the wipers. An envelope, letter-sized, unlabeled lay trapped under the wiper blade. Instinctively Ed looked around the garage. Nothing. No sounds, no persons, no cars moving. He recalled the last thirty seconds: the car had been locked; the concrete floor looked dry and undisturbed from activity, the tires appeared normal, lacking any object pressed against the tires waiting to be backed over. He pulled the envelope from beneath the wiper blade and carefully removed a folded sheet of blank paper except for the typed words: *Announce for President and you die in the thirty days following.*

Ed took several seconds considering the message and its timing. Was he being followed, targeted, or simply given a hollow threat? He turned and began walking back to Charley Rhodes' office when he muttered to himself, "Maybe it's someone on Charley's team—or Charley is part of the threat. No, that's stupid. Maybe it's just a prank from a misguided soul." He stopped, pointed at the Audi, and pressed the remote start, trusting his instincts. The Audi growled to life and purred quietly with all the interior lights on. Ed shook his head at his vivid imagination and jumped in his car. The ride to his Maryland suburban home went by quickly, as his mind churned with possible scenarios for the note. He struggled with how to tell

Irene—and then to find Dalton Crusoe and revive a few trusted NSA connections he knew would help.

◆◆◆

Late May, Canada, Eighty Miles North of Ottawa

The five mile trek to locate, evade detection and surround the target took the better part of three hours. Heavy cover, rolling terrain, open patches, and frequent water crossings made the second day of the trip difficult. The sniper shadowing Dalton found him in his scoped R700 LTR 308 rifle, ranged him at three-hundred-eighty yards, and followed his slow movements. Weeks of preparation had paid off as Hasid Khamal lightly caressed the trigger and watched as he relived his near death struggle with Dalton Crusoe thirty months earlier in the Caribbean. He could still recall the pain of the deep, near lethal knife wound across his chest he received when he fought with Dalton. The incident soiled Khamal's reputation: *guaranteeing to quietly complete each and every contract.* Presumed dead by all but a handful of prior clients, Khamal cheated death, spent months in recovery and now had a chance to fulfill his new contract; and he realized he could finish an open one—the Iranian contract on Jameson Dalton Crusoe. He relished the chance to eliminate a second man in Abboud's photo, the one standing next to Ed Kosko, the one circled. Dalton Crusoe was the second man, standing next to a smiling Ed Kosko, taken several months earlier. Having studied the relationship and interaction between Kosko and Crusoe, Khamal felt Kosko would be an easier target with the formidable Dalton Crusoe eliminated. Khamal's revenge was close at hand.

◆◆◆

Dalton paused, dropped to his knees and slowly scanned the forest-sheltered, small crescent bay on an oddly shaped lake from behind a dense cluster of aspen. Eight men all dressed in green and brown camouflage, sporting back packs and weapons settled in quietly behind Dalton and waited. The small, broken-down log cabin some seven-hundred yards away on the northern shore appeared empty. "Here Brad, what do you think?" Dalton handed the ranging binoculars to his friend and superior officer— although not for this mission. Brad Ronet dropped to the ground and crawled two yards to a narrow break in the small pine treeline protecting the shore. He studied the distant cabin across the lake.

"Too easy. If our hostage is there then a trap may be waiting for us. If it's empty, then our intelligence was wrong and we've wasted valuable time today. I'd bet he is not there. The hostage site is too visible—even if remote." Colonel Brad Ronet looked back at Dalton and waited for his response.

"Yeah, it does look and feel too easy. Besides our latest intel suggests they are four miles northeast in dense cover. Let's launch a mini-drone and get some images of the area."

"Right. On it now." Brad Ronet had become a close friend and combat comrade over the past five years. More than once Ronet had covered Jameson Dalton Crusoe's back when danger was descending on him. By his own choice Colonel Brad Ronet, a marine and clandestine Special Ops team leader for former President Jerome Conner, had asked to join Dalton on his current assignment. Dalton's mandatory active duty assignments were largely waived following his graduation from Annapolis years earlier. After President Conner was termed out and his party lost the White House and the Senate, Dalton felt it was time to complete his remaining active duty requirement. His experiences since graduation profoundly demonstrated his skill set and had garnered him a Lieutenant Commander rank. The seven-day campaign in the Canadian wilderness would satisfy his outstanding field duty obligation.

Ronet felt a strange protective attachment to Dalton, beyond the personal friendship, and he helped select several of the men on Dalton's team. The tragic loss of the Ranger team, twelve days earlier in Afghanistan, had left Ronet furious and desperate to expose the treasonous actions of the President—Ronet then joined the Crusoe team. He needed Dalton's help and couldn't wait for the "field campaign" to end, so he requested permission to join the team and personally update Dalton.

After Ronet made a few simple hand motions, Sergeant Patterson nodded and proceeded to open a backpack and assemble the small reconnaissance drone. At less than eight pounds the computer-controlled device had a transmitting camera, guidance, and an infrared package all powered by a quiet propane-fueled engine. The drone could operate up to eight miles out for thirty minutes before running out of fuel. In less than a minute, Patterson had the craft programmed for a "hand-thrown" launch while Dalton watched his wrist-mounted monitor of the camera images. The drone took off and quickly rose to three hundred feet sending detailed images back to Dalton's team. After adjusting the images for maximum resolution, Patterson opened his hardened military tablet for the entire team to follow the images.

"It looks like the cabin area is clear sir. No equipment, vehicles, men or lights coming from the cabin." The GPS software confirmed the cabin was 711 yards away on the far side of the lake.

Dalton looked at the larger screen and said, "Let's have it circle in from a one-half mile radius and tighten in on the shoreline before returning. It could be a trap. If they found it earlier they could be waiting to ambush us and rescue Andy." Ronet stared at the screen and then looked an approving glance at Dalton.

"Yes sir, I'll start the route now." Patterson directed the drone in nimble fashion with the small "joystick" connected to his computer.

The cool air forewarned of nightfall in less than an hour. The pre-spring sky looked ominous. The woods were already dim and would soon be dark. The previous two nights camped out in the Canadian woods were mild for late May, melting all but shaded areas of snow. Still a storm front was pushing the cold northern air down to bring a brief frost overnight. Dalton had to decide whether to approach the small cabin in the next hour or so and, if empty, use it for night protection, or wait until dawn, sleeping in tents on the ground. Dalton had the final decision as team leader yet he always sought out Ronet's opinion. "Let's make camp for tonight near the lake back of the shoreline." Dalton looked for any objections—there were none—Ronet nodded his agreement.

The men with Dalton were all seasoned soldiers with deployments in either Iraq or Afghanistan, and advanced covert operations skills. The primary assignment to the teams was clear: locate a single booby-trapped dummy hostage tagged "Andy"; avoid contact, if possible, with the opposing enemy team; make a stealth live rescue and escape; and return within seven days to the base camp. Khamal's considerable sources confirmed a respected government contractor, "DarkHarbor", was selected as team "B", in a change from former missions, to provide the opposing force challenging Dalton's team. Primarily used for training and front line support for active NSA or CIA operations, this was the first time such a group was being sent on a training mission. Stealth movement strategies, minimal adverse contact and high tech surveillance were the secondary "procedural" objectives of the campaign. If successful, Dalton's team, "A", would earn special merit patches and possible promotion upgrades; whereas if they were the losing team then they would be forced to "enjoy" another week in a classroom setting studying the successful team's tactics. Unintentional contact between the two teams could be physical, yet not lethal, and live rounds were not provided. Neither Dalton nor Ronet wanted to spend another week in a classroom—rather they'd prefer to successfully complete the training campaign and move on.

Patterson continued to study the drone imagery on his tablet screen when he noticed movement. "Sir, I believe I've found something." Ronet looked over Patterson's shoulder and saw the heat signature of three men less than two miles away heading toward the lake.

"Dalton, take a look at this. All we know of team "B" is that they are eight men, just like us, yet here are three alone, and no others nearby." Dalton looked at the soft white images of men moving slowly in tight formation northwest of the lake. Seconds later the drone's camera moved on leaving the screen dark. Patterson directed the drone to return.

"They could be a scouting the area or setting up a perimeter for their camp." Dalton thought about his own reaction. "Or they could be escorting the 'hostage' back to their camp—maybe."

Ronet grinned as he considered the fertile mind of his friend and said, "Could be JD. Or they may have located our position and are coming after us. Or maybe it's some lost hunters." The long day's hike had taken its toll and Ronet was trying to break the boredom with humor. "I'm sorry. It's hard to get amped up on our "pretend" mission when we all know we're using non-lethal ammunition—right boys?" A smirk formed across several of the team member's faces.

Dalton joined in the joking and said, "Ok, we need a couple brave volunteers to check this out at daybreak—anyone?"

"I'll take that on sir," replied Sergeant Mason, who looked over to Kilmer.

"I'll join Mason, sir."

"Fine. Get some rest. Patterson, stand watch till 0200, and I'll take over till dawn." Kilmer stood and removed his heavy pack, freeing up thirty pounds of dead weight and spread his bed role. Mason checked his weapons and gear before turning in. The nine-man team settled into a small grassy patch not ten yards wide under a camo-mesh screen stretched between trees surrounding their small camp. By 1:45 a.m. the temperature dropped to forty-six degrees, the sky was clear, and the woods were silent. A storm front was coming within the next twelve hours. Dalton reasoned he could complete the mission early the next morning and return to the base training complex before the bad weather set in. Dalton moved over near Patterson who appeared wide awake, sharp, and watchful. "How has your evening gone so far sergeant?" whispered Dalton.

"Fine sir. Nothing to report except a small herd of deer, grazing slowly off to the west."

Dalton slung his pack against a tree and sat down near Patterson. "Ever been on a training mission like this one Patterson?"

The sergeant smiled and said, "No sir. Did one just three months after basic a year ago, near LeJeune...not near as high tech as this one...mainly just observing and testing survival gear, hiding in *enemy* territory."

"Get some rest. We have only two days left to complete the mission and get back to base camp." Dalton watched the star-filled sky and thought about returning to the DC area and meeting up with Carolyn. The decision to finally set a wedding date had been delayed almost two years as Dalton's assignments pulled him into several critical national security matters. Carolyn had been patient and now was ready to marry her best friend and love. She had advanced her career as a finance professor at the Wharton School, and had just received tenure. The improved status gave her the ability to better plan her schedule, think about becoming Dalton's wife and...motherhood. The cool air caused Dalton to tuck his head into his jacket collar and scarf, retaining his body warmth. He tried to think how to keep Carolyn focused on their engagement and wedding plans, and not on the vague death threat that Declan had shared. Minutes passed, he could not hold his eyes open and drifted off into a light sleep. Three minutes later, Dalton awoke to a noise—it was close. Now fully alert, he scanned the woods before him, and saw nothing...then more noise, a cracking sound...someone or something was approaching. Suddenly a hand grasped Dalton's shoulder. "It's me JD—Brad."

"What? Are you sleep-walking? You scared the hell outta me." Dalton was embarrassed that he dozed off as Ronet approached. The colonel sat down next to Dalton and began, "I need you to hear the full story on Barriman's actions." Dalton sat up, rolled his shoulders to remove some stiffness from sleeping in the cold against a pine tree, and then concentrated in on Ronet.

"You said he left a Ranger squad to die...right?" Dalton looked around his camp and confirmed the remaining team was asleep.

"Yeah, Operation SnagLift, but it's real complicated. General Watts directed me to oversee the operation from the *Carl Vinson* near the scene. We're friends, did a couple of tours together. He suspects a political objective led to their deaths. I think he was right."

"How's that? What political objective?"

"His re-election challenge—Barriman. He needs to improve his image, particularly as this damn Chinese financial aid package unfolds. The attack mission, targeting Aza Bashir, would have really helped. But when the Rangers were attacked and they failed to capture Bashir, they ordered a Hellfire launch to kill him."

"Did they get Bashir or not?"

"Not sure. That's their problem. If they claim he's dead and white-wash the bungled mission resulting in getting our guys killed, they risk Bashir appearing on a video telling the real story, along with showing seven dead US soldiers and embarrassing the administration."

Dalton began to see the whole picture. "The President failed to order the rescue of our guys—trying to hide the botched attack—damn it's hard to believe."

"Believe it JD. I have a complete mission record, audio and video of the entire operation—its right here." Ronet patted his chest cargo pocket. "People are really getting angry as hell over his Chinese financial deal as they learn more. I hear citizen militia groups are forming in many red states as opposition hardens against Barriman and his reckless policies." Ronet paused. "I thought you could...well...help me expose Barriman for what he is."

"How did you get the mission file...those are heavily protected?" Dalton looked at his friend for an answer.

"Ahh, that's another story." Ronet nudged closer to Dalton, "Everyone in mission control aboard the *Vinson* saw and heard the actual story. Barriman told them to secure all the records using executive privilege. The communications technician, Seaman Murray, made a copy for me."

"You asked him to do that?"

"Well I kind of gave an order, but he knew it needed to be done—so he secretly handed me the disk file copy minutes later. I've got it all right here...its treasonous JD. It has to get out."

"You're right. I want to see this file before I take any action...Ok?" Dalton's mind began to think through the ramifications of the file's exposure. Ronet then took over the watch earlier than planned, letting Dalton get some thought and sleep time. As Dalton crouched prior to standing he said, "Brad, I don't recall you so taken to politics." A smirk ran across Dalton's face.

"I hate politics—it always seems to get in the way of doing the right thing. So I shut it out. But this Barriman disaster and that damn Badge Demarche were just too much for me to ignore—particularly since the Nawa Pass mess."

"I understand my friend, I understand. Just checking your temperature." Dalton walked toward the camp center.

Khamal sat on top of a broad hillside rising sixty feet above the surrounding terrain. Wedged twenty-five feet up in the crotch of a stately pine tree, he surveyed the staggered rows of pines just below his elevation. Scanning the lake shore four hundred yards away he discovered Dalton's campsite. The camouflaged canvas shield above his perch hid his heat signature as the drone passed nearby earlier in the day. The sun had slipped below the horizon, leaving the forest dark, and the temperature was dropping quickly. The sky was clear with a faint sliver of fading orange hue stretching across the western horizon. He kept Dalton Crusoe in his scope until the darkness filled in—exhilarated with the chance to complete his assassination assignment for the Iranians, and settle a score. He could not resist the temptation to light his thermal aiming laser dot on Dalton's camo green field cap. Yet his primary assignment, Ed Kosko, already paid for and approved by the Adrestia unit, must not be compromised by his second chance at Crusoe. A rifle blast, even suppressed, might be noticed, revealing his presence in the area and alerting others in Dalton's team to his location.

Two hours after sunset Khamal rested motionless in his tree stand. A cracking sound caused him to freeze and listen. He shut his eyes to better locate the sound direction...behind him, to the left, coming closer. Twenty-five feet below, three men, barely visible were moving in stealth, flanking fashion away from Dalton's team. He caressed the rifle trigger one last time, thinking...*they've lost Crusoe...I've waited a long time...it doesn't matter...at dawn Dalton Crusoe will meet his fate.*

◆ ◆ ◆

Dalton remained awake for much of the four hours leading to daybreak and thought about the telling evidence Ronet apparently had in hand. He also thought about the deteriorating political and economic climate in the US. Still officially employed at the NSA his powerful connection with Ed Kosko was essentially gone. The new Director Sanborn operated with a different, aloof, compliant style under President Barriman. Dalton was on loan to the Department of Energy, mostly relegated to a desk job overseeing the implementation paperwork of a new energy discovery. The current President chose to not push the new energy discovery, dubbed EFA, on to poorer nations and appeared to withdraw from America's leadership role advanced under the former President. Dalton was frustrated and wanted to get back into the action he enjoyed under Ed Kosko and President Jerome Conner. The current field operation was his first mission, of sorts, since he broke up the corrupt Swiss bankers at QSB Privee. His thoughts returned to the training exercise as the first rays of sunlight broke through the scattered clouds and graced the tops of the trees. The sunrise stirred his memory. He fondled his smart phone while thinking; opening up pictures of him and Carolyn in St Martin months earlier. He stared at the short sunset video he'd taken of Carolyn hours after their first day on the island. Looking radiant in an aqua beach coverup, as she brushed her windblown hair aside from her perfect face smiling she had mouthed... *I love you.* He felt she was withholding a hurting heart at not yet settling on their marriage plans, but still allowing him to work through the challenges arising from Declan's story. He vowed to resolve the death threat facing him and Ed and not disappoint her again.

Mason and Kilmer took four minutes after waking to arrive fully prepared for their scouting mission. "We have the advantage—

we know their location and they don't know we're here—maybe. Head north slowly around the lake until your position is between the intruders and the cabin. Then remain in cover, continue surveillance and report back. Do not engage unless forced to. We'll be listening in and watching the lake cabin—understood?" Dalton revealed his cautious yet pro-active leadership style. Ronet sipped a hot black coffee, listened respectfully and admired the intellect of his friend. The two Army soldiers checked their gear, weapons and their squad communications once again before heading off into the forest.

Mason and Kilmer moved north slowly in close formation keeping the lakeshore a few hundred yards to the east. The trek was confounded by dense hardwoods, patches of small evergreens and occasional clear grassy areas only to close up again as the men moved north.

Kilmer dropped to the ground. "I'm getting a faint heat signature ahead, two hundred yards, four figures." Dalton and Ronet listened and watched the dull computer images of the advance from shoulder-mounted infrared cameras on the two.

"They made contact much sooner than expected JD." Ronet focused in on the screen as the screen resolution adjusted. Ronet broke a smile.

Kilmer broke the silence, whispering, "Wolves. Four of them, moving west. Not our targets."

Mason announced, "Moving out north."

Dalton settled back into his backpack jammed comfortably against a pine tree trunk and sipped his coffee slowly. "I expect we'll hear something in the next thirty minutes, when they approach the targets." Ronet nodded agreement, as he prepared a thought.

"Have you heard the latest talk about Kosko?"

"Maybe, maybe not—what have you heard?" Dalton warmed his hands around the coffee mug.

"He's getting into politics—maybe the New Libertarian candidate against Barriman."

"Yeah I heard." Dalton's expression grew serious.

"Think he'll do it?"

"Ed hates the political world. He's a true statesman and diplomat though—knows every major leader, good and bad. I doubt he'll be their candidate. I haven't talked to him in a month." Dalton studied Ronet.

"What do you think he'll do if asked?" Ronet was holding back a thought. Dalton stared into his empty mug.

"Damn good question. I can see him reluctantly jumping in—for the good of the country. Barriman is destroying us from the inside, dividing people and weakening our world standing. Then there's this latest fiasco—the blown SnagLift operation."

"Ed could build a huge following with the file we discussed last night. You gonna join in if he accepts?" Ronet could not stop a revealing grin as he asked the question.

Dalton rolled his eyes and shook his head. "You know I'm *really* not the political type, no way."

"Bullshit. You and Ed are an effective team. You'd join in some capacity, buddy." Ronet continued to grin, pointing his finger and staring back at Dalton. "And don't tell me you aren't mad-as-hell about these wacko libs systematically destroying this country."

A smirk crept across Dalton's face. "You know me pretty well don't you Brad?"

"Hell yes!"

Dalton's anger came out, "Fact is I'm sick about where we are heading as a nation and I fear unless this Convention of States takes control, it's all over. If this file you've got shows the President and his top staff deliberately leaving a special ops unit to die when he could have saved them, it's frightening—maybe even criminal, particularly if the decisions were guided by political motives. The problem is Barriman is a crafty politician—skilled at speaking eloquently about a subject he neither believes in nor understands, and yet can convince an audience he has the right answers for them and the country. He may be able to escape any blame if the claims of wrongdoing are not completely supported by the video. And don't dismiss his primary 'pit bull' Demarche—this guy is smart and ruthless."

"I understand, JD, they are corrupt, but Kosko and you make a formidable opposition. So you will get involved—right? Take the file to Kosko; he'll go nuts with what's happened." Ronet leaned forward, cupping his hand around his left ear, pretending to strain for an answer.

"It's premature to involve Ed in this until, and if, he makes a decision to run. Regardless the best way to get this out is through the conservative media. You can be sure the major networks will not cover it, and the administration will launch a full blown cover up blaming the right. If Ed is involved in the release he'll be targeted directly and attacked as a partisan hack."

"So what are we going to do JD—you going to help expose this bastard? Kosko's gonna run."

Unable to argue against Ronet's case Dalton admitted, "Yeah, maybe you're right, damn it. I'd have to unofficially join if asked." Dalton looked directly at Ronet and nodded yes. "I know a guy who could handle this and keep Ed out of it—though you might be exposed as the source."

Ronet stared at Dalton and said, "Do I look like I care about that?" A silence followed which allowed the subject to rest. They both turned their attention back to Patterson who remained fixated on his computer screen.

Patterson monitored the movement and route of Mason and Kilmer for twenty-three minutes when a communication came in. It was Kilmer. "They're gone. We can't detect them anywhere near their location last night. No tracks, camp site indicators, nothing."

Ronet heard the call and motioned to Dalton, who spoke, "Hold for one Kilmer."

"They could have continued to the cabin after we withdrew the drone coverage. I'll check the cabin for activity." Ronet shuffled about, lying on the ground, to gain a clear view of the small cabin. "Nothing to see here. No smoke, lights, movement or personnel. Might be empty."

Dalton took the microphone, stating, "Kilmer, hold your position. Settle in and we'll join you in thirty. Then we'll approach the cabin as a team."

"Roger that, Out." Seconds later a loud blast, then another, came ripping through the woods, screams followed. "It's Kilmer. We've been hit by a trip wire land mine, Mason down, badly injured. I'm hit but Ok. Need medical help now." The forest shuddered with the concussion wave that knocked both men to the ground. The shrapnel cloud ripped through the leaves and tree trunks at lightning speed and left Kilmer groggy. "It's Kilmer. We've been hit by a trip wire land mine, Mason down, badly injured. I'm hit but okay. Need medical help now."

Dalton and his remaining team jumped to their feet after the twin blasts, weapons drawn and scanning the area—nothing coming in. Patterson responded, "Stay down, radio open, we are coming." He began to close his computer link as the remainder of Dalton's team was updated on the plan of approach. Dalton signaled his team to move out slowly. Forty-five seconds later, Dalton's seven-man team moved out led by Ronet to find Mason and Kilmer.

Ronet held back, Dalton noticed. "Here we may need these." Ronet flipped one of two .223-calibre full clips at Dalton. "This training mission just went live." Dalton caught the clip, and slapped it into his Barrett REC7 rifle.

None of the Team B members were in the area. Ronet radioed in to the Operation Commander, who ordered a halt to the training exercise until an investigation could reveal what had happened. Once on the blast scene, Patterson triaged Kilmer for a ripped left calf muscle. Ronet found Mason, twenty feet away, dead from a frontal blast ripping out his neck and chest.

Dalton halted the team's movement, ordering, "Form a perimeter and stay low—report any movement or sound." Ronet pointed to a nearby position and slowly moved out, rifle at shoulder level scanning the woods. Dalton nodded.

Seconds later, Ronet whispered to Dalton, "This damn setup was meant to take out our whole nine-man unit. Look at this JD, two directional mines and a bounding mine between them—each one set off by the same trip wire rigging."

Dalton studied the sophistication of the mines' arrangement, and its positioning at the only logical spot for his team to advance. It was *meant* to kill the entire team. He scanned the perimeter slowly though his rifle scope. He pondered the questions of *why, how and who*.

Khamal heard the explosion. Then he scanned the terrain from a mile away looking for a glimpse of Dalton's unit as it moved silently over the shallow ridges and draws covered in a mixture of pine, aspen and dense low brush. A small debris cloud lifted above the treeline; exactly where Khamal had set the trip wire land mines hoping to kill Dalton Crusoe and his team in their morning advance. Khamal was skilled at complex assassinations, where he could obscure the actual target, by taking out many more than the specific objective. In Khamal's view "collateral damage" was a useful method to disguise his primary goal. After two minutes scanning the blast area, Khamal saw no movement, no sounds.

Ronet examined the scene and said, "JD, this was set as a trap. The trip wire covered the only logical spot for our advance today on the cabin. The device was large and meant to kill as many of us as possible. Who are they after and why?"

Dalton spoke in a whisper, "Brad, is that another trip wire?" He then pointed to a thin clear line stretched from near Ronet's feet to the north. It was a single clear thread, twenty feet long, hidden less than a foot above the ground and just beneath the short ferns growing everywhere around the lake. The early sun managed to sporadically penetrate the tree cover and the ferns to reflect its presence.

"Yes, a second mine was set just beyond the first setup JD. This was meant for serious killing." Ronet looked back at Dalton in bewilderment. His team still stood at point holding the tight perimeter. "I'll disable this damn thing before we stumble into another trip line connected to it."

Dalton pondered the situation just as he received a text message on his private satellite phone: *Dalton, we need to meet asap. It's about the NLP slot. I need your advice on my decision...and a death threat! Ed.* The unexpected text from Ed Kosko crystallized several thoughts Dalton was mulling over. He took a moment, studied the text again and closed his phone.

Dalton looked over to Ronet and said, "Wait. I have an idea who may have done this. Maybe."

"Oh yeah—who?" growled Ronet.

"Not *exactly* sure yet, but dust the sides of the directional mine for prints. Be careful not to detonate it. Watch where you step." Dalton felt compelled to warn even a skilled soldier like Ronet. The rest of the team stood in a tight motionless formation waiting for Dalton's next order.

"I'll try to remember that." Ronet quietly nodded his agreement and found two partial prints, a thumb and finger.

"I've got two close up high-res images stored—maybe we'll find a match. You think you know who this might be?"

"Maybe, but it's a long shot. Yet if I'm right I think I must die to find out." Dalton could see Ronet's mind working too.

"Let's move out of here—by the way, looks like Ed's seriously thinking of running." Dalton signaled the team to quietly move out. Kilmer was assisted by Patterson; Mason's body was carried by Ronet on his back.

Khamal continued to watch the debris cloud disperse, when a final third blast rumbled through the forest. The fresh blast, a directional glass fragmentation mine, triggered by a hidden second trip wire had detonated. He tucked his binoculars away; smug in the belief his death trap was successful.

Khamal felt a sense of accomplishment believing his twin detonation arrangement had worked as planned and killed Dalton Crusoe and his team. He withdrew to locate a canoe, hidden in low brush two miles away on the border of a long chain of small inland lakes. By early afternoon Khamal had paddled to where he left his SUV, near a rural road cutting through the wilderness. Next on his agenda was a trip to Dallas Texas and the contract on Ed Kosko.

CHAPTER FIVE

Early Evening, West Virginia, Four months before the Presidential Election

The sun had set twenty minutes earlier creating a brilliant fiery orange sky on the western horizon. The four car limousine entourage left the rally site in West Virginia hill country and was making its way back to the turnpike. The short countryside tour and twenty minute speech at a local high school football stadium drew six thousand blue state democrats, concerned about their country. Governor Willy Boone was a vocal and flamboyant supporter of the President and knew how to bring out the big liberal donors. The visit and speech were a payback and photo-op for filling a vacant senate seat with a liberal, hand-picked replacement Barriman wanted and needed to pass his agenda. Every few hundred yards a state trooper vehicle was stopped, flashers on, armed officers beckoning to the limos. President Barriman sat comfortably in the back seat of the second, Presidential limousine, loosened his tie and studied the sunset reflection on the smoked glass partition before him. "How do you think the crowd responded to me today, Badge?"

"They loved seeing you. It didn't matter that you spoke mostly in platitudes and slogans. Your timing and delivery was fine, as usual. Right now they want to know you're focused on keeping the economy from collapsing. I think you were strong, convincing." Brandon (Badge) Demarche, the President's articulate, senior economic advisor, Chief of Staff, and *de facto* personal medical supervisor and friend looked directly into the President's face—as though he were performing an evaluation.

"Well, I hope so. This Chinese deal is going to stir up the right into frenzy—without the left's support it might not prevail. I'm really getting worried about the NLP. Originally they were a small nuisance, without much influence, but now with the old Republican organization in shambles, they are filling a void on the right. We need to slow them down, before the Chinese start making their own demands to us to stop them." The President cocked his head and met Badge's eyes.

"We close the China deal in ten days. Once that financing is in place you can announce the start of your stimulus plan. More manna for the masses, right?" Badge tried to lighten the President's mood.

The President began again, "Have you heard any blowback on the botched Asadabad operation?"

"No blowback, but it's only been sixteen days, still I've got a handle on that issue as well." The men gazed at each other for a moment silently acknowledging the economic and political challenges that lay ahead. Badge had seen the symptoms before...mild anxiety, loss of confidence and focus. The President sighed and rubbed his forehead.

"I think you may need a boost—a little extra to keep your focus and energy up." The President nodded passively at the suggestion. Badge reached for his briefcase. He withdrew a small leather case, which opened like a zippered eye glass case except smaller. The President sighed again, rolled up his right sleeve and extended his arm towards Badge. After disinfecting a spot just below the elbow, the small needle penetrated the President's forearm into a large vein. Badge injected about 2cc's of the clear liquid, before stowing the needle in its case. "We'll talk privately more tomorrow, privately, at out luncheon meeting," Badge stated with a hint of a smile. He could sense the President's mind was drifting toward indecision—a condition he and other powerful forces could not allow.

A moment later the front security limo flashed its taillights as it slowed to turn and cross a two lane bridge. Agent Simmons driving the President's limo began to turn just as it sped up and crashed into a short guard rail post on the bridge. Simmons fought but failed to right the car. The torn metal rail slashed the right front tire which blew out followed immediately by the right rear tire. The car vaulted hard, blasting through the guard rail and sliding off the bridge into river water thirty-five feet below. The limo went over and straight down, the engine racing, Simmons still trying to turn the steering wheel to no avail. The car sank slowly in fifteen feet of water, first filling the driver's compartment and trapping the driver and a Secret Service guard. The headlights, still on, created just enough light to track the limo's movement in the river. Badge and the President lay dazed and bruised, semi-conscious as the water rose higher in the passenger section. Eight Secret Service agents ran from their cars and drew their weapons creating a protective shield around the bridge. Press vans following the motorcade remained back, and tried to get footage, video, and comments on the events uploaded as the security perimeter formed. The nearly submerged Presidential limo moved slowly downstream as the front bumper dragged along the river bottom. Three agents ran down the hillside and jumped into the water to rescue the President. Agent Eric Walters was able to escape through the front seat passenger window, clinging onto the rear door handle on the passenger side. "I can't get the door to open. POTUS looks to be unconscious—water is rising." The limo began to spin slowly allowing the water flow to ease pressure on the rear door. Walters was losing his grip and fighting the current.

Jenson arrived alongside Walters and together the men were able to unlock and open the door. The President remained motionless, bleeding from the forehead. Demarche appeared to be unconscious. Walters looked at both men and made a tough decision—*who should he save.* As he reached for the President he said, "I've got POTUS, he's not moving. Demarche is nearly under water—hurry."

"I'll get Badge—just pull POTUS from the car." Al Jenson swam in just as Walters removed the President from the car seat and pulled him to the shore. Badge coughed and sputtered, trying to get a breath. "I've got you sir, just let me pull you back to shore, relax." Jenson managed to drag Badge near the shore where both men sat surrounded by agents.

"Where's the President!" yelled Badge. He then saw the President with several agents as they ushered him close to the third limo. Badge looked over to see Walters staring back at him while assisting the President. Another senior agent noticed the odd interaction between Badge and agent Walters. When both men were in the limo it roared off with Secret Service, helicopter, and state police escorts.

Jeffery Crandel, Press Secretary, was at home when he looked at the caller name on his private cell phone—it read Alan Jenson, lead Secret Service agent for the Presidential detail.

"Yes Al, what's going on? The Virginia Governor had a report of an accident on the route back to DC. Is that right? News coverage is confusing."

"Right. Yes, there was an accident, or so it seems. Had two odd tire blow outs on the POTUS limo, after it crashed into a bridge guard rail, after which it broke through, and fell into the water. An FBI team just arrived to work the crash scene, talked to all of us and is retrieving the car for examination."

"Is the President all right? Any injuries?"

"The President is stunned but alright. He has a gash on his forehead just below the hairline. He was close to drowning as agent Walters grabbed him. Badge Demarche also shaken up but he's Ok and tending to the President."

"Any sign this was an attack?"

"Not clear, but agents are on high alert—POTUS and Badge were being moved to another limo and a military helicopter is flying in from Andrews as escort. We did lose one man—the driver of the Presidential limo agent Simmons. Gotta go now."

"Understood. Update needed. Report back." The phone call ended and Crandel checked his watch...10:10 pm. EDT.

♦ ♦ ♦

The senior Secret Service agent had holstered his weapon as the third limo prepared to leave with the President and Badge. He scanned the perimeter looking for anything suspicious, then turned aside from the scene and retrieved his private, secure cell phone, opened the "contacts" menu and found "Flask". He entered a text message: *Re-routing accomplished. Two casualties. No joy.* After ending the call he tried to understand the odd visual interaction between Badge Demarche and agent Eric Walters. No explanation was forthcoming.

The President and Badge arrived on the bridge, wrapped in blankets, surrounded by Secret Service and looked back at the floundering limo in the river. They'd been able to walk under their own power to the third limo preparing to drive off. Agents in cars in front and behind the President's limo kept a tight formation as the vehicles moved out—lights flashing. Two state police vehicles also joined the caravan. The President tried to relax as the motorcycles and limousines moved out in a tight formation toward the interstate.

"Hell of a way to end a nice day, don't you think Badge?"

"At least we didn't drown. I was worried and kinda foggy as they pulled me out. Did you know Agent Simmons died— actually drowned, couldn't get out?"

"Damn, that's horrible. Did you see Simmons fighting with the steering wheel as we sped into the bridge rail?"

"Yes, that's right. I did notice him struggling just as we went off the bridge."

"Get Al Jensen on this immediately, and the FBI. We need to know if this double blowout was a freak accident or a planned attack on me. Until we are certain, this was an accidental event for purposes of any press coverage." Badge nodded his head in understanding and approval.

"Mr. President, I don't believe this was an accident—no way. Still the press will be forced to portray you as a *survivor*."

"Are you convinced of that—with all that's going on?" The President gave a glance of disbelief at Badge.

"Yes Mr. President, I will personally see that this event, whether it's an accident or an attack it will build your image. I've got that covered. We'll put the focus on the loss of Agent

Simmons." Badge Demarche did not like surprises and the incident at the bridge was a *real* surprise, requiring feeding the press a coverup story and finding a saboteur he felt certain had penetrated the administration.

◆ ◆ ◆

As a young prodigy medical researcher and psychiatrist, Brandon Demarche, had developed numerous patents involving medical treatments for dementia, epilepsy, and schizophrenia. Advanced trials quickly followed with strong interest among from big US pharmaceutical manufacturers, yet the results left patients in vegetative states—and research was abruptly defunded. Demarche was disgraced and ignored as a medical researcher. Agitated and angry, but a skilled speaker, he ran for elective office winning a vacant Democratic senatorial seat from Virginia while espousing populist views and an expansion of the socialist state. After one term, and with political credibility, he was named Ambassador to China, a role which allowed him access to Chinese drug manufacturers, amidst an endless supply of patients for live testing. The special relationship between Brandon Demarche and the Chinese leadership had started to develop eleven years earlier. Tan Zhang had studied in the US at American University for a year while in a foreign exchange education program. Badge and Tan were near the same age and became friends, which eventually led to the Chinese leadership providing support for Badge's research. After his original research failed, it was quietly taken over by the chemical industry in China and new discoveries were revealed. The technology was improved, expanded and provided surprising results.

Not only had Demarche's original theories been verified through the applied research, which greatly advanced the treatment for dementia, epilepsy, and schizophrenia, they also found the regimen of drugs improved cognitive powers and made for very compliant subjects. The Chinese saw an opportunity to use the discovery for political purposes and never approved the treatments as a prescription drug. The big Chinese pharma and the national leadership began a program to quietly introduce the drugs into Chinese society. They created custom cocktails as food additives for the military, then college-age youth, and mid-level party members. The results were impressive: fewer conflicts, less insubordination, and better productivity. The royalties, which accrued in China, specifically Hong Kong, made Demarche a wealthy man, yet unfulfilled. He desired to be in charge and in control. The realization of his goal came after he entered politics, was elected and gained national exposure all with Chinese funding and political operatives assisting him. The Chinese accommodated most of Demarche's financial needs to insure election success destroy the opposition and muzzle the press. With Badge Demarche now *managing* the President's policies, the Chinese were able to leverage their massive financial support for America to gain access to rich mineral and oil lands, influence international policy and move the country toward a Chinese model.

Now as Chief of Staff, consultant/advisor and close confidant to the President on major policy issues, Badge used his access to prepare the President on economic and political decisions. Demarche's privately organized Chinese pharma group eventually perfected an modestly addictive cocktail that normalized behavior and improved communication skills yet left the patient highly susceptible to programmed thinking under light hypnosis. Secure in the DC political arena he seduced many liberals to his agenda and was maintaining partial personality control over the President. Big Chinese pharma developed their relationship with Demarche introducing him to the highest

Chinese government officials. The sinister triad, funded and manipulated by the Chinese secretly financed US elections, infiltrated the press, discredited opponents, and promoted Demarche's broad agenda so long as their interests were furthered. The Chinese patiently waited over eight years for a weak, socialist driven President like Harold Barriman to emerge while assisting Demarche in clearing the path for him to ascend to the highest office in the land—with Brandon (Badge) Demarche at his side. Now the Chinese were about to claim their reward: America as a client state.

◆ ◆ ◆

Oval Office, the Morning following the Crash

The wall clock outside the Oval Office was poised at exactly 10:10 a.m., forming a perfect "V" to the eye. The only word that kept repeating in Badge's mind as he stared at the dial was *vulnerable...*suggesting that the opposition to the President's agenda was strong and growing militant. The next moment found the young assistant press secretary trying to get Badge's attention. "Mr. Demarche, sir...the President is waiting for you."

"Of course, thank you. Sorry for my day dreaming." Badge smiled to cover his concerns and entered the Oval Office, shutting the door behind him.

"Good morning Mr. President, how are you feeling?" Badge shook hands and sat down on one of the opposing couches beyond the desk. It was the typical setting the men used to conduct the discussion and semi-hypnotic sessions that Brandon Demarche, MD and PhD, orchestrated a couple of times a month.

"I feel tired and sore all over, but nothing broken—just bruised I'm told. I spoke with Simmons' wife—it was tough, two young kids. How about you?"

"Right. I feel the same—aching but moving." Badge could sense the President was struggling to stay focused. Have the FBI determined anything about the accident?"

"I met with them earlier this morning. They cannot accept the locked up steering and dual tire blowouts as coincidence. Yet they have ruled out gunshots, or a road device to destroy the tires. They feel it was a real assassination attempt yet, maybe...I guess we should not call it that without evidence. Jenson confirmed Simmons was a fine young agent with no hint he deliberately drove off the bridge. Until further evidence appears they suggest we inform the press it was an accident caused by unforeseen road conditions. Jeff Crandel has his talking points." The facial expression on the President confirmed he had slipped from his focused level a day earlier before the West Virginia rally.

"Mr. President I sense you are having trouble concentrating...would you agree?"

"Yes, I just feel confused and a bit dizzy." Badge recognized the symptoms: loss of focus, inability to organize thoughts, poor eye contact during conversation, and clear indecision.

"Let's get you back at the top of your game. The accident may have shaken you up more than I realized. Can we get into this issue now? Is that all right with you Harold?"

"Yeah, I guess that would be best. I want to understand what this all means."

Badge began by asking the President to close his eyes and listen only to his voice. The skilled psychiatrist spoke in soft, calming tones, freeing the President of all thoughts except his voice. Badge used powerful word signals and triggers to relax and make the patient receptive to strong declarations about the decisions and agenda Badge and his associates needed to become reality. Badge repeated several common phrases: *"you are the President and know the right course for the country; you can rely on me to give you the best advice; I will always have the answers you need; the plans we've developed for rescuing the country are good; we can and must complete the aid package with China; you can be assured your actions will be well received by Americans."*

The sessions which represented mild, brief psychotherapy, never lasted more than twenty minutes, sometimes ending in a fresh injection to boost the suggestive powers of the mild hypnosis. Badge so loved the effectiveness of the drug he occasionally injected himself with a low dose—it seemed to make him more convincing to the President and himself. He knew from the Chinese research that certain individuals were more susceptible to the drug's effects. Knowing a full personality profile of the patient allowed a custom formulation to achieve optimal results. Harold Barriman had been fully evaluated by Badge and the drug results were consistent and predictable: his mind sharpened, focus increased, and his ability to speak with conviction on matters improved, particularly those issues where Badge Demarche framed the arguments. It was as though Badge controlled a *"live puppet"*.

The President typically awoke rested, alert and affable. Badge transitioned the President out of the light sleep and moments later asked the President when he was ready to continue the "road campaign" to promote the party's agenda. The

President had a fresh attitude, an *"in-charge"* demeanor and a confident look.

"Next week we'll be out at four stops in two days, right? Isn't that enough to satisfy your *associates*?" A slight tone of irritation hung in the President's voice. Badge immediately recognized the slight deviation from the President's usual mood after a psychotherapy session. The messaging was clear—*I am the President, you work for me.* "I'll meet you tomorrow for lunch—we'll discuss how to deal with this NLP group promoting the Convention of States and I'll update you on the Chinese meeting in a few days."

Badge was taken aback at the abrupt dismissal by Barriman. "Very well Mr. President—until tomorrow at noon." He feared the increasing irritation foreshadowed him losing power over the President—and that would not be tolerated by powerful international forces.

◆ ◆ ◆

Three days Later, Lake Geneva Switzerland, Lausanne Palace and Spa

Badge Demarche read his meeting notes for a third time minutes ahead of when he and President Barriman were to meet with their Chinese counterparts for a signing of the China American Solvency Pact ("CASP"). He felt very uneasy—an unusual emotion for the crafty, intelligent, political operative. The Chinese President, Lei Zhang, representing the National People's Congress in the second year of a five year term, was a well educated multi-lingual man of small stature, and an easy smile. He'd arrived thirty minutes earlier and was surrounded by his advisors and negotiating team in the Chinese wing. Weeks earlier his staff had met with the Barriman team to rough out the "deal points" of a financial aid plan for the USA. It was a tedious negotiation as the Chinese knew the US must capitulate on many positions to keep the talks alive. The final document was tough; a serious blow to America's power and prestige.

The top floor of the prestigious Lausanne Palace and Spa was exclusively reserved for a month as diplomats and negotiators worked in secret to structure a deal. Badge Demarche led the American team and injected himself directly into the details as the proposal took shape. Having spent the last two days preparing the final documents totaling only sixty-two pages, Badge was exhausted and awaited the arrival of President Barriman for the signing. A vibration in his vest pocket alerted Badge that the President had arrived at the hotel. He muted the BBC Network on the large LED flat screen he'd been watching earlier on the BBC network and then touched his smart phone to accept the call.

"Where is he?"

"He's coming up elevator II now—and needs to meet with you immediately." The lead Secret Service agent was abrupt.

"I'll be in the west side antechamber to the Ambassador Conference Room." Badge sat down in a soft chair and organized his thoughts...*brief the President, check his focus level, confirm the parties are prepared to sign the "CASP", sign, and get back to DC.* Moments later the door swung open and the President walked in. "Badge are we ready? Any last minute problems?"

"A few, yes." Badge excused the entourage of agents and staff from the room. The President sat quietly, unbuttoned his suit jacket and said, "Let's hear it."

"The Chinese want to issue a "recovery currency," a twenty-five dollar bill—guaranteed directly by...the Chinese government."

"Why? Our currency isn't good enough?" The President showed the start of rage.

"It's more a statement of fiscal superiority, I think. Their money will be more secure than ours, and therefore more desirable to own." Badge paused to let the message sink in.

"Damnit. Are they firm on this?" Barriman rose and began to wander the room, his frustration growing.

"Absolutely. They informed my team of this last demand early this morning. Non-negotiable is how they presented it." Badge reached for his attaché. He withdrew a colored photo of a $25 bill, handing it to the President. "This is what they are proposing—the image of Chinese Party President Lei Zhang must be on the note."

"Oh this will never fly even with our solid progressive Congress. We can't do this." The President tossed the photo image on the small table separating the four chairs set for conversation. Taking a hard turn against Badge, the President snapped a look at his Chief of Staff and said, "I thought all your deep connections with the Chinese while they were perfecting your drugs would have provided a less punishing agreement. What happened?"

"They are opportunists. Just as they saw the advantages of carrying through on my research protocols, the also see the advantage of loaning the US trillions when our risk of default kept increasing. Now they are extracting their rewards—at our ultimate expense." The President remained fixated on Badge's words. "We have no choice Harold. Zhang will walk and refuse to buy anymore of our debt." Badge could see the President losing focus and reacting with anger rather than logic. "If that happens rates will soar, the economy might collapse and we could be faced with de-valuing our currency making the problem even worse—we have to take this deal."

"Do you think this Chinese deal will lead to my impeachment? The international disgrace alone will be devastating." The President had clearly lost focus and shifted from the nation's dilemma to his political survival. Badge paused and calmly said, "I don't know sir—but I'll manage it."

"How exactly can you do that?" A note of cynicism hung in Barriman's words.

"You know what I'm talking about. The folks we *don't* talk about, but use when needed—the Adrestia Unit." Badge instinctively looked about the empty room for any forgotten visitors.

"Really—I know they are good and made the elimination of Renkin and Garrison look like a mechanical failure rather than a disturbed solder gone terrorist, but how can they stop millions from organizing a Convention of States?"

"I'm already working on it. I can control this issue, trust me."

"Actually maybe I trust you too much. I need a *boost* before the signing session." Badge sensed the irritation and distracted tone in Barriman's voice, the second time in just days. The thought returned that he might be slowly losing control over the President's behavior. The President rolled up his left sleeve and received a shot from Badge; his first in three days. The two men then settled down to reviewing the final draft of the historic agreement, taking the full twenty minutes before they met the Chinese delegation. Twenty minutes later, the President completed his review of the draft agreement, checked his watch, and said, "Well, this is as bad as it gets, but you're right Badge, we have no choice. Next month I guess we all start learning to speak Chinese. I'll head to the signing platform."

"At least we've staggered transferring the title to development and mineral rights on western lands until thirty days after this signing when half the financing funds are provided." Badge tried to soften the stark reality of America's plight, which in reality he welcomed to ease the gradual movement to Chinese control.

Badge directed several staffers to accompany the President and then withdrew his encrypted cell phone, scrolled for a name, Tan Zhang, the younger brother of the Chinese President, and pressed call. "He's ready to sign. He should be arriving for the signing ceremony in a minute."

"Excellent. The press is ready also...right?" A pause came. "We should talk next week about the NLP."

"My staff will release a propaganda press release extolling the great benefits to both our countries through this agreement. Yes, agreed, we'll talk next week."

Badge and two staffers left to join the President and the remaining twelve members of the US negotiating team already assembled in the Ambassador Conference Room. The press was severely limited and given access only to the actual signing, and no questions were allowed. Officially on vacation for five days while between assignments for Adrestia, Declan decided to gather more data, if possible, on the Barriman administrations plans for the country. Once he escaped from Adrestia and went dark his ability to help Dalton stop Barriman's agenda would be limited—and dangerous. Lingering in the lobby floor hallways Declan Crusoe pretended to be a political reporter talking to his office. In fact he was reviewing the video he had remotely downloaded of the President and Badge in the antechamber discussing the Chinese aid package. Declan used a "heads-down-type-sometime-asset" of the Adrestia Unit, skilled in hi-tech communications, a drug abuser easily compromised for fast cash, to reconfigure the camera/audio on the 46" LED TV screen to transmit to Declan's encrypted email. The minute device was mounted into a USB port behind the TV screen, which was still muted and set to BBC News. The clandestine video confirmed that Badge was Lars Nevins' DC contact in the administration. Declan's earlier instincts were correct and caused him to think...*it's time to disappear...connect with Dalton....expose Barriman...before Adrestia discovers my intentions.*

CHAPTER SIX

Four Days Later at Jameson Dalton Crusoe's Funeral

THE crowd was building to around a hundred people in the small North Carolina rural cemetery—next to where Dalton's father lay. The limousine had arrived with a handful of former and current NSA workers assisting in the casket's transport to the burial site. Local friends of Elizabeth Crusoe, many of whom had met Dalton, mingled in the gathering. The mood was very somber. The funeral parlor staff gently carried Dalton Crusoe's casket to the burial site where a small open-sided tent covered the grave and seating for Carolyn, Elizabeth Crusoe and the Kosko family.

Only a select few knew the real plan. Carolyn McCabe resisted any involvement in the ceremony until the last minute. It was crucial that she be present and convince the crowd her emotions were real. The turning point came when Dalton, Kosko and Ronet decided not to inform Elizabeth Crusoe of her son's faked death—Carolyn had the task of comforting her throughout the proceedings. Dalton finally convinced Carolyn to undertake the ruse, which she despised, for the sake of *"making it real"*. Ronet also persuaded a trusted, retired Navy Chaplin to assist in the deception. The reaction of Dalton's fiancée, Carolyn, was crucial, as was that of Elizabeth Crusoe, in order to convince the killer that the man in the closed casket was truly one Dalton Crusoe. Kosko and Dalton felt the charade, might entice the killer out to view the funeral—a final validation of his success. Disguised video cameras were placed to cover the entire site for later facial recognition efforts.

Dalton felt the death trap set for him and his men along with the death threat against Ed Kosko, were just too coincidental. The nearly simultaneous events were likely related. Ed Kosko would deliver some brief, flattering remarks about Dalton and his life being cut short by a madman. Dalton sat in a van parked nearby recording and evaluating all the faces as the crowd arrived.

"How does it feel knowing you're just fifteen minutes from your own funeral and burial?" Ed Kosko reached for his black suit coat as he waited for Dalton's response.

"I feel quite alive for a dead guy. I may wish I were dead when I tell my mother why we did this." Dalton shrugged as he studied the camera monitors.

"Yeah Carolyn may never forgive you for this trick. I know Irene will have a few questions too, after we drop you in the ground."

"I know Ed, I know. I flew out from Canada shortly after your call came. Ronet and I worked on this funeral ruse. At least I met with Carolyn in person to explain my 'death'."

"I hope it works to uncover your killer. You still feel it's connected to the threat against me?" Kosko had suspicions the two incidents were truly related.

"But our twin threats have to be related—tied to your political future and the fact our friendship and careers are overlapped. I just hope my hunches produce a face or finger prints we can act on. Ronet is armed and connected to me through his Comsat gear; he will be your close security if this killer gets bold enough to try another killing. Don't worry."

"Ok. I'm not worried, just off to say a few kind words about my deceased friend. Let me know what you think—you know, for the real day and time." Ed tried to keep the mood light even though the visitors were largely solemn. Finding the one face without a genuinely solemn look was the task at hand.

Carolyn McCabe looked tired and somber. The effect was exactly as Dalton and Ronet had hoped for: she was gorgeous and devastated at the same time. Elizabeth Crusoe was the strong one between the two women walking arm-in-arm to the burial site. Ironically Elizabeth Crusoe had taken the news of Dalton's death with enormous grace, showing the expected pain only a mother could know, quietly mourning with tears yet pulling herself together for the benefit of Carolyn. Watching the two of them approach the growing crowd, Dalton grimaced and said, "Damn I hate doing this to Carolyn and my mom. I hope all this drama is worth it."

As Ronet checked his Glock 9 and prepared to follow Ed, he shot a look back at Dalton as they followed the multiple recording videos staged to cover the entire site. "Look JD, this guy, or group, had to have intelligence from deep in the NSA or the Navy to pin point your whereabouts. The wilderness in Canada was ideal for the lethal overkill he set in place—and it could easily have taken us all out. That tells me he, or they, have an emotional *need* to make certain we are dead."

"I understand, this killer is smart and determined—I sense he cannot accept failure. My guess is he's a professional under contract, right? If he appears here, at *my* funeral, it could be his need to confirm a success—or it could mean he is here to target Ed. Either way we have to take precautions."

"Yes, and that is why we have to carry on this charade as proof you, or we, are gone. What better proof than seeing your fiancée and mother grieving?"

"I know you are right. It's just painful seeing all this grief over my death while I'm here watching it all looking for a clue as to who killed me. What a crazy twist." Dalton sighed, and continued, "Regardless, of what happens today I have some serious comforting to provide Carolyn and particularly my mother. Damn I'm glad she's so strong."

"Right. Your ladies will understand in the end. I gotta go Ed's about to speak over your casket."

Khamal could not resist the lure of visiting the Dalton Crusoe funeral to verify his contract with the Iranians was finally complete. The formal looking announcement and agenda for the day's proceedings was nice but seeing Dalton's "women" in mourning was powerful evidence. The disguise was clever and extraordinary: a dated, full dress navy uniform styled to fit loosely over an artificially aged body pretending to be a retired Vietnam veteran. Khamal's facial effects revealed a weathered skin, with dull eyes, narrow lips and stained teeth. The antique cane, aiding a faux arthritic hip, added to the desired effect—an older, fellow naval officer paying his respects. Khamal sat in a back row of folding chairs, outside the large white canopy tent protecting the grave and speaker's platform from the sun and any potential rough weather. After Elizabeth Crusoe and Carolyn walked up and touched the closed casket one final time, Elizabeth broke down in an uncontrollable release of tears and cries. Ed Kosko, along with Irene, came to assist Elizabeth take a seat and regain her composure. Carolyn also broke down, not for the bogus funeral but for the pain and loss she knew her future mother-in-law was undergoing. The tears were real. Dalton choked up watching the last TV images of the two most significant women in his life bear the *reality* of his death. As the crowd began to break apart, Khamal drifted toward the casket and stared at it. As he turned to walk away, he met Carolyn's tearful eyes. He held her glance for an awkward time and then nodded, lowering his head as he slowly walked away. Carolyn initially sensed nothing but as Khamal disappeared into the dispersing crowd she felt a strange uneasiness—dismissing it as part of the stress of the day.

The only local TV news coverage dispatched a reporter and camera man to capture thirty seconds of film and commentary on the theme of a "local fallen hero's" death. Dalton was watching the live television feed as it came across the early afternoon news. The young female reporter panned across the crowd just after Ed Kosko finished a few minutes of praise and admiration for Dalton. That was followed by a distant shot of Carolyn and Elizabeth Crusoe holding hands, seated just before the open burial spot in front of the closed casket. The coverage played while a photo of Dalton, taken at his graduation from Annapolis, was notched into the screen during a brief rundown of Dalton's short, yet impressive, career. Dalton felt an uncomfortable tension as the TV coverage scanned the crowd full of NSA workers, college friends, local leaders, Carolyn and his mother, and several military veterans. A haunting sense of danger left him perplexed.

◆ ◆ ◆

Cove Production Studios Outside Washington DC

THE lead cameraman raised his right hand revealing three, then two, then one finger to alert the host, Wren Cove that the final minute of the *Cove Connection* was about to continue following the commercial break. The hour long show lured thirty-seven million viewers each day, a record for a political opinion show— one sharply tilted to the right. Nevertheless, the host invited liberal and conservative guests to share their thoughts on the topics of the day; namely the growing angry opposition to President Barriman's progressive liberal agenda which many felt was unconstitutional and leading the country into a steep decline. Wren thanked his guests and then took the camera alone, looking directly at it, and spoke to America.

"My friends, I have obtained video and verbal documentation which proves, I believe, serious crimes by our highest leaders against our nation. I intend to release this damning information for the nation to examine and judge the actions of the Barriman administration. When America views the material I believe its citizens will fear for the fate of our nation, and consider whether we shall maintain our nation or give it over to extremists. Our President Harold Barriman, and his close advisors, appear to have committed high crimes against the Constitution which may subject him to impeachment. As we all know the Congress, and most particularly the Senate, has been unwilling to make this case against our President. Yet I believe that once the information I have is verified, the Senate will have no choice but to act. Stay tuned for my three day special series beginning Wednesday next week which will reveal these discoveries. God bless you and thank you for following the *Cove Connection*. Have a great Labor Day."

Wren left his camera studio and headed back to his small office with his production manager, Max, trailing in hot pursuit. "Wren, what do you have? I hope you're right or we are done.

Governor Tippen stayed around after his roundtable talk and blew a gasket. He's pissed and intends to make our lives miserable."

Wren woke his computer and entered a few key strokes—whereupon a video began to play.

"Right. Tippen's the new head of the DNC, and a huge supporter of the President—he'll make some noise." Wren took off his sports coat, tossed it onto his office couch, and flopped down in his desk chair, glancing between his computer and Max.

"When were you going to let me in on this? If you start this series next Wednesday I've got lots of work to do." Max gave Wren a stare and strained at the video playing on the computer monitor. Wren clicked the ESC button and the images disappeared.

"I'm meeting a contact in an hour with some final details—when he leaves I'll meet you for a drink at the Peninsular Club, say about 730 p.m. Today was just a tease. You won't believe what I've got."

"Is this one of your secret sources that always gets the scoop on Barriman?"

Max didn't expect an answer, but Wren responded, "No this is actually a source I've met only once. Yet the material is unquestionably real."

"How do you know it's *unquestionably real?*"

"The material, at least a brief snippet of it, shows the President admitting to serious wrongdoing—impeachable stuff. This edition is protected by a program prohibiting copies and scraps the entire file soon without a password" A second reflection on Max's question caused Wren pause. "I'm supposed to get access to the full recording tonight."

"You'd better, because unless you can support these claims, we're toast. I just wish you'd warned me this was coming."

Dismissing his concerns, Wren grinned at Max, "Hey! We knew what he was; now we can expose him." Max nodded and waved as he walked away. "I hope you're right, because if you're wrong, we'll never broadcast gain. You can close up---see you later."

◆ ◆ ◆

Seventy Minutes following the Cove Connection Program

Wren Cove sat at his computer and viewed the compelling seven minute teaser of the full twenty-two minute video. A muted TV had four split screen views all following the main news networks. His remarks had soon spread all over the world. He thought about the next steps to editing and developing the narrative to present the material. He switched screens and checked social media for comments. Twitter was receiving 1500 tweets a minute, and Facebook showed thousands of "likes" and new followers for his Cove Connection site.

Outside in the cool evening air Declan Crusoe stood a hundred yards from the Cove studios building and watched the traffic. Minutes earlier the man known as Max had left the Cove Production Studios, and stood on the street, looking either way just before he made a very short call on his mobile phone and walked away. Declan checked his watch: time to meet with Wren Cove, answer a few questions and give him the password to remove copy protection on the video. The material Declan had gained at the CASP signing sparked Wren's interest and he was prepared to go public with it only after he viewed the entire recording. The afterhours meeting was to confirm the video's details only—Wren promised Declan's name and face were strictly confidential, protected by the freedom of the press. Just as he began to move, a dark GMC Denali with blacked-out windows slowed and two men jumped out, surveyed their surroundings and entered the floor level of the building. Declan's thoughts ran through a half dozen explanations—none very comforting. He held back and waited in the shadows.

The office and studio were quiet now, with only the street sounds three stories below breaking the office silence. Wren's computer was getting flooded with hundreds of emails. He closed the video storing it in an inconspicuous file. He thought again about Max's reaction: *a soft complaint from an overworked technician, or a feeble attempt to gain confidential source information known only to Wren Cove?*

Then the clicking of leather heels on the tile corridor floor revealed that his contact had arrived. "I'm in my office—end of the hall." Wren stood and as he opened his large oak office door two men came crashing through, knocking him to the ground. The first man pushed a damp rag onto Wren's face.

"Stop—what are you doing? I can't ..." Wren slumped into the second man's arms who gently dragged him to the office couch and laid him down.

"Get the needle. Hit him in the right arm, just below the elbow. Make sure it all gets in." The first man pulled up Wren's shirt sleeve and the second man found a vein and pushed the entire syringe of fluid into Wren's arm. "Check his heart rate." The first man made several more puncture marks along the prominent vein.

The second man withdrew a stethoscope from his coat jacket pocket and pressed it against Wren's carotid artery. Wren opened his eyes, seeing nothing, flinched and shook for several seconds, before falling limp. The second man said, "Now pulse slowing...slower...stopped."

The two skilled "field operatives", posing as private security men took their orders from Badge Demarche and their paychecks from Adrestia. Thirty seconds later the first man had located the entire critical video file. "I found it—his material on Barriman is in a video."

The two men watched as the seven minute video clearly showed the President and Badge Demarche discussing the disturbing elements of the CASP agreement. The President's secret plan to push the US toward a client Chinese state was both evident and comprehensive. The men wiped emails and documents from Wren's computer's memory. As they tried to copy the video, the protection codes flashed a screen message onto the screen ...*Video Copying Prohibited.*

The second man said, "Damn it. The file is protected. We'll have to take the entire computer."

Seconds later the screen flashed with another message...*Enter the Protection Removal Password.* The screen showed an active cell for entry of a password, with a timer nearby counting down from thirty seconds. The second man yelled, "What's this?"

"It's a time dependent code...a 'sunset' auto destruct command. Without the password it will probably erase the video...damn!" Ten seconds later the screen went blank and the file containing the video appeared empty. "Grab the computer, we gotta go."

"Leave the heroin vials in his desk. I'll get our listening bug." The second man listened to the audio bug recordings through his ear bud and said, "He was going to meet Max at 1930 or 730 for a drink."

"Is that a problem?"

"Maybe—Max may have seen the video. I can't be certain. Also there is a note on Wren's desk calendar with the letters DFC penciled in at 7:00 p.m. That was seven minutes ago." The men looked in silence at each other. "I'm gonna check with Command."

Badge walked slowly from outside the Oval Office and retrieved his buzzing cell phone. "Yes?"

"It's me. A video of you and the President talking just prior to the CASP signing was on Cove's computer."

"What? We were alone. Does it reveal much that's damaging?"

"Let's just say, it's a good thing we moved quickly on this issue."

"What about the former owner...*gone*?"

"Yes owner gone. We have the computer but the video file was protected with a sunset destruct command. We lost it without the password."

Do the letters 'DFC' mean anything to you?" Badge swallowed hard, his chest tightening.

"What? The letters mean nothing, why?"

"Cove had a meeting scheduled exactly at the time we arrived—yet he was the only one here. The letters DFC, probably initials, were written on his calendar desk pad at 7:00 p.m. It was just a couple of hours after he made his claims of corruption and impeachable acts to his audience on national television."

"I just saw the comments. It's all over the news. We are preparing a strong, brief denial claiming partisan politics."

"Also Cove's production manager, Max, may have seen the video. Is that a problem we need to fix?"

"No I can manage Max. You're sure it's *safe*? Any other issues found at Cove's offices?"

"No. Still a cautionary thought. Cove hadn't used the password to free the video for use when we arrived, so likely he hadn't received it, and the source may be the same person out there with the original video—probably this DFC character."

"You think the video may reappear?"

"Yes, very likely."

"The servers are now clean though, and you have his computer, right?"

"Absolutely."

Badge began to breathe again. "I'll check out the initials DFC."

Badge Demarche knew he had escaped a political "bomb" had the video of him and Barriman discussing the real impact of the CASP agreement with China ever made it to the news wires. With Wren Cove now gone, a new attempt would surely be made to publish the video. He struggled for the better part of an hour to guess where and when the next announcement would come. His private secure cell phone buzzed with a distinctive sound tagged to a particular caller. Looking about to assure he was alone, he answered the familiar caller. "Yes Max. Where are you?"

"I'm not far from Cove Studios, waiting to have a drink with Wren. Now there are cop cars all around the entrance, news media are here and it appears Wren has been attacked...maybe killed. What's going on?"

"Did you learn anything about the video he referenced in his broadcast tonight?"

"Well, he had it playing just after the show. I came into his office as he was viewing it, but I didn't learn much. He shut it down when I asked about when he was going to let me in on what he had. He promised to meet me later here at the bar and discuss the program planning for next week. That's when I called you, as I left?"

"So you never saw the video and Wren didn't call or show up to meet you?" Badge inquired.

"That's right. Do you think the source he was planning to meet with backed out of releasing the video...and killed him to get it back?"

"That's exactly what I think happened. You need to stay low, out of sight for a few days then head to Dallas. Contact me when you arrive."

"Ok, really—what should I do in Dallas?"

"Attend the Convention of States."

CHAPTER SEVEN

Dallas, Texas, Five Days before the Convention of States

Ed Kosko sat in one of the soft cushioned director chairs in the cigar room of the Renaissance Executive Center, a luxury mixture of lodging rooms, conference centers, meeting rooms, bars, lounges and restaurants. The pre-convention energy was growing every hour, centered on whom, if anyone would announce their candidacy for President and offer a real alternative to Harold Barriman. The backroom talk leading up to the convention primarily dealt with amendments and clarifications to the Constitution, yet the whisper talk increased about a NLP ticket announcement by Ed Kosko on the final day.

Kosko's rock glass of Famous Grouse scotch, neat, had come close to empty when Jameson Dalton Crusoe finally arrived. "Where the hell have you been? I expected you yesterday when I arrived. You look like shit JD." Ed could not contain his composure looking at his friend.

"Sorry Ed. I was delayed yesterday leaving North Carolina. It took the better part of a day apologizing to my mother about the funeral; Carolyn was next in line and it also took awhile."

"So were you forgiven?" Ed sipped the last of his Famous Grouse.

"Forgiven yes, forgotten no. On top of that, I couldn't get booked on commercial until early this morning. We'd better get these threats neutralized soon." Dalton was dressed casually and in full disguise.

"Nice disguise. You're idea? Are the mustache and glasses real?" Ed inquired.

"Absolutely not and I want to get rid of them soon, the colored contacts, the glasses and this ridiculous black hair color." Dalton paused and began again, "Remember I'm not here. I'm dead. Ronet talked me into this for my time here. You're very upset, remember, even grieving. Call me Bill...Bill Wright."

"Have you thought how you're going to explain that you are alive, now that you're dead, to those who follow this sort of stuff?"

"Actually, Ronet did have a great remedy for that issue. It was a mistake. The funeral home, which provided the empty casket, and produced the brief obituary materials, intends to issue a simple, concise correction next week—the whole thing was a mistake. We gave them a nice financial incentive to gain their full cooperation. So I'm alive, or will be next week." Dalton said smiling.

"Really, who was buried?"

"No one—they checked, it was empty." Dalton couldn't help but find the dark humor in the ruse designed to attract the assassin to the funeral setting.

Ed chuckled and nodded his amusement, grinned, and then got serious. "What, or who, do you think is behind this threat left on my car?" Dalton made no direct response.

Dalton surveyed the room for familiar faces, then said, "You have suspicions—correct?"

"I don't have a damn clue, except that it's likely from the group hoping I don't run against Barriman." Ed looked to Dalton, holding up his glass, "Care for one?"

"Yeah, sounds good." Dalton meant to speak to the attractive young female bar attendant approaching when Ed pronounced, "My friend has decided to join me—please bring two more. Thank you."

Dalton's eyes caught the attention of the barmaid and nodded his agreement with Ed's selection. The relationship with Ed Kosko reached back a full twenty years, when Dalton was only fifteen. Ed Kosko knew almost everything about his young protégée, including his favorite brand of scotch.

Dalton had graduated from the Annapolis Naval Academy at the top of his class. His well-connected mentor, namely Ed Kosko head of the NSA, with the Navy Secretary's approval, offered Dalton a chance to forgo active military service for five years if he agreed to participate in a new curriculum for exceptional individuals in an accelerated training program in the governmental arena. Dalton agreed as long as he could pursue his MBA concurrently. When his father died suddenly during Dalton's first year at Annapolis, it had hit JD hard. His sorrow turned to anger, then mellowed to determination to be the best at all things he pursued. He had committed himself to making his parents proud by exceeding their expectations. His mother remained a forceful advocate for her son. After his thesis work was accepted, he was done and ready to move into the quasi-private sector as a consultant to his friend and professional mentor. Kosko saw Dalton's potential and used him for specialized assignments in the NSA, where he excelled.

The drinks arrived in a flash, due to the near empty cigar room nuzzled off the lobby bar. Dalton smiled, took his glass and raised it in salute to Ed. "Here's to the next President of the United States."

"Damnit JD, I haven't made a decision yet—I think."

Laughing aloud, Dalton said, "What does that mean Ed?" Kosko chomped his cigar before setting it down.

"That's what I want you to help me sort out. I was pretty much committed to staying out of this mess, but your call last week and then this death letter just pissed me off. I'm thinking of running. Is that nuts?"

"Ed, there is a lot at stake here—for the country, you and Irene. I will support you in any decision you make. I will say that with the issues facing the country; runaway government, constitutional breaches, political unrest, and of course this damn aid agreement with China— you'd be my choice to lead us out of this mess." Dalton took a sip of his scotch and settled back in his chair awaiting Ed's thoughts.

Ed Kosko *was* a serious player on the world stage and a key asset in the prior Conner administration. Yet he had never aspired to be the chief executive of the US—he preferred to be a *"power player"* operating just behind the political scenes in an advising, managing, negotiating role. After first serving President Conner as Energy Secretary and then as head of the NSA Ed Kosko was well qualified for the highest office. While he had no elective office experience, it had allowed him to stand aside as the opposing political parties broke and fractured against each other. He was an *"insider"*, but not one easily attacked based on a voting record. In Dalton's mind, Ed's decision to run as the New

Libertarian Party candidate, following a strong mandate from the Convention of States, would be merely a matter of compassion for the country he loved, and have nothing to do with political ambitions.

Ed listened carefully to his friend Dalton and grew serious as he formulated a response. "You know JD, this is a big deal for me and Irene, yet that's not the reason I would take it on. I feel someone has to lead the effort to save this great country from these crazy liberal nutcases—and if the support Charley Rhodes claims is real and they really want me...well, I'm in."

"Great. I'm glad you're going to run—and I'm here to help." Dalton was concerned about the death threat to Ed and had some clues to share with his friend. He had withheld the damning SnapLift mission video Ronet obtained until he knew whether Ed was inclined to run for office. "This death threat left on your car is interesting. Have you studied it?"

"Hell no! I'm trying to forget that note, hoping it is a bogus prank."

"I don't think so, Ed. Look at the structure of the message... *Announce for President and you die in the thirty days following.*" Ed adjusted his readers and gazed at it for a moment.

"Ok I don't get any other messages JD, except the obvious one."

"The words are configured in a way that implies certain sophistication. It sets up a premise...*Announce for President*...then follows with a result...*and you die*...then it ends with a time schedule...*in the thirty days following.*"

"Ok, I'm trying to follow your thinking." Ed remarked.

"Most jerks trying to get a thrill from scaring you might have written...*in a month*, or...*in thirty days*...but this guy adds...*following.* To write... *in the thirty days following*...suggests to me an intended clear precision, or clarity in the message. I feel that this guy had a timetable to follow and it found its way into this expression of a threat. You see my point?"

"Ok, right, I get it. So what does that mean?"

"To me it means this guy is educated, perhaps in Europe, based on the phrasing; and he is a professional working for someone, or some group." Dalton rested his head in his right hand and said, "Still it's all speculation, my friend. But...we must take it very seriously."

Ed Kosko thought about Dalton's analysis and was glad he had called his friend and confidante for help. The conversation stalled for a noticeable moment, waiting for a new topic.

"Ed, I lost a man on the training mission in Canada."

"What? Who? How so?"

"Sergeant Mason, a smart, technical whiz. He took the shrapnel bomb blast set to wipe out the entire training team. It may have a connection to me as well Ed."

"Really, how do you figure that?"

"Very few people knew of my training mission last week. But clues were available if one knew where to look. After the Asadabad fiasco, Brad Ronet made it very clear he intended to join me in Canada for the exercise, and the word had to move through a number of agencies. In my meeting with Declan he was very convincing that a rogue group had penetrated the US security agencies—including the NSA." Ed Kosko sipped his scotch with his full attention on Dalton.

"So what, where does that lead you?" Dalton grinned at his friend as he was about to reveal a finding, just a few hours old, that provided some *real* answers.

"Ronet captured two clear partial prints on the third mine meant to take out my team—and I now believe I was the *prime* target. My instincts told me to detonate the third mine—we did that after moving back to a safe area." Kosko nodded that he followed the logic.

"Last night Wilson called me and said he'd found an 82% certain match to prints we had on file. A file we both know well."

"That's not a positive confirmation, but damn close. Ok, you've really got my attention now—whose prints came up?"

"Hasid Khamal was the match. I believe he's alive and may have been sent to fulfill your death threat, assuming you announce your candidacy. It would be an easy step to connect you and me—and I suspect his Iranian client still wants me dead."

"Khamal is still alive? We searched those waters for days and found nothing—assuming the sharks got him. Yes, we had prints from his attack on you off St. Martin on that boat, right?"

"Exactly. When my training mission resulted in a serious assassination attempt, just as your email message arrived, I began to connect the dots. It was a long shot as we both felt Khamal was dead, yet I always wondered why his body was never found."

"Damn, JD, you may be right. If the guy picked to knock me off has an unsettled score with you, he sees the connection we have and targets both of us—perfect. And your assessment of the death threat note makes real sense now."

Dalton prepared to further explain his theories, fears and plans when a man approached. "Hey Ed, good to see you. When did you arrive...today?" Charley Rhodes beamed with enthusiasm as he shook hands with Ed Kosko. Charley nodded a glance at Dalton.

"Actually I got in around noon yesterday. Irene wanted to have dinner with a couple of her old college friends living near Dallas." Ed shrugged sheepishly.

"So Irene was able to join you—wonderful." Charley felt Ed had already decided on running on the NLP ticket and Irene's presence was a further positive indication.

"Charley have you met...Bill Wright?" Ed reached out to introduce the two men. Charley looked at Dalton, smiled broadly and said, "No, we haven't met," reaching out and shaking hands with Dalton.

Ed offered a seat to Charley at the casual setting within the massive twelve-story atrium lobby. Charley welcomed the chance to further probe Kosko on his decision. "Charley I've called...Bill...into my decision because I respect his opinion, and I have some security issues that may require a man of his skill and connections to resolve. You'll learn more about Bill in a day or two." Charley failed to understand the comment but smiled anyway.

Charley looked at Dalton for any clue to what Ed was referring and found no answers. Ed sensed the dilemma and offered, "I'm going to run for the NLP candidacy for President Charley. You, or a man on your staff, can manage my campaign—I just want final say on all ads, schedules and opinion pieces...agreed?"

Charley Rhodes lit up. He had hoped and expected Ed to become the NLP candidate and now he could really unleash the money faucet. "Excellent Ed. You won't regret this move. I can handle any campaign thrust Barriman attempts to undermine you. The NLP is ready for you and this Convention of States is the perfect stage to announce it. Are you Ok with that?"

Ed shifted his eyes to Dalton who nodded his agreement. "I'm good with that, Charley. I'll need some strong, concise talking points to make at the Convention on...when, Friday night?"

"Yes. That's perfect. We'll have thirty million viewers on four major networks, cable and social media." Charley had already organized a plan assuming Ed Kosko would accept the invitation to speak on behalf of the Convention agenda, and *now* also announce his candidacy for the NLP ticket."

"There's another issue...one that arose a week ago after I left your office." Ed grew serious. Charley seemed to hold his breath.

"I found a death threat on my car window in your office building's parking garage." Ed reached into his jacket pocket.

"What? A death threat..." Charley sat up and revealed true concern. "Do you have the police working on this?"

"No way. The police can't help if the threat is from powerful political foes."

Ed handed the note to Charley who looked at it for a full minute, repeatedly re-reading it. "This is bull-shit Ed. I can't believe this happened. Still, we can get candidate Secret Service protection you know...the moment you announce and receive the nomination from the NLP."

"That's all fine. Yet I am not sure the Barriman team, particularly that *'Oval Office overseer'*, Badge Demarche, wouldn't be inclined to corrupt that protection. You understand my concern?" Ed gave Dalton an uneasy glance.

Charley responded, "Yes, I can believe that. Badge is very bad news and carries enormous weight with Barriman. I believe he is blinded by some kind of world domination dreams."

"One reason I want Bill involved is to oversee the protection efforts. He's been effective in the past—right...Bill?"

"Charley, I'd appreciate it if you could spread the word that I'm involved only as a friend and no more? At a later time I'll explain more." Dalton made certain his request sounded like a command.

"Right Bill, I understand. Absolutely."

"Good. I have a number of concerns and clues there may be strong, shall I say illegal, opposition to Ed's announcement. I need time, confidentiality and privacy to work through these issues.

Dalton saw Ed Kosko reemerging again as his former self, before he was retired early from the NSA when the new Barriman administration took office. Replacing top officials was a typical move for incoming administrations, yet one that had left Ed unfulfilled—he was not yet ready to leave a position of high-level influence. The abysmal record of Barriman's policies were so destructive that those who had committed the bulk of their working careers to making America great felt compelled to reengage in the political process. Dalton felt this was the driving force in Ed's mind.

Ed stood to announce his departure to meet Irene at a classy downtown restaurant and tell her of his decision. "I have to leave gentlemen. Thanks for coming in...uhh Bill, tomorrow we'll discuss the plan going forward Ok?" Ed butted his cigar, slugged the last of his Famous Grouse and waved a goodbye.

Dalton gave a disapproving look at Ed as Charley followed him to the door gushing joy like a happy puppy over the decision to run against Barriman.

Mingling unnoticed in the crowd, a man, one of a very few who supported another named "Flask" stowed his mini-camera and followed Ed Kosko out the entrance doors of the Renaissance Executive Center.

◆ ◆ ◆

Next Morning at the Convention of States

The opening day event for the Convention of States began at noon on July 21. Thirty-six states had petitioned Congress to call and set the Convention of States. Following a reluctant Congress action, the convention was set in Dallas, Texas for the first full week in July. States formed their delegations from those faithful and committed to the process. The delegates, referred to as "commissioners", totaled 320 individuals; with most states selecting seven and others up to eleven commissioners to represent their states. Each participating state sent all or a portion of its legislative body to Dallas in support of the process. The open forum drew major political contributors, PAC's, and of course the news media. A number of states, not sending delegations to the convention, did dispatch their senior progressive legislators to offer counter-points through the news media coverage and attempt to rally a counter movement for most of the initiatives proposed for discussion and ratification. Still, the conservative legislators attending outnumbered the progressives by a factor of twenty.

The massive auditorium was near its official capacity of 8,000 people. Music and strobe lights fueled the high-energy crowd in the building. Large balloons, labeled with all of the thirty-six states names surrounded by stars and stripes bounced off the gathering as if a rock concert were about to start. Many people wore tall red-white-and-blue paper Top Hats reminiscent of what many of the founding fathers may have worn. The top five main television networks and their technical crews, anchors and "talking heads" sequestered themselves in the corner pockets of the arena. Every network displayed their signature logo and image on huge banners and electronic ribbon displays of the current news and happenings; each trying to impress their viewership with fancy podiums, interview couches and large wall touch screens showing the convention activity.

Once the crowd settled down the chairperson Governor Rob Welkins from Montana, took the podium and called the convention to order. The popular, outspoken, and charismatic governor looked out at the crowd, raised his arms and said, "Welcome to Dallas, Texas and the Convention of States." The crowd erupted into a roaring response, with chants of "America, America", "Restore the Constitution" and "Impeach Barriman." Banners were thrust upward in the crowd everywhere promoting the main agenda of proposed amendments: Term Limits; Balanced Budgets; Flat Taxation; Limited Executive Branch Powers; and Abolition of Gun Controls.

Welkins followed up, "I declare the Convention of States now open." The crowd erupted again with even more energy. Fifteen minutes of steady wild cheering and chanting followed. Dalton stood in a balcony wing next to Ed Kosko who surveyed the crowd below in amazement and remarked, "This is going to be one helluva convention JD—I believe these folks are serious about change for the country."

"Right and you'll help make that happen." Dalton was pleased to see his friend and mentor back in the *action*. Ed had been talked through all the major points and important "sound bites" by Charley Rhodes and his campaign team. Dalton had spent the morning taking Ed through the difficult to watch video of the SnapLift operation. Ed's reaction was predictable.

"This is so disgusting and un-American I can't believe what I'm seeing—a President covering up a botched black ops mission and refusing to rescue the team he sent in, all for political purposes." Kosko bristled as he listened and watched the Ranger's desperate pleas for help followed by the President's order to abandon them. Dalton shut down the laptop playing the time-stamped, password-protected video.

"Ed, the approval came through two hours ago that you are able to receive Secret Service protection now that you've delivered a written announcement as a candidate for President.

You're televised announcement here shortly will confirm that to the world as well."

"Does that really help JD? If this business threatening to kill me is real, they must have realized that I'd get that protection—which means they're likely to have a plan to get around it."

"You're right Ed. Ronet and I have talked about how best to stop them before you're overexposed. Brad is coming in tonight and he has a couple of helpers."

"Helpers? What are you talking about?"

"Wilson and Cotter are coming with him to assist in the protection." Dalton knew that the names of the two top NSA field agents he'd worked with before would excite Ed.

"Damn, that's great. I love those boys. How did they get sprung from their assignments?" asked Ed looking puzzled.

Dalton declared, "Even though Sandborn heads the NSA and is a Barriman stooge, he's detached and has left much of the middle operational management in place. They are the folks who will always do a favor for you...and me. Once Wilson learned that Khamal was likely a match with the prints Brad got, he said he and Cotter were coming to Dallas."

Ed studied Dalton and said, "Good JD, real good."

"We'll let the Secret Service arrange a protection plan, and examine it to see where there might be weaknesses. I'll have Cotter or Wilson check out each Secret Service man. If anything appears odd, it may signal an intentional gap in protection—or an oversight which is just as bad."

Dalton withdrew a powerful NSA issued tablet, stroked the screen several times and continued, "The message I took away from my meeting with Declan is that the bogus attack on Barriman could occur in the presence of one or more of his rivals. Once you formally announce—you are an *active* rival—still an attack could come anytime, anywhere. So let's look over the tentative travel schedule the DNC is suggesting for the three Presidential debates. If Declan's correct an assassination attempt could take place almost anywhere, yet at a debate site—is where the Secret Service coverage is supposed to be closest."

Ed decided to probe Dalton on his feelings about having a half-brother. "How are you handling this news about Declan?"

"What do you mean Ed? His explanations appear to be genuine, although some areas are disturbing—you know the nature of his work."

"Does he look like you or Jonathon?" Ed inquired.

Dalton shifted in his chair and lowered his eyes alerting Ed that the subject was unsettling. "Carolyn says she knew at first glance we were related; same eyes, bone structure, even hair according to her—just older by a few years. She summarizes it by saying he resembles a 'more-so' version of me." Dalton had held back his own questions for Ed about Declan for days, yet felt the discussion was about to lead there. "Ed in all your dealings with my dad, did you ever hear about a half-brother?"

Ed Kosko thought long and hard about the proper response. "Jonathon never mentioned it JD, although he did speak of Karin, his original Brussels marketing assistant. I never met her because the period when Jonathon and I became friends was years after his first assignment in Brussels. When he was there fulltime, during your final high school year, I never heard anymore about her. She was Irish and had to travel with him occasionally. He never spoke of a relationship beyond their working arrangement."

Dalton listened attentively and appreciated Ed's candor. "Declan was born a few years before me, so you're right, this all began early in dad's first European assignment. I was just starting college when he moved us to Brussels for a second time. I guess he decided to keep it from me. Dad was gone a lot, then he died suddenly and I never was able to re-connect as father and son. Mom never spoke of any of this."

"I don't believe she knew, and knowing your dad as I did, I suspect he was embarrassed and wanted to protect her and you from any scandal. Also your dad was not one to push off blame; I'm sure he felt he'd been reckless and accepted full responsibility." Ed looked into Dalton's face, and continued, "Long ago I made a promise to your mother. After your dad died I committed to help your mother encourage you to achieve great things—and you did JD. Jonathon would be very proud."

Dalton smiled as he tried to forge a pretend look of irritation, "Yeah, you and mom were a tough act—pushed me hard all through grad school. But I do appreciate all you *both* have done for me Ed."

Ed threw his arm around Dalton's shoulders and said, "JD, you did it with the skills you got from your parents. I just saw your potential and tried to be a supportive friend. When you became a man I decided I could use you on my team—so I pushed you—on assignments and your education. What I did was no more than encourage you as your dad would have. I still miss your dad to this day." A pause followed before Ed's next question. "Do you plan to tell your mother?"

"I don't know yet. I want to discuss it with Carolyn." Dalton shrugged at the thought.

"You're a great friend Ed. I'm so sorry you're caught up in this assassination thing with me. I really thought Khamal was dead and gone." The relationship with Ed Kosko had grown from a "friendly uncle" form of relationship to one of a confidant and mentor. Both men admired each other and relished the friendship.

"JD, I have full confidence in you and Ronet. With the help of the Secret Service, you will find and stop this bastard. I'm not worried. Still I fear Carolyn is shook up far more than she shows in her beautiful face. Is she alright?"

"Carolyn is doing what she always does—stands by me in all things, even though it tears her up inside. I really love that woman."

"No decision on a wedding date yet?"

Dalton looked up at his mentor and knew the feelings were genuine, prompting him to say, "No decision yet. She wants the threats behind us before we set a date."

A pause followed, "I miss dad too Ed, I really miss him. As to mom, I don't know what to do. I must discuss it with Carolyn. Her instincts are better than mine on these matters. Besides, she is really starting to connect with mom as we look to a wedding date."

Ed smiled and said, "You'll find the right answer JD. You're right about Carolyn—she has great instincts and obviously loves Elizabeth. She's a great match for you, JD."

The threats against Ed were serious and credible. Ed's call for advice on the NLP candidacy option was both a "sanity check" on his decision, and a subtle plea for security from a man Ed trusted implicitly. Dalton knew the moment Ed announced his plan to run for office the death threat and the assessments of Declan would become real—and he had to protect the man. Meanwhile, the Adrestia unit was organizing teams for elimination of their list of "targets" by Khamal and others.

CHAPTER EIGHT

Second Day of the Convention of States

The atmosphere was electric with activity and energy. The country had been awakened to the country's problems and most blamed the Barriman administration's progressive policies. Dallas was the focal point for the rebirth of America, as many New Libertarian Party followers declared their support. The crowds grew each day beginning a week before when the press and support groups set up field offices, canvassed the area with brochures and held informational seminars on the choices for the country. The Convention of States gave the average American a tangible and emotional avenue to get involved and help alter the course of the country. Armed civilian militia, in full camouflage, made their presence very visible wherever large crowds formed to rally the NLP speakers. Sports bars across the country cut coverage of minor athletic events in favor of the convention. Every news organization capable of sending a satellite crew to Dallas was set up in the vast parking areas, cameras aimed at the convention center, and all frantically trying to snag interviews with the favorite convention speakers. Each speaking guest was expected to deliver a crowd-rousing discourse on restoring America's stature in the world and halting the rapid path to socialism under the Barriman administration. While the progressive opposition set up nearby Barriman reelection offices and hosted a few neighborhood petition campaigns to discredit the NLP and the convention, most were ignored by the local residents. The polling momentum was favoring the NLP. America was engaged.

Mixing among the crowd was a man, a special man with strong connections in the world of politics and the military. He blended in and kept a low profile yet he wielded enormous influence with a powerful group—operating quietly, secretly behind the scenes, committed to stopping Barriman from achieving a second term. As he walked about checking out the numerous news outlets he retrieved his phone, vibrating in his jacket pocket. "Yes, who is this?"

"It's Flask. Are you in Dallas yet?"

"Yeah, I arrived last night. The place is packed with press and NLP attendees." Devin McCord wanted to cover one more Presidential campaign before retiring at 62 years of age. As a senior Secret Service agent he had considerable pull with the lead agent to get in on particular details. The head of the Secret Service had anticipated Kosko's announcement to run and sent a team to Dallas due to the heightened tension surrounding the Convention of States. McCord had never been drawn to covering the candidates in a Presidential election, but he despised Barriman. Secretly he deplored the task of protecting him, yet did so when assigned, remembering it was really the office of the President he respected.

This election was different—in fact it was the whole ball game in McCord's mind. He revealed his feelings to Flask, who used his connections to get McCord assigned to the presumed NLP candidate, Ed Kosko.

"Devin when is Kosko planning to formally announce?"

"I don't know yet. He is here with a few friends surrounding him, and yesterday he met with Rhodes. I'm betting he will announce in the next few days."

Flask asked, "How many men assigned to the protection detail?"

"Five men including me. All young and mostly unknown to me—worked with one of them on a few assignments, Eric Walters."

"Walters. Isn't he one of the agents that rescued Barriman and Demarche from the river in Virginia a while back?"

"Right, he's the one who snagged Barriman and pulled him out. Good agent I'm told, but I don't know his political leanings."

"Find out the convention schedule of events and speakers just as soon as you can, and let me know. Keep an eye on each of the agents—I fear Badge Demarche may have a compromised agent in the group."

"Right. I should know more by tomorrow. I'll call then."

◆ ◆ ◆

The bar lounge at the west end of the lobby was large, dark and nearly empty—not unusual for a Thursday night. Most business travelers had left in the late afternoon to get home for the weekend, and the family groups simply never picked a place like the Colonial Heritage Hotel to stay with their kids. It was situated in an older part of Falls Church, mid-way through a re-development period and far from vacation attractions. Still it was a safe, convenient spot for Badge Demarche to meet with his *contacts*. As planned, Saul Abboud was sitting at a small table snuggled in a corner of the room, checking his watch...6:45 p.m. Badge saw him surveyed the room, walked over, and sat down.

"The down payment of $15,000,000 for the operation in Dallas was wired to Adrestia's accounts in Zurich an hour ago." Badge slid a copy of the Washington Post across the table folded to partially conceal a black briefcase containing $150,000. "Here is the cash payment for your efforts...thus far."

Abboud nervously fumbled handling the newspaper and case as though they were toxic. "Relax. With any luck at all, we should see all this mess wrapped up in ten days, and in two months the President will win in a landslide." Badge could see that his courier connection with Adrestia was concerned.

"Yes, it will be over soon, right?"

"Absolutely. Let's have a drink." Badge motioned to the barmaid, cleaning up after a patron just leaving the bar.

"Alright, yeah that's good idea." Abboud answered without thinking.

"I sense there may be a mole in the administration's inner circle. The tire blowout in Virginia that nearly drowned me and the President is still unsolved. I'm now suspicious that someone in the Secret Service may be a conspirator. Do you recognize this man?" Badge flashed a photo on his smart phone for Abboud to examine.

"He looks familiar, but I don't know his name."

"He's the only agent who specifically requested and was given approval to cover the likely NLP candidate at the Convention of States. He's Devin McCord." Saul Abboud looked confused.

"So you think he's responsible for the Virginia accident? What could he have done there?"

Badge looked directly at Abboud as he spoke, "It was no accident—someone orchestrated a clever dual tire blowout hoping to drown me and POTUS. It appears an explosive charge was hidden in both the two right side wheel covers and detonated remotely—the perpetrator had to be close and watching the limos route to time the blowouts. I've kept it out of the press—for now. McCord was there. Watch him and tell me who he's spending time with. I'm emailing the photo to you now. I may be wrong about him, but I'm suspicious."

Badge noticed that his contact of several years appeared tentative, tired and distracted.

"Do you have any new reports from your recent meeting with uhh...Mr. Thomas, concerning the target?"

"Uh, no. He may not call, unless there is an issue, until the contract is...fulfilled. I still carry the phone, right here." Abboud pointed to his coat pocket unable to hide his nervousness.

"Keep that phone he gave you in your pocket at *all* times. Understood?"

"Yes, of course." Abboud displayed the phone, as though he needed to confirm it existed.

Badge waited for the bar maid to set down the drinks and leave before saying, "My contacts at Adrestia suggest it may happen soon." He then waited to gauge Abboud's reaction.

Abboud starred at his drink and said, "That's good."

Badge doubted Abboud could handle the ongoing stress of the assignment to interact with Adrestia's premier contract assassin, Hasid Khamal. The stakes were far too great to allow a weak link in the communications. It was a concern.

◆ ◆ ◆

Early afternoon July, the West Wing of the White House

The President sat on the couch in the Vice President's office. He was casual, no suit coat, tie loosened. Badge Demarche found him and knocked on the open door. "You were looking for me Mr. President?"

"Yes, Badge. Come in and have a seat. You know that Garrison seldom spent time in this office." Badge saw an opportunity emerging.

"I did know that. But it was for the best—I recall how we talked about keeping the VP outside our discussions or memos on our Chinese discussions with the Chinese that led to the CASP agreement." Badge could see the President was losing his focus again.

"Did we really have to kill him along with Andrea Renkin? I understand Andrea could not be trusted to keep her mouth shut once this financing deal got negotiated—she'd have spilled her guts and run against me in the primary to unseat me. But Garrison—he was a good man just not progressive enough to fit in." Badge looked over to Barriman—his slumping shoulders, negative frame of mind, a grim look and the definite remorse in his words alarmed Badge.

"Harold, remember what we are doing here. We, you, are saving the country from economic disaster. This plan will work;

people will see that as new jobs are created and the fear of financial default is avoided, you will be credited with the success. Bob Garrison was a real liability to you as VP on the second term ticket. We were lucky Adrestia managed the double deaths as an awful accident." The situation was serious enough, and since they were alone, Badge spoke to him as a friend using "Harold" rather than "Mr. President".

"Maybe you're correct" A pause followed, "...Do you think I need a boost?" The President definitely needed a boost injection: it had been two days since the last one. Badge retrieved his small hypodermic and administered 2 cc's. The President remained silent and staring at a staged photo of him and Garrison shortly after the election.

Shortly the President settled down and regained focus. After a few minutes of needed silence, Barriman continued, "Who should be nominated to take the VP slot, Badge?"

"Actually sir, I believe that without a primary challenge so far, and the short timetable for any competitor, you can simply select a VP candidate to join you on the new ticket. And I think we can be assured now, with the Renkin and Garrison deaths, you will not now receive a primary challenge." The discussion was heading exactly as Badge and his Chinese associates had hoped. He proceeded very carefully with his next remarks—as though he were conducting a medical interview.

"We need someone we can absolutely rely upon—someone who will unquestionably support your decisions." The President was focused again, sharp and hanging on Badge's every word. The injection fluid, sometimes referred to by the Chinese as *"mood stabilizer"* was working.

"Well, who then Badge—who are we thinking of?" Badge held a tight focus on the President's face. Barriman was focused and ready to hear what his Chief of Staff had to suggest. The moment was ideal.

Using his most sincere, and compelling voice to the President, Badge said, "Well, sir, I think you need me as your VP."

The President's mind arrested, clearly churning over the words, while still staring at his Chief of Staff. The President's face was frozen on Badge, his mind working and his emotions in check. Badge knew to wait, leaving the enhanced cognitive and persuasive elements of the *mood stabilizer* to work their effects. The early signs of a decision were a mild grin appearing on the President's face—first at the eyes then the mouth. Badge smiled back and waited.

"Damn, Badge. That's a great idea! I hadn't even thought of it until now, but you're right, absolutely right, you'd be the best man for the job. Let's do it." Barriman stood and began to strategize. "Under the Twenty-Fifth Amendment you can be approved by a simple majority in the House and Senate, right? I could make you my Vice President right now."

"Yes, that's correct and we have the votes." Badge stood to model the President's energized behavior. "Thank you Mr. President. I truly appreciate your faith and trust in me. We will make a great team." Badge extended his hand to informally seal the understanding. "I'll prepare a press release."

"Yes, get the press behind this. Think about a replacement for Renkin whom we can count on." The President smiled with pride at *his* decisions.

Badge Demarche returned to his office, shut the door and beamed at his own resourcefulness—leading the President of the United States to a pivotal decision, initiated years earlier as part of a strategy to position the USA as a client state of China.

CHAPTER NINE

Third Day of the Convention of States

The early morning sky east of Dallas revealed a stunning sunrise, laced with red, orange and yellow hues as the rays broke through the fractured clouds just above the horizon. From the leased seventh floor of the Business Suites Center, the views were impressive, with the convention center a block away, surrounded by service roads and an adjacent woodsy exercise park, hosting dozens of early morning runners. Charley's thirty-person staff was busy, set up and operating twelve hours a day during the convention. Rhodes turned his attention back to the AP newswire printer, spewing out paper at his side. He ripped the newswire sheets from the tray, walked briskly back to his office, slammed the door shut and slid into his desk chair to study the latest White House Press release. It read:

The White House: The President announced this morning that he will select Brandon (Badge) Demarche, his current Chief of Staff, to become his Vice President to fill the post held by the late Robert Garrison, and to become his VP choice for the second Barriman administration following the election in November. The Senate Majority leader has promised a swift approval. Furthermore, the administration announced that Mr. Demarche will temporarily assume the role of Secretary of State to replace former Secretary Andrea Renkin until a new replacement can be selected by the President and confirmed by the Congress. Both Garrison and Renkin died recently in an apparent security and support helicopter accident in Egypt when both administration officials were there on a diplomatic mission to the region.

Charley picked up the phone and called Ed Kosko. "Ed, its Charley. Have you seen the newswire release by Barriman this morning?"

"No, I'm walking over to your convention headquarters office headquarters now, be there in ten. What's up?"

"Barriman is picking Badge Demarche to be his second term VP pick. I didn't see that one coming."

"Really. Is that good or bad for us?"

"It's both, actually. This will drive independents to your camp, but Badge is articulate and connected. It depends on how much exposure Barriman affords him. If it's minor then it's manageable. If he is a main stage player *with* the President, that is tougher. I've often wondered who controls whom in that relationship."

"I'll be at your door shortly." The walk gave Ed a chance to burn off the adrenalin rush hitting his system. Badge Demarche was formidable, but his presence whether as Chief of Staff or VP reinforced Ed's decision to run and defeat the duo. He believed as did many Americans—the country could not afford another four years of Barriman.

◆ ◆ ◆

Hours later in a special session of both houses the Congress approved Demarche as President Barriman's selection for VP. In a brief ceremony Brandon (Badge) Demarche recited the oath of office as Vice President on the west front terrace of the U.S. Capitol, accompanied by many high ranking Democrats. President Barriman was still responding to the last "boost" and smiled broadly as his friend, confidant and de facto medical overseer assumed the office. The news media smothered the President and Badge with shouted questions. President Barriman raised his hand and took the podium as the crowd settled down. "I want to congratulate my friend and new Vice President Brandon Demarche. He has and will continue to remain a critical member of my inner circle to run this great country. Shortly Badge will announce a replacement Chief of Staff to fill his former role, yet until the position is filled he will still oversee that office."

The press fired a few questions at Badge, who took to the microphones and pointed to a reporter. "Sir you were directing the President's election campaign. Will you now still direct the campaign for the Barriman-Demarche ticket for you and the President and yourself?"

"Clearly, I have more responsibilities now. Yet as I am already heavily involved I will oversee other persons, to be named later, who will manage the details of the campaign. Thank you and thank you Mr. President for your confidence in me."

Additional calls for answers were not acknowledged, as the two men walked away, waving to the collection of reporters and photographers. Flask stood beside the podium in a hand-picked crowd of thirty cabinet members, politicians, advisors and other officials and politely clapped thinking...*this is clearly a strategic move by Badge...I'm sure of it.*

◆ ◆ ◆

Saul Abboud was dressed casually with a collared light blue dress shirt, no tie and a summer weight tan sports coat with dark blue dress slacks. His bogus ID pass dangling on a red lanyard strap listed him as a political consultant for a little known, yet real, conservative think-tank. His lapel was adorned with three buttons displaying themes of the Convention. He looked like he belonged in the audience—part of the committed right, firmly bent on reversing President Barriman's agenda. Abboud's investigations had revealed a strong, solidarity among the participants—an unexpected alliance of traditional conservatives, libertarians and swing vote independents, tired of the Barriman administration's leadership. Abboud wondered if Khamal was in the crowd setting up an assassination of Ed Kosko or if he had avoided the event altogether in favor of a less populated and congested venue.

Abboud checked his watch and decided to update Badge Demarche. "It's me Saul. I'm at the Convention."

"What's the talk about the NLP? Are they planning to propose a candidate to run against Barriman soon?"

"I've talked to several legislators from Texas, North Carolina and Florida—they are very energized and the name of Ed Kosko keeps coming up as the favorite to challenge Barriman—and you—I'm just told. Is that right?" Abboud's first reaction was one of faux exhilaration, hoping Badge would reward his years of dedicated support and appoint him to a White House role, perhaps Senior Campaign Advisor, or running the final days of the current campaign.

"Kosko, yes he's being promoted by Charley Rhodes' group. I had hoped he'd stay retired from politics. Any indication he's going to announce? And yes, Barriman offered me the VP slot—was sworn in two hours ago. It will increase my exposure so I must limit my involvement with our friends in Budapest."

Abboud's sense of elation faded fast as he heard Badge clearly state he must distance himself from Adrestia—which meant from Abboud as well.

Saul Abboud swallowed his pride for a moment. "I understand. I'll see what I can find on Kosko's role at the Convention, and whether he's scheduled to speak. I have seen McCord, always near the Kosko camp—I'm still trying to position a bug. I was able to use a small directional receiver and eavesdrop on one conversation."

"Learn anything?"

"It was a short call and I only caught the first few seconds, which seemed to suggest his caller, who goes, by 'Flask', felt a Secret Service agent named Eric Walters may have been planted by you in Kosko's protection detail. Does that make any sense?"

"Flask? Interesting. Hurry this along—I need to know what our enemies are thinking. Saul, now that I'm VP, I've got to remain distant from our Adrestia associates. Understood? Call tomorrow."

Abboud closed his phone and looked around the huge auditorium. A sudden rush of anger, which morphed to fear, overcame Abboud as he considered his situation. He had to force himself to get back into character as a political consultant enthralled with the historic Convention of States. Each state's legislature had its own information station, all staffed with smiling young workers handing out flyers on its particular slate of amendments. The crowds were building for the afternoon speakers. Ed Kosko's name did not appear on the list of seven speakers slated for the hours from 1:00 p.m. through 9:00 p.m.

◆ ◆ ◆

Every state in attendance selected a legislator who was allowed to speak ninety minutes to make his state's case for a slate of amendments. Most states' slates were quite similar and focused on the main themes of smaller government, term limits, balanced budgets, states' rights and limitation of Presidential power. Certain states like Florida, New Mexico, and Arizona had different top priorities targeting immigration, border security, and voting issues over and above the central themes. Still the convention atmosphere was vibrant, with a strong sense of patriotism flowing from every speaker. Pathroads for America ran continuous polling, both at the convention and throughout the US. The sentiment for major changes to the way government works was growing every day, until nearly 58% of those polled felt a Convention of States was the best way to restore balance. By the evening of the fourth day thirty-two states had presented their slate of amendments to the assembly. Straw vote sampling by Pathroads showed all but four states were prepared to vote in support of the Texas delegation slate which encompassed most of the issues brought forth. However, if the Convention of States did not obtain the support from those four states in the final voting, it could mean that while the convention had produced a slate of proposed amendments, it ultimately might fail at reaching the three-quarters approval needed by the subsequent states' ratification votes. Ratification by three/fourths of the states' legislatures would be necessary to make them law. Political posturing began to take place in quiet corners of the auditorium to gain a solid consensus. Charley Rhodes saw Ed Kosko walking toward the glass door to his satellite offices at the convention. Ed waved to Charley as he entered.

"Here's a copy of the President's press release concerning his selection of Demarche as his VP and running mate. It's crazy stuff." Charley looked frustrated.

"I'll take a look at that if you'll take a look at this. Over the last two days I've taken a shot at my speech over the last two days. It's short and to the point—maybe your team can soften it up and add some zip to the message." Ed held a small flash drive which held his first draft.

Charley Rhodes smiled and said, "Yes Ed, we'll look it over and suggest some ideas...if needed."

◆ ◆ ◆

The fifth day of the Convention of States was a huge party. The commissioners from the thirty-six states which had called the convention all ratified the proposed amendments to the Constitution, thereby avoiding or eliminating the Congressional process. It appeared that the legislatures of all of the thirty-six states would also approve the amendments. Therefore the five broad initiatives comprising the amendments were to be placed on the states' ballots weeks before the normal November election date when Barriman and Kosko would compete. This was necessary to ensure that the wording in the proposed amendments had the approval of the respective State Election Boards and met all election laws,

The progressives had already launched an attack campaign blasting the "Governance Amendments" as they were dubbed, as un-American and undermining our basic structure of government. They targeted the ten to fifteen states where the *status quo* progressives felt they could defeat the amendments. New Libertarian operatives were just as responsive hoping to hold their slim majorities in the liberal leaning states.

Ed Kosko took the stage at 8:00 p.m. E.D.T. following a lengthy introduction by former President Jerome Conner. The message was short on Kosko's significant career achievements and long on his plans for the future of the country. Conner was a strong President, well liked by the conservative camp, and tolerated by the left. His conservative policies were working, but he was term limited out for Barriman's first election run. At the same time, the GOP ran a weak, controversial candidate that Barriman trounced by a 54% to 46% margin. Once in office the Barriman administration moved quickly and deeply to the left destroying the progress made in the Conner years. Ed Kosko presented a sharp contrast to Barriman and had the career record to persuade voters he would move the nation toward the path of conservatism and embrace the Governance Amendments. His final words to the audience, and the forty million television viewers brought a crescendo of applause:

I love this country. I love the opportunities in America, and I fear we are being led down a path which will eventually limit, or remove them. Time is not on our side, as our country has been so neglected and mismanaged. We cannot wait another four years to make a change. We need to act now, and the Convention of States proposal for ratification of the Governance Amendments is the first right step in the right direction. We need to take control of America away from progressive, career politicians and give it back to the people. I offer my candidacy as the New Libertarian Party nominee and hope to become your President to do just that. I welcome your support. God bless the United States of America.

Dalton watched from a mezzanine overlooking the vast arena along with Brad Ronet. The crowd rose to their feet giving thunderous applause, whistles, and chants of "Ed Kosko". A band in the orchestra pit beneath the speaking platform erupted into a rousing version of *"You're still the One",* as red, white and blue balloons fell from the ceiling. Network television coverage was universal, as even the liberal biased news sources gave the historic event plenty of coverage.

"Damn JD, Ed looks like he's been in the political spotlight for thirty years—he's good." Ronet glanced over to Dalton, smiled and said, "You know, I think you looked better with the mustache and glasses." Ignoring the second quip Dalton chose to answer the original remark.

"I agree. I always felt he could attract votes even though he regarded politicians as lepers. He just speaks truthful, no bullshit and is convincing. People are drawn to that." The applause and chanting continued as Ed waved a goodbye from the podium.

"I decided this being the sixth Convention day a Khamal appearance would be unlikely, and I've been backstage and on this mezzanine most of the time. Ed felt Charley Rhodes needed to know exactly who I was and what I was doing." Ronet just smiled back at his friend.

"How do you feel the Secret Service guys are doing on protection?"

Ronet offered an ambiguous look before responding, "Well...I've not found a break in their protocol or securing procedures yet, but I'm not declaring victory until this convention ends and we move to a smaller exposure profile. Still I'm going down now to take him with me once he comes off the stage. The Secret Service is down there now."

"Has anything surfaced in our search for Khamal?" Dalton feared the assassin was alive and the one contracted to kill Kosko.

"We have scanned hundreds of faces, body types, accents, credentials and more—nothing pops up saying *'here's Khamal'*. Carolyn was going over the images and film with Wilson earlier today."

"Keep Wilson and Cotter monitoring this crowd. We have thousands of folks here and he is skilled enough to have made it in."

"Right. I'll connect later with Ed in tow."

◆ ◆ ◆

Mixed in with a gathering of photographers was a man wearing an ill-fitting suit, thick glasses, and three cameras dangling off his arms and neck. He carried AP credentials and operated like any other *paparazzi* photographer, aggressively searching for the perfect image of the key players at the event. He watched another man, Saul Abboud, who stood alone, taking extensive notes and looking nervous.

Seconds later Abboud retrieved his phone and called Badge Demarche to deliver the news. "I just heard the speech from Ed Kosko—he's formally announced his candidacy for the NLP top spot."

"Was there any pullback, negative or contrary opinions on his announcement?"

"No, none. Actually he roused the crowd to a long standing ovation. He is supported by Pathroads for America, Charley Rhodes' group, and they've been preparing for this for a while. It was very well orchestrated and well received."

"As I feared the NLP is rallying around Kosko. That's a serious problem. You need to get that call from Mr. Thomas. Get back to DC as soon as you can." Badge reflected on his promise to Tan Zhang to stop the COS momentum.

"I'll leave tomorrow morning. Maybe we can meet when I return to DC." Abboud failed to get a response from Badge. He closed his phone in anger and nearly bumped into the AP paparazzi reporter as he walked away. "Excuse me sir, I'm sorry."

"Oh, my mistake, too busy looking through my camera lens." The minute listening bug, equipped with a GPS tracking tag, configured to appear as a button, was easily slid into Abboud's sport jacket pocket as they separated. Saul Abboud never recognized the man he knew as Mr. Thomas, disguised beyond any resemblance to the man he dealt with to arrange Kosko's elimination. Khamal walked away prepared to visit Abboud's location well after dark. It had been determined that Saul Abboud was destined to disappear soon.

CHAPTER TEN

Budapest, Hungary, Adrestia LTD Headquarters

Declan Crusoe sat in the sequestered conference room along with four other members of the Adrestia special unit group. His mind kept replaying the night he was to meet with Wren Cove. His instincts had told him to vanish after the two men rushed into Cove Production Studios just before his scheduled meeting with Wren. When it was announced two days later that Cove died in his office of a heroin overdose, he was suspicious. Declan's original copy of the damning video of Barriman and Demarche had yet to be seen by Dalton, but he worried Wren's copy was missing or destroyed.

The conference room was one of four locked, secure wings, each connected to a central lobby atrium, affording the only natural light into the complex called the "Operating Center Unit". This structure was attached to the main office of engineering and project offices for Adrestia LTD, and supplied all the project financial control, along with other secret functions for the "unit". Lars Nevin entered after a few minutes through a side door, normally locked and guarded by his personal security men. He handed out large sealed manila packets of individual mission assignments to the field operatives. Declan let his packet, labeled Declan Faden, lay unopened as Lars sat down and began his usual update on the unit's activities. As he studied the Faden name he thought of his mother, known only through photos and letters Jonathon Crusoe left with his adoptive parents until a later time. He was nervous fearing Lars' highly skilled intelligence team had discovered his true identity.

Lars Nevin looked at each man in attendance, including a penetrating stare at Declan, before saying, "We have a target list. My contact in DC has confirmed the men in this packet are the final targets and must be eliminated within the next two months. The funds are expected to arrive this afternoon, and then we will be active on this assignment." Lars then opened his mission folio and began to sort out the pages. "Open your mission packets gentlemen."

Declan's pulse rate increased and his body felt warm as he ripped open the mission envelop. He removed four photos, a map, several newspaper articles dating back two years, a cash deposit of $30,000 against a $300,000 contract payment, and a full page biography on *his* target. Declan struggled to control his reaction—Jameson Dalton Crusoe was his target—his worst fear was now a reality. The extensive material made it obvious Dalton Crusoe was considered a major threat to the President's agenda. Dalton's history and friendship with Ed Kosko left no doubt he represented a formidable asset to Kosko's campaign plan. It was clear Declan had been selected to not only set up the attack, but then personally carry out the assassination of Dalton. A sickening tension began to overtake Declan. A nameless, brief mission statement explained he was left to work out the specific timing and method, yet making it appear as a mugging gone deadly. Beyond the standard covert combat rucksack, Adrestia would secretly deliver any special weapons, bomb materials, secure communication systems, and provide for Declan's extraction following the mission.

Lars Nevin let the group study their respective mission packets and finally spoke. "Are there any questions about your individual missions? Anyone want out?" Declan followed the others lead and accepted the contract without comment. He wondered if anyone ever survived outside the closed conference room after declining an assignment. Lars' two reclusive, well armed, security guards made a menacing image as they strolled by the small sidelight glass at the door. An unmistakable ringtone came from Lars' satellite phone lying atop his leather portfolio. The group sat attentively as Lars took the call and said, "Excuse me a moment men. I'll be right back."

The other three men all accepted their respective assignments, and the hefty payments, yet no one knew the others' targets, except that all were threats to the current administration. Lars returned to the conference room after a minute. "Gentlemen, you have your assignments. Be careful, and be successful. Our client needs these men eliminated. You are dismissed."

The men stood and began to leave when Lars said, "Declan remain here a minute."

"Of course." Declan answered yet he feared the worst— perhaps he had been discovered or was going to be questioned on his assignment.

"The call I took was from one of our contractors, working on the same mission we just discussed." Lars studied Declan like an examining physician. "It relates to your assignment." Lars pointed to the mission packet with Declan's name on it.

"Yes sir. What is the issue?" Declan felt trapped, awaiting his death.

"The caller confirmed, through his own actions, that Dalton Crusoe is dead. He died three days ago in Canada. His funeral was two hours ago. So your target is eliminated and your assignment cancelled." Lars paused, showing no emotion, no expression.

"Really, that's interesting. Had Crusoe been under another's contract? I don't understand why my assignment was sanctioned." Declan tried to look misled, hiding his shock that his half-brother is dead.

"No Crusoe was not under a kill contract from us until last week—however it appears there was an older unfulfilled contract by another group that has long wanted Crusoe eliminated. Another of our contractors personally carried out the assignment—he apparently found an opportunity to get it done before his assignment with us. I don't exactly know the circumstances, but nevertheless, your assignment is withdrawn."

Declan shifted about in his chair, before saying, "Well I guess that means I'm sitting this one out then, right?"

Lars Nevin calmly stood and walked to the only door serving the conference room. "No, perhaps not. I have a call to make to DC about the Convention of States project. My client contact feels he may need a specialist to investigate a suspected mole in the Barriman administration—and eliminate him. Are you up for that?"

"Yeah, I'm ready; I'd welcome the action and need the money." Declan rose and delivered a forced smile at the new possibility. Lars gave a stone-faced glance at Declan.

"Stay here today and I'll confirm if we have a new assignment." Lars left the room, shutting the door behind him. As the door closed, a stocky, muscular security guard glared at Declan through the window glass. Declan shook as he reached for a cigarette. The morning dragged on waiting for Lars Nevin to return to the sequestered "operations" room adjacent to his secure office. Declan took a seat in the lobby and used his company supplied smart phone to access the internet. He paused and considered the idea all his searches, calls, emails and texts were run through Adrestia's impressive intelligence wing of the communications center. He rationalized a search for "Dalton Crusoe Funeral" would not be unexpected, in light of the information Lars just provided. Within seconds, a link appeared for a brief North Carolina news release...*Local Residents Attend Funeral for Dalton Crusoe, Annapolis Graduate, Former NSA Agent, Killed in a Training Mission.* The two paragraph article highlighted Dalton's brief, yet high profile career, and referenced his mother and fiancée. It seemed a weak tribute to an extraordinary man in Declan's mind.

Declan's mood turned somber, reviewing the first and only time he met his half-brother, the warning he'd given him, and the information he'd wanted to give Dalton. He imagined the shock and pain Carolyn must have felt at the news. Suddenly without a hint of his presence, Lars Nevin approached him, and sat down across a small coffee table in the outer lobby area serving the communications center. The stocky, muscular, security guard followed behind Lars and stood at a comfortable distance, saying nothing while he scanned the area, every angle and every movement. Declan tried to remove the gloom that had spread over his face.

"I've had a long talk with my DC client. He's very concerned there is a mole in the Barriman administration, and that he may have arranged a near fatal accident for the President and him. They both survived but it was close. He's contracted the *unit* to investigate and find, if he exists, this mole. Are you interested?"

Declan took notice and saw the assignment as a way to effect his exit from the unit. "Yes sir, I'll take it on. What is the timing and what clues do they have as to where to look in the administration?"

"I'll start a file through our intelligence team and get it to you in a few days. Get a flight into DC late today if possible. All we know so far is that one name has come up as a possible lead, and it may have a military connection."

"Really, Ok what's the name?" Declan appeared eager and committed, hoping to convince Lars that he had made a good choice.

"The name is 'Flask', obviously a code name, but it's a start. Keep me informed; this is a high priority with the client. Good luck Declan." Lars shook hands with Faden and left the lobby.

Declan began to breathe a bit easier, and thought to himself... "Flask".

◆ ◆ ◆

Dallas Texas, Sixth Day of the Convention of States

The late morning crowd was more active than expected. The powerful speech given by Ed Kosko the evening before continued to resonate with the various state delegations. The New Libertarian Party took the unprecedented step of inviting the various state delegations to pass a unanimous consent resolution to declare Ed Kosko as the party's nominee for President. The fractured remnants of the Republican Party had neither the candidate nor the money to promote a contender to Kosko. The resolution was adopted and passed by enough states to assure Ed Kosko the nomination, uncontested. The plan was to avoid a painful and fractious primary contest which would only weaken the surviving candidate. The "Kosko for President" banners, newly printed and distributed among the delegations were waving everywhere. The news media, even those of a liberal bent, were rushing to Dallas to cover the historic rise of the New Libertarian Party, now championing Ed Kosko. Barriman strategists were looking at a new calculus with the strong message and formidable challenge of Ed Kosko. Charley Rhodes and his team were rolling on the momentum of Ed's speech and the fund raising skyrocketed.

Just as the convention's closing was announced a call came in for Ed Kosko. The communications technician covered the phone and said, "Sir, it's the President...President Barriman."

Ed Kosko set his water bottle down, looked to Dalton and said, "I wonder what this is all about?"

"I'll wager a tidy sum, he's calling to congratulate you on the NLP nomination." Dalton smirked and motioned to his friend to answer the call.

Ed took the phone, and said, "Mr. President, this is Ed Kosko."

"Ed, I wanted to call and congratulate you on your impressive speech and the resulting unanimous nomination by the NLP to become their Presidential candidate. Perhaps we can get together in a social setting with our staffs and settle on timing for a couple of moderated debates."

"Thank you Mr. President. I appreciate your call. I think establishing some understanding as to how we proceed during the campaign season would be fine."

"Excellent! I'll have Badge connect with Charley Rhodes as I hear he is managing your campaign. Is that alright?"

"Yes that would be fine. Thank you Mr. President. Goodbye."

Badge Demarche watched the President as he recited the prepared comment, and sensed he was nearer to satisfying Tan Zhang's demands—eliminate Kosko, and stop the New Libertarian Party.

◆ ◆ ◆

Carolyn was disturbed, looking for Dalton, Wilson at her side. They moved over to the mezzanine where Dalton and Ronet had set up a semi-enclosed vantage point amid massive lights and cameras for the visual effects of the Convention.

"JD, there you are, I've been looking for you." Carolyn was visibly shaken.

"What's the problem? Are you all right?" Wilson had a serious look on his face. "We've found something important, we think, Dalton."

Dalton directed them to a small table, behind the cameras and lights framework. Wilson began to spread out two dozen photos taken at the funeral ruse days earlier.

"He was there. He was there JD." Carolyn began to tear up and Dalton moved close to hold her.

"Who was there honey?" Carolyn dropped her face into her hands and fell into Dalton's chest. "Khamal was there, he was looking at me—right into my face. I felt uncomfortable at the time but I know now it was him."

Wilson spread three photos before Dalton. "Here are two photos just as this guy left the casket and walked by Carolyn and your mother. This close up we cropped and expanded to show a direct frontal face image. She took one look at it and knew it was Hasid Khamal." Dalton looked at the photo and searched his memory of the funeral crowd. He pulled Carolyn close and kissed her face as he whispered, "I'm so sorry honey. Don't worry, Brad and I are ahead of him and will get him." Carolyn tried to compose herself, and looked deep into Dalton's face saying without words...'*please save me from losing you to this killer*'.

Dalton glanced at the photos Wilson had provided and remarked, "I remember this guy. He was an old Navy veteran, I thought. Are you sure it's him?"

Wilson spread more photos before Dalton. "This one right here got me wondering. The uniform didn't look right, nor did the service ribbons on his chest."

"What exactly do you mean, Wilson?"

"The ribbons were from many areas—not just the Navy. Several of them are Army and Air Force, a few from the Coast Guard and one Canadian ribbon. The uniform and medals were fakes." Wilson noticed Carolyn ready to speak.

"JD, the facial photo did it. The moment I saw this man's eyes, I recalled the encounter at...your funeral...and was thrown back to the Caribbean, where he pushed me onto the bed, held a rag over my face and his other hand on my throat. I will never forget my fear or those eyes—I stared into them and saw death."

Dalton tried to comfort Carolyn while he held her tight. She regained some composure and straightened up. Wiping her eyes, she said, "I'm sorry. I want to be helpful, and I *know* this is the man I thought you...killed...after he attacked us a couple of years back." She smiled for a split second and pointed at the face photo. "That's him—I know it—that's him."

"Ok. That's what we were trying to confirm at my...'funeral'...that Khamal might appear to verify I was killed in Canada. Do we have anything else, Wilson, that supports Carolyn's assertion?" Dalton gave Carolyn an assuring look—he believed her. She sat down in a nearby chair and sipped her water bottle trying to calm down.

"Actually we have some interesting security images on file from the Marigot marina in St. Martin the day of your sail that led to the attack on you and Carolyn. The man believed to be the assassin Khamal wore sunglasses, but the body size, and facial structure is a good match, allowing for the obvious disguise Khamal surely wore to your funeral. Since we never found Khamal's body following the earlier attack, we have kept the file open, looking for him. He never appeared until now when his prints, combined with these photos, likely confirm he's most likely alive—and set on completing his contract with the Iranians to...kill you." Carolyn shuddered at the thought.

"Right. The question now is whether he's here to assassinate Ed, or me—or both of us. If he's the assassin contracted to fulfill the thirty-day threat against Ed then we have exactly twenty-eight days left." Dalton contemplated the situation. "We need to draw him into a trap that looks too attractive to pass by for an assassination attempt." Dalton looked to Wilson who got the message.

"I'll start working on that, Dalton." Carolyn tried to control and disguise her current panic attack.

◆ ◆ ◆

Saul Abboud got the message that an "operative" was headed to the COS to aid in the search for the suspected mole that Badge Demarche felt was in the administration. He waited in the large entrance lobby just outside the security checkpoint, and obsessed over a mental outline of talking points he'd use when he'd meet with Badge. The time was 5:43 p.m. less than an hour away from the time when the majority of prime time television coverage would begin on the event speakers, analyses and interviews for two hours.

Declan was told to identify Saul Abboud based on his slim 5'-11" frame, nominally 165 pounds, darker toned skin, and a distinct bright red lanyard strap holding his credentials. Declan noticed Abboud immediately after entering the outer door to the arena. As he approached, Saul stepped up and said, "Mr. Faden, I'm Saul Abboud."

Declan looked the man over and felt convinced he was in fact Abboud. Still he needed confirmation. "Dallas seems nice. Have ya ever been here before, Mr. Abboud?"

Saul grinned and responded, "Why, yes, I was here in *April 1998*." That was the correct answer to the test question Adrestia's unit had set up to confirm identities once the men connected.

Declan smiled and said, 'Thanks that's a good answer. Please call me Declan."

Saul gave Declan the authentic looking, but bogus credentials claiming he was a political consultant for the same conservative think-tank. They walked through security without issues and Declan was given a wristband identifying him and giving him with access to the main floor, the press section, and the General seating areas.

"So what is it that yer man...Demarche suspects—a mole in the Barriman administration right?"

"Yes, weeks ago the President and Demarche were nearly killed in what appeared to be an unusual double tire blowout following a fundraising event in Virginia. Later investigations strongly suggested this was an assassination attempt made to look like an accident." Saul offered Declan a slim file detailing the event and the findings. "This just came in a download from Adrestia."

Declan took the file and asked, "Saul does the name 'Flask' mean anything to ya?"

Abboud fought to control his reaction to hearing the name Flask twice in two days. He thought carefully and answered, "No, means nothing to me. Why?"

"It is the only clue we have as ta the possible identity of the mole—not much ta go on."

"How are you expecting to uncover this 'mole'?" Saul held his breath waiting for Declan's answer.

"Adrestia has given me names of some possibilities, ya know, folks that Demarche suspects. I'll do some footwork, plant some bugs and see what comes up." Saul Abboud listened with intense interest to Declan's words.

"I'm goin' ta walk about this place for a while and pick up a sense of what's going on. Maybe learn something interesting. When da we fly ta DC...late this evening?"

"Yes, it's a charter that some of the news media arranged— you're a contract photographer working with me through my political consulting group—PRS, Political Right Solutions, ever heard of them?" Declan shook his head indicating—*no*. "I'm going back to my hotel room and connect with my boss, then we can get together this evening go to the airport. I'll try to help you with your assignment."

"Fine. See ya later."

◆ ◆ ◆

Hasid Khamal sat in a small coffee bistro sipping a strong dark roast Columbian blend that was meant for only the hearty. He was outside the main arena, in an open setting allowing smoking and some sunshine. As he picked at the plate of tapas supplied with the coffee he listened to the conversation Saul Abboud carried on with Declan. The bug was extremely clear and the miniature earpiece resembled a music player. Khamal's smart phone GPS monitored the movements of Abboud as he left the complex to return to his hotel. On a small note pad Khamal wrote the word "Flask", studied it for several minutes and then wrote two more names—Saul Abboud and Declan Faden. He next sent an encrypted email through Lars Nevin for Badge Demarche through the Adrestia server. The message was brief: *As feared Abboud denies knowledge of the code name Flask, to the requested operative (Lars) sent to working for you. Concerns? Actions?*

Less than an hour later Badge Demarche read his encrypted email from Lars Nevin which contained the concerns and observations of Khamal. The email ended with: *SA likely connected to "Flask". We recommend risk elimination. Respond.*

Badge was alarmed to read the reactions of Abboud when told of the suspected mole known as "Flask" He struggled to see how Abboud could have played a role in the Virginia tire blow out episode. Still he had trusted Abboud implicitly and may have left opportunities for his friend and operative to betray him. Nevertheless, Abboud's denials and lies indicated he could not be trusted. He simply couldn't ignore Lars' opinion, and risk any blowback from the Chinese. He emailed back to Lars: *Expand contractor's assignment to eliminate new risk. Funding adjustment forthwith.*

♦ ♦ ♦

Declan felt convinced Abboud believed he was just another "foot soldier" in the Adrestia unit sent to get information, and evidence if possible, on a mole in the administration. His escape from Adrestia had to come in the next few days, when he would go silent and try to find a way to stop the contract on Ed Kosko. Declan began to browse the various state legislature booths, reading some of the literature and listening to an endless string of scheduled speakers each adding their personal twist to the agenda for the COS and their support for the new darling of the NLP— Ed Kosko. Dalton remained in his mezzanine perch studying the crowd and looking for a certain face. Ed Kosko had left for a meeting with Charley Rhodes to plan details of his campaign. Carolyn remained with Dalton and sat nearby in a chair sipping a fresh coffee, trying to calm down after confidently identifying Khamal in the photo search Wilson had provided. She could see a large part of the convention floor and casually listened to the speakers and the ever present music which played loudly between speeches and as soft background support during applause moments. Carolyn found her eyes focused on a man, walking the floor and strolling between the delegation booths. "Dalton come here a moment."

Dalton looked back at her, left his laptop keyboard and smiled at her as he approached. "What's going on—you OK?"

"Look at that man, right there." Carolyn pulled Dalton into her line of sight and pointed directly at a man some hundred yards away. "Do you recognize him?"

"No not really, should I?"

"Yes, it's Declan." Dalton stood up to get a better view and stared at the man.

"Carolyn I think you're right, he's here." Dalton started to head down to the main convention floor, when Carolyn said, "What are you doing?"

"I'm going to talk to him. He must have made his exit from Adrestia." At that point, Dalton realized his recklessness as he looked into Carolyn's eyes.

"No you shouldn't go down there. First of all you're looking for Khamal right? Secondly, you don't look like Dalton, right?"

Dalton failed to consider that Declan might not recognize him in disguise, and his identity might become compromised. "Yes, you're right, damn disguise is a nuisance. This is the last day of the convention...I'll take the chance." Dalton removed the mustache and glasses; the contacts and dark wig had already been retired the day before.

Carolyn said, "Don't go down to the floor, I'll get him." Dalton knew the comment was a command not a request.

"I'll go down to meet him and take him to the conference room in Charley Rhodes' administrative center. Behave, Ok?"

She looked with delight at the *"original Dalton"* and walked away with a wink.

Dalton smiled at the clear thinking and cool demeanor Carolyn produced after having been upset earlier at the recognition of Khamal. "Smart girl! See you at Rhodes' camp."

Declan strolled along the perimeter of the large arena main floor unaware of Carolyn's approach. Carolyn considered the possibility Declan had not heard of Dalton's *"funeral"* and chose to present a smiling face rather than one of remorse—the truth could come later.

"Good morning Declan. I'm surprised to see you here." Carolyn looked stunning in a fashionable navy blue short jacket over a sleeveless cream blouse, matching a tight skirt stopping just above the knee and in four inch heels. Declan finally noticed her when she was less than ten feet away.

His instincts took over and he grabbed her in a firm hug and said, "I'm on my way out o' the unit, I'm on a new assignment." Carolyn reciprocated and embraced Declan. He pulled back and released Carolyn.

"I am so sorry to learn of Dalton's...passing. I was sickened and shocked...how are you doing?" Declan struggled to understand her happy expression, so he asked, "How is it you're here at the Convention o' States?"

"I can best explain that in private, please come with me." The start of a smile spread across Carolyn's face again and Declan looked bewildered.

Dalton had made his way to Charley Rhodes' convention headquarters and steered his way through two dozen energized staffers working the phones and organizing appearances for Ed Kosko. Rhodes was in his office, meeting with Kosko, Ronet and several campaign specialists. Kosko saw Dalton coming without disguise and informed Charley that Bill Wright was really Dalton Crusoe—another target for assassination. Charley understood, noticed Dalton's arrival and made a hand motion to join him in the conference room. Ed Kosko took note and followed along. Once together Dalton said, "I've got someone I want you all to meet. Someone who can help us protect Ed as this campaign moves forward."

"Really, what the hell are you talking about, JD?" Ed shuffled through his sport jacket pockets for a cigar.

The door to the conference room opened and Carolyn entered first. "Ed, Charley, this is my...brother, Declan Crusoe."

Declan looked at his brother and walked up and hugged him for a long moment. "Thanks ta God, brother yer alive. I was so shocked and fearful when I was told ya were...killed...in Canada. I dunna understand." Dalton introduced his half-brother to Charley and Ed.

Ed Kosko shook Declan's hand and said, "I understand you were the one who first alerted JD that I was targeted by— Barriman's invisible operatives. Is that right?"

"Aye, sir that would be correct. Pleased ta meet ya, and I'm sorry for all this mess."

"It's alright Declan. You did the right thing in the end. I knew your dad—he was a great friend. We've got a strong team on the problem, led by JD. Sorry about faking JD's death—Ronet's idea to draw out the assassin." Declan glanced at Dalton revealing his love and respect. Charley Rhodes held back and tried to absorb all the new information and faces. Ronet smiled at Ed's teasing.

Dalton took control of the conversation and asked, "How did you learn of my *death*? It was not heavily covered." Before an answer came forth, Dalton remarked, "By the way Declan, friends and family call me JD." The quip lightened the mood and Declan smiled at his brother.

"I learned fifteen minutes after I was assigned ta assassinate ya on a contract through Adrestia. I immediately knew I had ta *really* make me escape from the unit. While I struggled with that news for fifteen minutes, Lars Nevin, pulled me aside and withdrew the contract stating ya'd been killed and were buried in a funeral...a few days ago. He'd just been alerted ya were killed days earlier. Turns out the assassin is active on another contract on Mr. Kosko, here. He claims ta have confirmed yer death as well. "

Kosko broke in, "Damn JD, you and Ronet were right; Khamal went after you before he set sights on me."

"How was it you were selected to...kill me?" Dalton was fearful Declan's origins were revealed.

"I'm sure it was a random choice mate. They knew I needed the money, and was available. I feared they made our connection as brothers but it never surfaced or I may have been killed on the spot."

"So why are you here now?" Dalton had his suspicions.

"I was asked ta come here, meet with some bloke, Saul Abboud, and gather information on a suspected mole in the Barriman administration."

Charley Rhodes piped up, "I know this Abboud character—works for Badge Demarche, usually on dark, undercover stuff, always in the shadows."

"Is he an assassin, working for Adrestia?" Dalton asked.

Charley Rhodes quickly answered, "I don't think so. He's an opportunist, more of a mid-level contact to those types, and an intermediary to the real power players like Badge. Should we inform the Secret Service?"

Dalton thought a moment and said, "I don't think so. We still don't know whom to trust. A mole in Barriman's administration, interesting—I wonder who he is."

"He goes by the name of 'Flask' I'm told...that's all I know so far." Declan shrugged his shoulders.

"I wish he'd identify himself to us; he may have some helpful information on the Barriman-Demarche plans for Adrestia." Dalton looked to Ronet for ideas. Ronet delivered a blank stare.

"There's somethin' else Dalton. Ya've heard o' Wren Cove's death?"

"Yes, we all have. He was a strong conservative voice. You knew him didn't you Charley?"

Charley Rhodes added, "Yes, I knew Wren Cove—worked together years ago as cub reporters. He was no druggy. But he had enemies because of his outspoken stances and conservative audience. It's strange he dies days before he planned to reveal stuff on Barriman and his man Badge."

"Well brother, I've got another bit o' video you might like ta see. It shows Barriman and Demarche fixing to set America as a Chinese client state—using this CASP deal. My guess is Barriman's team went after Cove's copy, which means me former employer is aware and looking for me."

Dalton exclaimed, "You had the video material Cove mentioned?"

"Aye, I set it up and got the video. I offered it ta Wren. The night he died I was ta meet him prior ta his TV coverage of it."

An enraged Charley Rhodes spoke up, "Dalton let me help you with these two videos. If they are as revealing as Declan and Ronet claim then it goes way beyond political jockeying—it suggests a breakdown of the federal government system. We have to get it out on every media site soon. They blew it off immediately as a fabrication. You can bet Barriman and Demarche will try to suppress it coming out and try to portray it as a conservative forgery." Charley Rhodes was not about to remain non-responsive to Wren Cove's death.

Dalton considered the facts: Barriman was corrupt, his direction for America was hugely unpopular; and his plan would sacrifice the country's sovereignty, and his tactics were criminal. He then said, "Declan you are clearly the top priority for elimination now that Abboud is gone."

"Aye, brother. That's exactly how I see things lining up." I best stay low a bit and see what I can learn from hiding in the shadows. Right?"

Dalton looked at his brother, then Ronet, and replied, "Yes. I have the perfect assignment for you over the next couple of days."

The entire group waited to hear more, but Dalton simply said, "Later."

Carolyn sat quietly—confused and hoping Dalton could stop Khamal and protect his brother.

◆ ◆ ◆

Khamal's tracking bug he'd tucked into Abboud's sport coat pocket led him to the Sheraton, near the Convention Center. He had received a brief response from Lars Nevin through Adrestia: *Confidence Lost. Exposure risk great. Make Correction Immediately per prior Understandings.*

The premier assassin understood the message—eliminate the risk per your usual fee. Khamal opened his briefcase and found his special phone dedicated to communication with Saul Abboud, if needed. The time was 8:20 p.m., an hour before his flight back to Washington DC. Khamal entered the number for the burner phone he'd provided Abboud. Saul heard the unusual ring and had to search for the phone in his briefcase. He thought Khamal may have just completed his assignment on Kosko and quickly opened the phone saying, "This is Saul."

The phone made an unusual click, and followed with the words, *'Please listen for a private message'.* A second later a powerful electrical charge blasted into Abboud's right ear. He fell to the floor and held his head grimacing in pain. Moments later his breathing labored and his heart stopped. The modified burner phone then heated quickly and began to emit smoke as the memory was rendered inert.

Khamal determined the opportunities were not great at the Convention of States to complete his contract on Ed Kosko. In deliberately sparse words, Khamal sent an encrypted email through Adrestia to Lars Nevin who passed it on to Badge Demarche. It read: *Exposure Risk Eliminated. Original contract strategy is revised, yet timetable still intact.*

CHAPTER ELEVEN

Dallas, Seventh and Final Day of the Convention of States

The nation had increasingly become focused on the meaning and importance of the Convention of States project. Beyond a poorly-defined but well-accepted political strategy to restore the country to its founding tenants and structure, it had crowds identifying with the message of the New Libertarian Party and its candidate Ed Kosko. Over the days that followed the start of the Convention, news coverage had grown and the rally that had begun in Dallas spread to twenty-two cities, where thousands hit the streets, in generally peaceful, yet spirited support for the movement to prepare a slate of amendments for presentation to the states for approval by their legislatures. Nevertheless, opponents on the left, including governmental unions and many in the entertainment industry, rallied against the effort labeling it a *"trick"* to weaken the constitution and harm the country.

The crowds had essentially deserted the arena the night before, yet a number of commissioners remained the next morning to coordinate the approved amendment slate for adoption by at least forty-one states—more than enough to incorporate them into the US Constitution. The floor was quiet except for the cleanup and work crews dismantling booths all intended to restore the area to a useable surface. Charley Rhodes kept over a skeleton staff of six to update the commissioners on the talking points for the Kosko campaign. First on the agenda was a fast six week "whistle-stop" journey to most of the states participating in the COS with brief speeches from Kosko to put a face on the new messenger for their amendments. Pathroads for America had purchased radio, television, and billboard space for the promotion of Ed Kosko, New Libertarian Party candidate for President. It seemed incomplete without a VP selection yet the energy was high following the COS, and the voters needed a name, a man, an image to add life to the staid process of approving amendments to the Constitution. Ed Kosko understood and began to sharpen his considerable speaking skills.

When Charley Rhodes offered five possibilities for the VP slot, Ed took little time in making his first choice—General Jack Watts, head of the Joint Chiefs, a loyal Army soldier and smart leader. Watts had been a member of the Joint Chiefs the final year of the former Conner administration and was kept on and promoted by Barriman. His credentials were impeccable and his loyalty was unquestioned, at least toward the office of the President. Kosko and Watts had worked together years earlier on crises that crossed agency lines between the NSA and the military, specifically involving Colonel Brad Ronet, a special military assignment which reported directly to past President Jerome Conner. Even though Watts and Kosko had not connected in months, Ed knew the General detested the way Barriman was running the country. He was certain the failure to protect and rescue the SnapLift team in the Nawa Pass area of Afghanistan would have repulsed Watts. Ronet confirmed his suspicions and the decision was made to talk with Watts.

Charley Rhodes set up a conference call with Watts, Dalton, Ronet and Ed in the remains of his Dallas operations center. The phone rang into the General's office assistant. "General Watts office, may I help you?"

"This is Ed Kosko calling for the General." After two clicks the General answered.

"Hello, Ed, I see you are all over the news the last couple of days. You gave up fishing for politics. What's the hell's the matter with you?"

"Hey Jack. Well you called it correctly. I've got you on speaker phone with Dalton Crusoe, Colonel Ronet and Charley Rhodes, head of Pathroads for America—in his conference room on a secure line. Can you talk awhile?"

"You've got Brad in there? Is he in camo fatigues or a suit?" The group chuckled, as Ronet shook his head at the humorous shot.

"General this is Charley Rhodes and we have been doing some spot polling since Ed announced his candidacy on the NLP ticket. We have learned that by a strong margin you lead all other prospects by eight points or more to be the favored choice for Ed's VP. We'd like to talk with you about your interest in joining the ticket." Charley almost hyperventilated at his bold request to a man he'd never met before.

"Spot polling huh? I'm surprised anyone knows who I am."

Ronet couldn't resist and spoke up, "General, I know you hate politicians but you are known and respected particularly by the voters likely drawn to Ed Kosko. We'd like you onboard."

"You still drinking before noon, Brad?" The crowd broke into a laugh at the friendly sparring. "Ed, have you thought about this? You know me and I'm likely to say something, well very 'military', if I get pissed off at some reporter or journalist."

"I know exactly that feeling Jack. Yet I'm betting you're just as fed up as I am with the direction of the country. And I know you had a hard time stomaching the actions of Barriman in the

Nawa Pass recently." The room grew silent and the mood somber.

"Right! I damn near snapped Badge's neck as he told me to stand down against the President. I almost quit that moment—but didn't. Brad did you follow my last instruction to you that day?"

"Yes sir I did. I have an hour's worth of ops coverage, video and voice—even though Barriman ordered all files protected under executive privilege." All but Rhodes knew the background behind the remarks.

"What do you propose we do with that data gentlemen?" Watts inquired.

Dalton spoke up adding, "General we also have a video of Demarche and Barriman discussing the CASP deal moments before the President signed the final agreement. It's pretty damning—more corruption."

Ed took the question and said, "I think we need to wait, check the progress of the campaign, and if necessary call for release of the mission files through the House Armed Services Committee. Let Badge and Barriman squirm to avoid an impeachment based on their actions."

Charley Rhodes emotions grew and he followed up with, "If the Nawa Pass disaster doesn't stir the country, then we can go with the CASP video and folks will link it to Wren Cove's death. He can then try to explain away that away as well."

Watts listened carefully. "That sounds reasonable, as long as there is a day of reckoning. Barriman's actions were criminal and, I fear, influenced by the Chinese. You really want me to do this Ed—join the campaign as your VP?"

"Yes I really do Jack. I promise you I'll handle the bulk of the political stuff, if you'll handle the defense, military and security parts." Ed looked to Dalton and added, "Dalton can be of help in all of that as can Ronet." A long pause followed, causing Charley Rhodes to fear the coming answer.

"Ok Ed I'm in as your VP. But I am not going to be a *'grip and grin'* political type. I need to stick to my field of expertise." Rhodes jumped from his chair and yelled. "Excellent General, my group will help you get up to speed. When can you submit your resignation?"

"I'll meet with the President tomorrow and tender my resignation effective later—maybe give him a week to promote another Joint Chief to be the Head and announce my departure."

Ed thanked him and added, "Jack, Dalton, Ronet and I head to DC next week Tuesday. I'll call to set up a meeting to acquaint you with the COS initiative, if you haven't followed it much."

"Fine Ed. You just might be surprised how acquainted I am with the NLP and the COS initiative. See you on Tuesday." The phone line disconnected and all three men struggled to understand Jack Watts' last remark. Dalton had some interesting theories.

◆ ◆ ◆

Norfolk Virginia, Norfolk Naval Station Ship Yards

The Enterprise class super carrier, *Enterprise*, was engulfed with structural engineers, welders, marine contractors, naval weapons specialists, and a contingent of ten Chinese military leaders, all in business suites to avoid attention. The intense activity was unusual as the *Enterprise* was scheduled for decommissioning in a year and was awaiting defueling efforts. However, the CASP financing deal included a few amendments in the final days which went unnoticed by most Americans. The sale and recommissioning of the *Enterprise* under the Chinese flag, and a new name, *Varyag II*, was on schedule. A handful of skilled Chinese naval engineers and technicians worked around the clock supervising, in the shadows, the modifications and upgrades. The new nuclear Chinese nuclear engine plant was installed and now in dry-dock trials, the navigation and communications had been totally updated and were in beta testing, and the aircraft comprised of fifteen Chinese fighter aircraft that would call the *Varyag II* home were scheduled to fly in once the *Varyag II* set to sea.

The $400 billion purchase of the carrier was a much welcomed, and needed, early payment, weeks before the official signing of CASP. The US Treasury found few buyers for its debt and the Barriman administration needed to avoid a fiscal panic during the Convention of States and the approaching November elections. The sale was originally explained as a scrap sale for Chinese steel mills causing little stir in the American public.

Walking with the Chinese military party were Badge Demarche and Tan Zhang, brother of the Chinese People's Party President. Badge used these ceremonial occasions to have confidential talks with the Chinese leadership.

"It appears the progress of reconstruction is ahead of schedule Tan, would you agree?"

"Yes, it is well along and I expect within two weeks we will deploy the ship to the Atlantic and head to the west coast of Africa."

"What happens there if I may ask?"

Tan Zhang stopped and smiled at Badge. "We will stock the ship with aircraft, drones, missiles, supplies, and a crew and wait to see how you and the President handle this Convention of States matter."

"Really, what does that mean?" Badge tried to display a non-threatening interest in the answer.

"It means, sir that my brother and I do not believe our interests, and therefore your interests, will be promoted by the presence of this growing political group. Do I need to remind you we have a major loan package in place for your country, and have spent years supporting your private research to your benefit and have perfected it for many interesting uses? Should the New Libertarian's take control of your Congress, and your positions— and if they adopt many of the proposed revisions to your Constitution, our relationship will be compromised." Tan gave a stare that left no doubt the Chinese would not tolerate a change in leadership this soon after a financing deal. Tan then addressed another concern, asking, "Do you have a plan to deal with the rising vocal support for the Convention of States? I notice this movement has now grown to include street rallies, and in some instances armed protesters...calling themselves militias. This cannot stand."

"I understand all that, Tan, and I assure you we are working on those concerns. The crowds are growing yet they are peaceful, so far, and when the President and I enter the debate stage and make appearances the opposition will weaken. As you know I'm now Vice President, and can manage the President even more effectively in this role." Badge left unsaid the underlying actions, known by both men, preceding his ascendancy to the VP slot.

"Then I can be assured our funds to engage the "Unit" will soon to yield results?" The unspoken reference to Adrestia was crystal clear; Tan expected Ed Kosko and the New Libertarian Party to be destroyed.

"We're doing what we can, but you must remember we are a nation of people governed by a popular vote, and we cannot predict the vote with absolute certainty. We may have to deal with the agenda of the New Libertarian Party for a few years if they win in November."

Tan Zhang slowly turned to face Badge before saying, "Mr. Demarche, we are not going to allow a change in direction for the USA unless it is heading toward a MORE compliant role as it relates to Chinese interests. Is that perfectly clear?"

Badge Demarche swallowed hard and responded, "Yes, I understand, as does the President. We are going to neutralize the NLP initiative."

"Good, Mr. Demarche. You recognize China is now your *most* favored partner in all matters."

"Yes, of course I understand."

◆ ◆ ◆

Ten Days later, off the West Coast of Africa

The large cargo carrier finally docked alongside the *Varyag II,* and began to unload munitions, drones, weapons, fuel and sophisticated communications hardware. Large cranes lifted supplies and personal transport equipment to the side-board loading portals on the *Varyag II*. The full complement of 5300 sailors, officers, and pilots boarded the new Chinese warship.

Fighter aircraft flew in every three minutes to load the lower bays with the war birds. One of the new Type-096 Chinese submarines parked near the aircraft carrier; its mere presence creating deterrence against any provocative actions by other naval vessels. On its maiden voyage, the submarine carried twenty-four ballistic missiles capable of being launched underwater from the new sub variant and delivering multiple independently targetable reentry vehicles (MIRVs) each of which carry a nuclear warhead and allow a single launched missile to strike several targets.

This conjuncture of Chinese naval vessels was confirmed by NSA satellites that had been positioned directly over the meeting site and taken multiple photos. The Chinese now held the strategic, first-strike advantage over the USA after it had consented to the conditions of the "CASP" agreement which required United Nations approval of any US military action. NSA reports of the rendezvous flooded the White House and landed *only* on Vice President Badge Demarche's desk.

Badge Demarche read the latest satellite report and feared his relationship with the Chinese leadership was tilting away from the balance he had known for years—they now acted as though they had the upper hand. Unknown to the administration, a copy of the satellite report found its way to the man known as... 'Flask'.

CHAPTER TWELVE

August, Outer Banks, North Carolina

The evening sail aboard the thirty-seven foot C&C, named *Trending*, was smooth and slow, tacking modestly at a steady three knots. It was Charley Rhodes' boat on loan to Kosko for the evening. The setting of the sun, still some two hours away, was preceded its steady journey to the western horizon, casting long shadows of the boat and sails on the water. The pleasant offshore breeze tempered the 79 degree air toward a refreshing 73 degree feel. The sky now completely clear except for a string of thin, cirrus clouds directly above, began to change to a rich, dark blue as the light weakened. On the stern deck sat Dalton and Carolyn, and Ed and Irene Kosko, sipping fresh mojitos as Dalton steered the sleek single mast vessel south. The trip was a last minute getaway for the couples following the fast-paced, high energy schedule at the Convention of States.

Dalton had spent hours apologizing to his mother and Carolyn about the ruse faking his own death. The strain of misleading his mother was too much for her and Dalton decided to postpone the revelation of Declan Crusoe. Carolyn forcefully argued her future mother-in-law should be told, and felt she should be present when Elizabeth learned of Declan. Their relationship was maturing to one of trust and support. Ed Kosko had to admit his complicity in the plan to Irene. The quiet evening sail was intended to further heal the intense pain and sorrow all had been forced to endure. Elizabeth Crusoe had excused herself from the sailing venture to allow the couples some private talking time. Ed Kosko had made his candidacy announcement for President on the New Libertarian ticket the final day of the convention, just before the closing remarks. The reaction from attendees was unbridled enthusiasm for the candidate and his plan to restore America. Charley Rhodes had jumped into action the next day and begun the promotional campaign activating his skilled fund raising team to get the message out—the New Libertarian Party had a winner at the top. The campaign coffers were rapidly filling with donations.

Carolyn and Irene strolled around to the starboard bow as Dalton manned the wheel and Ed pondered campaign strategy going forward. "Have you come to accept the fresh scrutiny you and Ed now face Irene?" Carolyn knew Irene to be a strong woman, who ran a charitable foundation outside Richmond Virginia for two decades. While privately conservative, yet apolitical in her career, Irene knew how to avoid controversy.

"I guess so. Ed's been vetted several times during his career. Still the stakes have never been higher, so it will likely be a rough ride. But there are no skeletons in his closet...I hope." A smile spread across Irene's face as she tried to make light of the coming intrusion into their lives.

"It's really the threat on Ed's life that has me most concerned, although Ed is almost dismissing it—probably for my benefit. Still I have faith in Dalton and Colonel Ronet." Irene continued, "How are you and JD handling the apparent threat on his life?"

"Dalton is acting predictably—calm, logical, focused and unafraid. I'm scared to death, but will get through it. I just want to get this business with his half-brother Declan Crusoe behind him and settled. Right now, all JD can think about is Ed and Declan. So I've decided to let the wedding matter slide a bit." Carolyn's eyes glistened with the start of tearing while she smiled caringly at Irene.

Irene saw the loving concern Carolyn had for her man. "I'm so sorry dear. Be patient. He loves you very much." She reached over and held Carolyn's hand.

Carolyn related to Irene like she was the big sister, or aunt, she never had in her life and cherished her support. "Thanks Irene, I'm trying to be calm, and optimistic. I just can't get my hopes up too high with Dalton—he always seems to be dragged into these dangerous crises. Still he is the one I want to be with, so I'll be patient as you suggest. Thanks."

The two sipped their wine and watched as the sunset started to color the distant horizon sky. The water was calm and with a very light offshore wind *Trending* slid along with only one sail raised, about half billowed out and heeling the boat only three degrees. The eastern view displayed a few other boating craft including a few sailboats tacking gently in the soft breeze. Dalton had spent the last two days exclusively with his mother and Carolyn. To his surprise Elizabeth Crusoe, recovered quickly after Dalton appeared following the *funeral*. The adjustment in attitude involved a severe reprimand, lasting most of the evening, for not trusting her upfront with the plan. The three stayed at Elizabeth's condo on the North Carolina shore. However, next morning Dalton made them both breakfast and saw his mother ease back toward her normal self. Carolyn however, remained hurt, moody and scared even though she knew the funeral was a sham. The evening sail was a comfortable way to allow the two couples to "reboot" their sense of reality.

Ed Kosko seemed rejuvenated and near his former level of energy and engagement when he ran the NSA and was a top confidant of former President Jerome Conner. Dalton held a steady course of 240 degrees SSE, three miles offshore and near the outer bank of barrier islands protecting the distant shoreline.

He, too, was relaxing and trying not to spoil the evening with discussion of the upcoming campaign and Khamal's plans. Ed, however, was still on a *high* following his announcement to run on the NLP ticket.

Ed sipped his Famous Grouse and thought about his powerful speech at the Convention of States. "JD, what was your impression of how well my candidacy announcement came off?"

"I thought it was perfect—maybe the high point of the Convention. The cheering lasted seven minutes if you recall. The main stream news media actually reported it as a bellwether message tilting the uncommitted toward the New Libertarian Party."

"Really, that good?" Ed smiled shamelessly begging for more adoration.

"Yes, that good. And Charley Rhodes feels fund raising and poll ratings will jump."

"Well, what do you suppose the next big issue will be then?"

"Now that we have a VP pick. Charley's working on a small press conference to introduce him at your side—likely dressed in full military colors. Yet I'd say that the major issue is the need to uncover and eliminate this death threat against you." Ed nodded the logic of Dalton's remark.

"Remember my friend you've also already had an attack on your life. If, as we believe, Khamal is the contractor involved, and he learns he failed in killing you, he may take bold measures to get us both."

"I've thought of that, and Ronet's working up a comprehensive protection plan with the Secret Service guys as we hit the campaign trail. I know my bogus funeral will eventually be exposed. I just hope Ronet and I can stop Khamal, and others, before that happens." Dalton twisted his back slightly to sense the Beretta 380 tucked into the rear waistband of his shorts, further covered by his long windbreaker.

"Has Brad found anything on the funeral video yet?" Ed stood to refill his glass with ice and scotch. Dalton sipped his glass of cabernet.

"I expect he'll connect with me tomorrow, nothing has popped up yet. Wilson and Cotter are helping with lots of NSA data and analyses". Changing the subject, "Are we ready to have some food?" Dalton felt they needed to re-engage with Irene and Carolyn before they felt ignored.

Ed caught on to the subliminal message and responded, "Absolutely, JD, I'll gather our ladies."

Dalton surveyed the smooth water disturbed only by the mild wake the hull created as it slowly pushed south. A school of dolphins played with the faint ripple left behind the stern some fifty yards away. A handful of boats, mostly sailboats, were seen, including one large fishing boat seemingly floating without power a few hundred yards to the port side. He pulled up his binoculars and saw nothing on deck or in the captain's upper steering deck. The yacht appeared to be about thirty-five feet long with a high flying bridge, drifting towards Dalton's course. A small dinghy was tied off the stern. The red and white *"Diver Down"* flag hung limp off the swim platform....Dalton concluded...*divers.*

The lower galley made a comfortable setting to enjoy some appetizers and snacks while Ed grilled up some small tenderloins. The mood grew festive and moved away from the trauma of the threats against Dalton and Ed. Dalton could see the *real* Carolyn personality emerging again—smiling, flirting, talkative and relaxed. The sky darkened just enough to reveal the first star of the evening set against a brilliant orange hue on the horizon stretching to a deep dark blue in the east. Dalton headed up to the deck, with Carolyn in hand. He needed to check their heading and trim the lightly fluffed mainsail to dump wind and drift. After a brief hug and kiss Dalton pointed out the last of the sunset to Carolyn. "Ed's ready with those steaks, let's eat." Carolyn responded with another firm kiss and a nod, followed by a broad smile as she whispered, "I love you JD."

Dalton grabbed her in a tight hug and kissed her passionately before saying, "I love you very much too. We'll set that wedding date soon, Ok?"

"Yes, of course, there is nothing more dear to me, except having those threats gone from our lives. Get that done first."

"Agreed."

The men aboard the lingering yacht sat quietly, dressed in full black wetsuits, scuba gear, light weapons and satellite communications equipment. The time was near. The lead commando aimed his long lens camera and shot numerous photos of the sailboat and the passengers and then uploaded them to a special website portal Adrestia established for the activities of its unit. The three men tracked the sailboat route and set the yacht to intercept the *Trending*. Khamal sat in his sixth floor hotel room, on the North Carolina outer banks shore, near the Hatteras inlet, got on the password-protected website and opened the files. He studied each image seeking to be assured his target, Ed Kosko, was present. His careful research along with an audio bug in Charley Rhodes offices determined that he had offered the evening of sailing as a pause between Kosko's candidacy announcement at the Convention and the rigors of campaigning set to begin in a week. Lars Nevin expedited the three mercenary commandos to the States in support of Khamal's new plan—death by an apparent accident.

Khamal studied the two dozen photos, in order, enlarging and cropping each, for clarity. Kosko appeared relaxed and comfortable, his wife Irene, reserved and contemplative. The ninth photo was a clear facial shot of Carolyn McCabe, smiling, looking radiant as the setting sun cast a flattering profile of her. Khamal studied the photo and thought...*Carolyn McCabe...why is she there...why so happy...could this be someone else?* The brutal memories of his struggle with Dalton returned, and Carolyn's fear as he smothered her with a chloroform-soaked towel leaving her unconscious. His anger grew as he considered explanations to his question. He skipped through the remaining photos quickly and there in the three final photos was Jameson Dalton Crusoe, at the wheel, and speaking with Ed Kosko, and another with him holding Carolyn close. Khamal flushed with anger as he muttered to himself... *"Crusoe's alive, faked his own funeral. He should not have joined Kosko on the sail."*

The lead commando read the incoming email from "Client 26771", Khamal's ID on the Adrestia web site: *Proceed after sunset with the intercept plan. Target confirmed. Report results.*

The yacht was drifting, nearly motionless, as the three men slid into the water with their breathing equipment, fins, knives and nautical rope. Each man pulled a line tied to the front cleats on both sides of the bow, and directed down through an eyelet just above the waterline and into the water. The three men swam at a depth only five feet below the surface, pulling the lines in unison. The *Trending* had its navigation lights on but was generally dark on deck. Carolyn, Dalton Ed and Irene were enjoying the meal Ed had cooked onboard. The gentle movement of the drifting boat was a soothing sensation for all onboard. The wine was flowing and the conversation was brisk as soft music played in the background.

After swimming for several minutes the yacht floated twenty yards behind the stern of the sailboat. All the lights were off and the engine shut down. The lead commando quietly slid onto the sailboat stern and looped the lines through the low railing posts protecting the back seating behind the wheel station. The men untied the small dinghy dragging behind the yacht, and began to paddle away while holding the lines secured to the yacht. As they paddled the dingy away from the *Trending*, the pull lines drew the yacht to within five feet of the sailboat stern. Fifteen feet away in the lower cabin area Dalton reminisced on Ed's stunning nomination speech and the crowd's robust reaction.

The lead commando looked back at the yacht tracking directly behind the sailboat and opened his communication mic. "Release the pull lines, start the motor and head to shore. Start the detonation timer, set at twenty seconds." Khamal listened in through his Satcom gear and watched in the General direction of the sailboat with his binoculars. The timer, wired to two canvas bags of C4 tucked into the bow cabin of the yacht started its countdown. Khamal called the count in his mind and studied the water two miles out. The twenty seconds seemed like twenty minutes to Khamal whose attention was riveted on the two boats. A fast, bright fireball erupted on the water, which was followed by a secondary explosion throwing flames fifty feet into the air. The mainsail disintegrated into a waving flame far above the water, and then began to tilt downward finally entering the ocean after a minute. The flames quickly subsided to scattered burning debris floating at the explosion site. Khamal watched for another half-minute until the light from the flames dispersed. He felt satisfaction that he had now completed both contracts. The lead commando called into Khamal, "Detonation accomplished—Destruction complete—Survivability zero."

◆ ◆ ◆

The blast was a fast detonation blowing out the sailboat's stern up to the steering wheel. The side walls of the stern ripped apart and blew flaming debris out and upward. All four aboard the sailboat were thrown into the water scant yards from the hull, which was sinking rapidly into the water along with the smoldering fishing yacht. Carolyn's last memory of the event was Dalton screaming *"get down"* as he jumped forward to cover her and Irene. The swirling orange flames on the sail above the water allowed Carolyn to see Irene struggling nearby to reach the surface. Dalton reached the surface and swam to the raft. As he was towing Ed, when he noticed Carolyn pulling Irene to the surface. He struggled to push Ed into the inflated life raft. Carolyn, a strong swimmer, but shaken, reached the other rope rail and hung onto the edge along with an exhausted Irene Kosko, gasping for air. "Are you alright Carolyn?"

"Yes, yes. But Irene is so weak she can't pull herself into the raft. I'm keeping her alert but she needs help. What happened...fuel fire?"

"I've got Ed, he's unconscious, but alive." Dalton did not answer immediately but managed to get Ed into the small raft. He then swam around to aid Carolyn and help her load Irene onboard. The burning fishing yacht nearby had flooded through the bow and was listing to the port side as it continued to sink, gushing air from the cabin areas, as the flames sputtered and then reignited.

Carolyn revealed a look of bewilderment as she held Dalton in her stare and waited for an explanation. Dalton pulled himself onboard the four-person, non-motorized raft and looked back at Carolyn. "I heard a strange wave slapping as we were eating and worried we were drifting too much. So when I went up on deck to check it out, I expected to feel a mild wind shifting our course. Instead I saw a yacht tied to our stern, and a powered dinghy moving away at high speed."

"What? A yacht tied to us?"

Ed Kosko began to cough and spit up water as he regained consciousness. Carolyn helped stabilize him just as he asked, "What the hell happened, JD?"

"I noticed the yacht earlier. It appeared to be a group anchored and diving. I was wrong. They were likely part of Khamal's team, and they set the yacht on our stern to blow up and take us with it." Irene began to move and grew alert.

"How did we survive the blast? The sailboat is gone," Ed observed.

Carolyn continued to stare at Dalton for a full explanation. Her face strained to fight off the fear of another deadly attack from the killer Khamal. Dalton took a deep breath and began, "I knew we had little time when I got on deck. I first threw the top deck safety raft overboard as I pulled its inflation plug, and dove into the galley pulling the door shut as I came down. Luck was with us. The door minimized the blast in the galley but still blew out the starboard side on the stern. I feared we'd all be killed. As we rolled starboard, mostly in shock, we were thrown out into the water. The sailboat went down in about eight seconds—stern first."

"All I recall is you yelling, *'get down'*, and then the blast." Carolyn began to realize that crucial seconds had saved their lives.

"I hit the water, came up, grabbed Ed who was near me and looked for you two." Irene was now fully awake and listening to Dalton. "'Thank God, honey, I saw you pop up beyond the flames and grab Irene. The raft inflated and we both swam towards it. The rest you know."

"Carolyn threw herself at Dalton and screamed, "This has got to end. How can this be happening again? You've got to stop him, JD."

Ed straightened himself, wiped the water out of his eyes of water and said, "This SOB will not stop me. I can still pull a few strings at NSA—we'll nail his behind."

Without any oars the raft floated aimlessly except for the hand paddling Dalton provided. In the dark distance, the lights and sounds of a small powered craft came closer. "It's Ronet. I had him waiting at the shore with a Coast Guard rescue craft nearby, just in case we needed help. I thought it might have been for more wine, not an explosion." The quip, helped relax the tension among the four, although the near death experience felt very real.

Ed reached over and slapped Dalton on the back as he remarked, "Good job JD, good job. Thank you." Carolyn dropped her head down to hide her tears and fear. With the sail abruptly ended, the beautiful sunset had expired and left the water dark and foreboding. Minutes later Ronet arrived with the Coast Guard rescue team and took the inflatable dinghy and passengers aboard. Ronet pulled Dalton aside and whispered, "It looks like you were right—an attack at sea was too tempting, after failing to get us in Canada. Khamal has to be behind this."

"Exactly. Have Cotter and Wilson found anything on the scans of phone calls to and from the intracoastal?"

"Yes, five minutes after the attack a phone intercept referenced the explosion. It sounded very much like a confirmation by the attackers to their command."

"Did we get a fix on the land location?" Dalton hoped his instincts would be rewarded with a clue to Khamal's whereabouts.

Ronet looked about to make certain no one was able to hear his next words. "Wilson got the fix—four miles north near the beach. They are in surveillance waiting outside near a beachfront condo project. What's your call JD?"

"I'm going with you after I alert Ed to keep the Secret Service team close and on high alert."

"I figured as much. Your gear and light-combat pack are in my SUV."

CHAPTER THIRTEEN

North Carolina Shore, Elizabeth Crusoe's Beach Condo

Ronet took control of the situation and organized a security team to create a protective barrier two hundred yards out from the condo. A dozen agents, plus a number of state police, surrounded the site and shoreline. Dalton quickly updated Kosko who knew he couldn't discourage Dalton from joining Ronet.

Elizabeth Crusoe hugged her son for over a minute, ignoring his still wet clothes. She finally released him, looked in his eyes, kissed his cheek, and said, "Enough with the near death experiences and bogus funerals. Can you promise me and your fiancée that, JD?" Carolyn took note and seemed to make the same request through her facial expressions of stress and fear.

"I understand Mom. I'm sorry for all this, really I am. We've got a strong team on the trail of this assassin. We'll stop him, I promise." Carolyn sighed and came to hug Dalton just as his mother stepped aside. Brad Ronet stood nearby listening to several voice mails he'd received.

As he closed his phone Ronet said, "JD's right, Ma'am, we will stop this bastard. Sorry for my colorful language, but we do have a good team working on this problem."

Carolyn sat down next to Elizabeth, held her hand and offered, "Brad and JD are the best at keeping us all safe. I know that from my own experience." Elizabeth seemed weary and drained from the stressful evening yet she smiled at Carolyn's uplifting words. Carolyn prayed her past horror at the hands of

Khamal did not show on her face as she tried to comfort Elizabeth.

Ronet motioned for Dalton to join him and Wilson in the small den off the living room. Wilson was busy tapping away at his powerful NSA laptop securely connected to the agency's computer center. His communications head gear was monitoring the Secret Service team covering the perimeter. Cotter reported in, "The Secret Service team found a dinghy two miles down the beach, punctured and abandoned. Here's a photo they shot. We should check this out now."

Dalton agreed and directed Ronet, Wilson and Cotter to meet him outside in their SUV's momentarily. He told Carolyn only that he needed to "debrief" with Ronet and would return shortly. Carolyn was not convinced but knew Dalton had to follow his instincts.

Dalton jumped in the second vehicle with Ronet and sped down the coastal highway. They linked their headset ComGear headsets to continue their conversation. He studied the photo and offered, "It was dark and things were happening fast, but it sure looks like the size and shape of the one I saw leaving the yacht."

"They are dusting for prints but I doubt they'll find much to help us."

Ronet jumped into the discussion. "If this was Khamal's doing, you won't find any prints, or any clues linking this attack to him. He probably had operatives under his control tasked with loading the explosives, on the yacht and moving it alongside the *Trending*. Once positioned to take you all out, they pulled away and remotely detonated it."

"Khamal must have been nearby, watching to confirm, just as he did at my *'funeral'*, that we all died." Dalton thought about the situation. Wilson and Cotter came in through their headset communications gear with an update.

"Colonel, we just saw three men come up from the water and load scuba gear into one of two Escalades. The second vehicle has a man behind the wheel. It appears they are beginning to move out together, heading north."

Ronet rounded the curve revealing the resort's dark rear parking lot and the two SUV's. "These could be the attackers. We'll hold back a minute and see what they do."

Dalton raised his night vision binoculars and saw the three men stow their wetsuits and gear and get into the vehicle. "These have to be the guys Khamal was directing from the shore. Stay back and follow them until we are out of this populated shore area and we'll try to jam them into a roadblock with the state police."

The two Escalades pulled out slowly and began to head north on highway NC 94. Wilson alerted the state police who set up a roadblock six miles ahead, near an active crash site. From a half mile behind Dalton and Ronet saw the vehicles suddenly leave the highway on a two track road into heavy wooden terrain. Dalton reacted, "They know were behind them. Speed up and follow them into the forest."

Once off the main road, the dark misty forest hid the SUV's from sight. No lights, moonlight, noise or movement. Ronet and Wilson held their mics open. Dalton waited before speaking. "This could be a trap if they suspect we've found them. We're out here alone, and perhaps outgunned."

Ronet spoke up, "Yeah, but if we delay pursuit they could escape on foot through the woods. Its three hours 'til sunup." Dalton weighed the options as he remembered how skillful Khamal was at clandestine attacks and his strong survival instinct. "Let's all get in one vehicle, move forward slowly without lights, and see if we can catch a glimpse of them through the night vision binoculars before they see us. Agreed?"

The team agreed and swiftly gathered in the front vehicle driven by Ronet. They had light assault weapons, ComGear, 9-millimeter hand guns, vests and survival packs—still in basic civilian clothes. The "two track" was rough and winding, heavy ground cover including palmetto bushes, pine, and oaks blocked the view. After three hundred yards, an abandoned farm house, chicken coop and small wood shed stood on a partially cleared lot being overtaken by the forest. Dalton held the night vision glasses up scanning the area, as the team stood two abreast, separated by ten yards front to rear. From near the house a spray of gun fire erupted. Dalton hit the ground as he felt a round graze his vest near the waist. The shots were widely scattered and failed to find any of Dalton's men. All lay flat on the ground and withheld fire hoping to get a visual on the targets. None appeared. Moments later, the sound of movement of men, crashing through brush, twigs snapping, and leaves slapping, revealed the General direction of the targets.

Dalton stood, still scanning the forest ahead looking for something when he spotted two men, running further into the woods seconds before they disappeared. "They may have split up. Two have moved out at one-o'clock from our position. Be alert." The team moved ahead very slowly. As they approached the old house it was clear it had been vacant for decades; the roof was all but gone, fallen in, and a large dead oak had collapsed the rear wall. Gunfire erupted again; from near the wooden shed and hit Cotter in the vest and right calf. He fell to the ground and returned fire along with the remainder of the team. Dalton held his last sighting of two men moving fast and low into the dark woods and fired a burst of six rounds in their direction. After ten seconds and thirty rounds fired, a lone gunman fell into palmetto bushes behind the shed. Wilson looked to Cotter's wound which was superficial and easily wrapped. The fallen attacker was dead, still carrying a sheathed knife strapped to his right calf, as divers frequently do.

"I sure wish we had some damn light to work with. We got too close." Wilson remarked.

Ronet said, "We were lucky here, this guy could have gotten us all—if there were more light."

Dalton responded, "We've evened the odds a bit with one man down, let's keep pressing."

Dalton's team moved out slow and low again. He studied Cotter who was on his feet and motivated. "You alright? Fall back if necessary."

"Hell no—I'm good and ready to finish this." Cotter was determined to capture or kill Khamal and his team. Dalton looked to Ronet who confirmed with a "head nod" he felt Cotter was stable and mission-ready.

Fifty yards ahead Dalton could see the broken ground where Khamal and his remaining men had run. Ronet held his hand up and the team stopped. He pointed to the ground. A major fresh blood trail had sprayed the ground and low brush. Dalton whispered, "Careful he may be alive and nearby. We must have hit one or more of them in the last gunfire exchange."

The pre-morning sun lit the hazy sky just enough to improve visibility to around twenty feet. Still, Dalton's team had covered only one-hundred yards the next ten minutes when Cotter, moving in a flanking position to Dalton, signaled a halt. He pointed to the ground, and there lie a dead assailant, shot through the liver and left thigh resulting in massive blood loss. Dalton rolled the man over to see his face, "This is not Khamal—he and one more are still out there. Let's spread out to avoid them circling behind us."

Ronet agreed and headed to Dalton's left some forty yards with Wilson. The foursome now moved in a stealth fashion alert to the possibility the two remaining assailants could have split up or backtracked to get behind them. The mist hung low and dense in the damp forest, when suddenly two tear gas smoke grenades exploded near Dalton. Two men wearing gas masks rushed in; one clubbed Cotter with the butt of his assault rifle, sending him unconscious to the ground, the other pouncing on Dalton jamming a pistol onto his neck. Ronet and Wilson strained to see movement in the advancing tear gas cloud, coughing as their eyes started to burn. They moved aimlessly toward the center of the cloud barely able to see.

A voice yelled out, "Stop, drop your weapons or your friends die now. Move slowly towards me." The voice had a chilling effect on Dalton. It was Khamal's voice, altered from the spoiled French accent he recalled from his previous lethal encounter with the man in St Martin. Ronet and Wilson could see the shapes of two men: one standing holding Dalton in front of him with a 9-millimeter Beretta forced against Dalton's throat; the other on his knees with a pistol aimed at Cotter lying unconscious near Dalton's feet and an assault rifle's red laser dot centered on Ronet's forehead.

Ronet stopped and studied the situation from twenty-three yards away. "Alright. We're lowering our weapons." He looked to Wilson, only ten feet to his right who also dropped his weapon.

Khamal smugly announced, "It's so nice to meet you again Mr. Crusoe. I so enjoyed your funeral display. Now I'm here to assist you in a real one." Khamal jerked on Dalton's collar and kicked him hard in the ribs. Dalton slumped in pain, coughed and spit some blood out.

"I'm sorry I missed your funeral Khamal, after I hoped you were dead in the Caribbean." Dalton could recall every second of the nighttime struggle and final deep cut Crusoe struck across Khamal's upper chest before he fell into the water.

"Well, you did slow me down, but I have never failed on a contact assignment and today I intend to restore that record." Khamal was obsessed and disgraced by his failure to complete the Iranian contract on Dalton. Now he felt he could regain his stature.

"Well you may have the upper hand now but the Secret Service and others know you are trying to assassinate Ed Kosko and slow the Convention of States efforts. They will find and kill you." Dalton spit another mouthful of blood, his side aching.

"You misunderstand Mr. Crusoe. I couldn't care less about the political maneuvering in the US. I just enjoy the challenge— and the money this profession offers me."

"Well it's all soon to end for you and Adrestia." Dalton tried to unsettle Khamal with the mention of Adrestia.

"Oh, so you think you know something?" Khamal made a feeble attempt at a dismissive quip, yet Dalton sensed he had startled the assassin.

Ronet looked extremely troubled. He was unable to help Dalton, in the sights of a serious killer, and no options coming forth. Dalton felt the identical dilemma—caught off guard by a master assassin and his elite mercenary force. Dalton knew he had to initiate something very soon or watch himself and his team die like dogs. He glanced down at Cotter, who had quietly regained consciousness, despite a bleeding head and his oppressor's gun pushed against his neck. Cotter shifted his eyes twice toward his boots; Dalton noticed and recalled the 5-inch combat knife in its sheath, strapped to Cotter's calf just above his boot.

Khamal forced Dalton down to his knees, cocked his Beretta for an easy trigger pull to fire his weapon, and said, "Tell me what you think you know about Adrestia and I promise to kill you quickly." Ronet and Wilson kept their eyes focused on Dalton with hands held high as they walked slowly towards Khamal. Dalton glanced at Ronet who held Dalton's stare and made an imperceptible nod to Dalton. Wilson tracked the non-verbal signaling. Dalton leaned forward slightly and turned his face upward to Khamal, "I know all about you and Adrestia."

"And how did you learn this...Mr. Dalton Crusoe?" Khamal was curious, concerned and smug all in the same moment. He awaited an answer.

Dalton stared directly into Khamal's face, smiled and said, "I learned from my brother Declan...who worked with Lars Nevin."

Khamal's anxious reaction was just enough of a distraction for the quick attack. Dalton grabbed at the knife, just as Cotter yanked his pant leg up revealing his weapon. Dalton grasped the knife and swung around beneath Khamal's gun and thrust the knife deep into Khamal's right side. Blood spewed as he screamed in pain. Khamal fired instinctively, missing Dalton's throat by inches. He started to fall on Dalton with his pistol aimed at Dalton's face. Simultaneously Ronet and Wilson dropped to the ground, withdrawing their Glock 40's secured in their rear belt holsters and fired five rounds. Two hit Khamal in the neck and upper chest, three more hit and killed the mercenary over Cotter.

Khamal dropped on the ground and lost the grip on his hand gun. Dalton grabbed it and held it over Khamal starring at him as blood gushed from his wounds. Ronet and Wilson joined to watch as the life of the secretive, deadly and formidable assassin slipped away. In his final seconds, Khamal met Dalton's eyes and whispered with his last breath, "I underestimated you Crusoe,—I doubt my successor will." Dalton stood over his nemesis of several years, which he had assumed was dead, but in fact had survived and relentlessly pursued his contract for the Iranians. A sense of relief and triumph flooded over Dalton as he eyed the assassin's face.

Ronet holstered his weapon and said, "Well it's finally over with this maniac—you and Carolyn can rest a bit easier now I'd guess."

Dalton looked at Ronet and reminded him, "Khamal may have been after me, but he was also after Ed Kosko, along with the Adrestia organization. They will not stop. That's what Khamal's last words meant."

Dalton checked his watch, it read 4:44 a.m. Ronet noticed and offered, "JD, you and Cotter need to head back in one of the SUV's. Calm down Ed, his wife, your mother and Carolyn. Wilson and I will stay, call in some of the Secret Service guys and clean up this mess."

Dalton looked exhausted, Cotter was weak and still bleeding. "Thanks, Brad. We'll take off, but direct all involved to keep this out of the press until we've know exactly what else may be heading our way. Declan can help with that—I *hope.*"

◆ ◆ ◆

The hazy morning light revealed no further useful information where Adrestia's commando unit had come ashore or went. Charley Rhodes was informed about the *"boating mishap"* and successfully diverted the press from serious inquiries with an alternate explanation. Without any casualties the media had nowhere left to go and quickly dropped the item from their twenty four hour news cycle. Kosko was cleverly portrayed as the resourceful warrior: decisive, focused and courageous— brilliant use of a tragedy for political gain. A short press briefing was scheduled later the next day at Rhodes DC offices where Ed Kosko would appear, obviously healthy, casually dressed, and energized, ready to take on Barriman.

Dalton slipped into bed with Carolyn without arousing her except for her subtle caressing of his shoulder and neck with her hand following by a whisper. "Good night darling." Dalton kissed her forehead and fell asleep hoping a full night's sleep and he at her side would lessen the impact of his late evening activities.

Ronet and Dalton pulled Ed aside early the next morning and explained their pursuit followed by Khamal's death. "My God JD, I'm trying to catch up. All this happened after the boat explosion?" Kosko was amazed.

Ronet walked in and said, "Catch up on what Ed?"

"All your excitement last evening. You're damn lucky you weren't all killed."

"Yeah, well we had them in reach and we couldn't let the opportunity pass." Ronet seemed dismissive. Dalton looked humble. "Besides Dalton needed to settle the score with that animal sometime—last evening seemed just fine." Ronet grinned and winked at Dalton, who just shook his head while thinking how close he had come to death.

Ed paused in reflection, then asked, "Have you told Carolyn all this?"

"Yes, although I waited till morning, over a cup of fresh coffee, with the TV on, to minimize her digging into the details. She was very glad to hear of Khamal's fate."

Wilson stepped into the room, then summarized what he and the Secret Service team had found.

"This guy, Khamal, was hired by and reported to the Iranians. He was also apparently hired recently by Adrestia to remove you Ed, on behalf of Barriman contacts. With Khamal dead, and you alive, the group behind all this may just get reckless. We might be able to lure them in."

Ronet let Dalton know he approved, "I like it JD. How do we do that?"

Ed spoke up, "Charley can set it up for us."

"Yes, Charley Rhodes. We announce that Ed, his wife and family friends are fine after an unusual boating accident. Charley schedules a brief press conference tomorrow and standing alongside him is...me. Adrestia should feel tons of pressure to complete the contracts."

Ed added, "I'll call Jack and let him know he needs to be available for the press session."

Carolyn listened, unseen, from the outer hallway and prayed Dalton was not exposing himself to a new inevitable attack.

CHAPTER FOURTEEN

North Carolina, Outer Banks

On the morning following the near death attack on the Outer Banks waters, Rhodes arranged, as planned, a brief yet image filled press conference, outside Elizabeth Crusoe's beachfront home. A handful of reporters, mostly the local variety, covered the event. Ed took to the microphones and stated, "We all had an exciting evening sail, yesterday." He smiled, signaling upfront the ending was fine. The small crowd gave a subdued chuckle, and then jumped directly into questions.

"What time did this explosion happen, Mr. Kosko?" Ed looked to his left side where Dalton, stood, his mother and Carolyn behind. Irene Kosko was at her husband's right arm. "Do you recall the time Dalton?"

"Right. I think it was perhaps an hour after sunset, say about 8:50 p.m." The camera crew focused in on Dalton as he smiled and made his remark. Charley had suggested that despite the scary events of the prior evening a calm and relaxed presentation by all would be best not only for Ed's image but for provoking the assassin group involved. As viewed on one of the nation's ubiquitous television screens on that evening's news, while Dalton spoke a television banner ran beneath his facial image... *Dalton Crusoe, friend of Ed Kosko, NLP Presidential Candidate.*

◆ ◆ ◆

Half a world away, and ten hours later, at a small Budapest river front café Lars Nevin watched the local TV coverage of North Carolina and ate a continental breakfast. The BBC was presenting highlights of the events in the US surrounding the robust coverage of the upcoming Presidential election. He feared Khamal had failed and now worried he was lost to him. His animated full-face smile helped offset his secret distress with the images of Dalton and Kosko, alive, and dismissing Khamal's attempt to kill them both as an... *"Unfortunate accident"*. As Lars finished breakfast he noticed his secure mobile phone buzzing, alerting him to an incoming alert...the screen read, *Important Message for Contact 26771 from Contact 26000*—Lars Nevin had an incoming text message from Badge Demarche.

Lars opened his Adrestia portal and found the new encrypted file. The message to Lars read... *'must proceed immediately to complete the open assignments. Please provide details on timing'.*

Lars thought for a moment and entered a text response. It simply stated...*Understood.* He added more text which contained a photo, and a name. It announced *'we've lost a contract operator, Declan Faden'.*

◆ ◆ ◆

Washington DC, Later That day

Cotter arrived early to his NSA desk in DC. Wilson took notice and asked, "You feeling up to our normal work schedule?"

"Of course," snapped Cotter, "The wounds were nothing. I'm ready to get on with finding the rest of this assassin group."

He tried to access data from a satellite that was near the outer banks the night of the explosion. The recorded images failed to reveal anything of consequence, yet in his browsing he discovered the unusual activity off the west coast of Africa.

Under the cover of night, days earlier, the *Varyag II* had left Norfolk and motored out to sea. Intelligence explaining the activity indicated the carrier was heading to China to be scrapped for its steel. Cotter grew suspicious and tasked other satellites covering the eastern Atlantic, expecting to find the carrier heading to the Suez Canal; instead it was parked near a Chinese missile sub 110 miles off the west coast of Africa. Fighter aircraft were stationed on its flight deck and were arriving every thirty minutes. Cotter shut down his search efforts, thought for a moment and left his station, exiting the building. Outside he called Dalton on his private satellite phone.

"It's Cotter Dalton. Where are you now?"

"I'm in Charley Rhodes' personal DC limo with Ed heading to a meeting at Pathroads for America. We just landed. Why?"

"I stumbled across something that is hard to explain. A decommissioned carrier has left Norfolk, reportedly heading to China for a scrapout. Yet I see it on satellite coverage off Africa being fitted with crew and aircraft. No one in the agency has mentioned this event. I fear its being covered over by Barriman's handpicked stooge heading the NSA."

Ed Kosko bristled as he listened in on the conversation Dalton had put on speaker phone. "These idiots are covering up for sure. This smells like Badge Demarche is involved."

Cotter said, "You're right, Ed; I can see that all reports are directed exclusively to Badge—no one else outside the agency under an executive privilege order. Badge Demarche did this it appears."

"Can you get a copy of the file without it being discovered by others in the NSA?"

"It's tough, but I think I can—once if I send a blind copy to a dummy file next time Badge receives an update, usually each day at 8:00 a.m., then I'll have minutes to quickly download from the dummy file to my device and then delete any record of the duplicate copy on the server. Do you want me to try?" Ed thought for a moment, glanced at Dalton for support, and said, "Yes, but be really careful."

♦ ♦ ♦

On Barriman's orders the Treasury began to distribute the Chinese $25 dollar currency through the banking system, directly following the Convention of States event. The reaction surprised Barriman and Demarche. The issue grew to national attention when Texans called an impromptu gathering of 1200 supporters who torched a large metal bowl filled with the new rescue currency. Badge watched from his office the local TV coverage of the event now shown on national TV. Josh Gaines stood nearby. "Are these folks nuts? Burning money like that—they look stupid."

"No they're not nuts—they're detractors—committed detractors.

CHAPTER FIFTEEN

Washington DC, American University, the First Presidential Debate

President Barriman had practiced his delivery and body language for several days with his debating coach, Max Budent, an old political consultant with an impressive record at polishing a good speech into a classic masterpiece. His best skill was training candidates to listen carefully to a tough *"trap-question"*, and sincerely address it with a *"non-answer"* which the candidate wanted to get on the record. The content had been prepared by Badge Demarche, of course, and it was power packed with populist themes, false claims of administration success, and glowing predictions for the future if his policies were allowed to play out. Other image consultants were busy tasked with the suit style and color, the tie selection, lapel pins, the shirt collar shape, cuff links or buttons, light stripes or a plain pinpoint oxford white variety. The President felt prepared and ready, but nervous and fidgety. Badge took notice and asked the President, "Harold, do you feel like you need a boost just before the debate?"

"I'd rather not, but I need to be sharp. Kosko has shot to dead even with me in the Real Clear Politics poll after his formal announcement to compete. Even your news about becoming my VP didn't help." Badge could see the President losing focus, doubting his abilities, and concerned about an embarrassing stumble before the cameras.

The Lincoln-Douglas format for the first debate was reported in the press to help the President more than challenger Kosko. Charley Rhodes felt differently, pointing out that while the discussion content was comprehensive, it was a unique opportunity to blast Barriman with a flood of damning facts, including hidden details of the oppressive "CASP" agreement with China. The selected moderator was a low impact, courteous news anchor, well into his twilight years, known for his apolitical interview style.

The twin podiums were massive and allowed for a protected sloped surface beneath the oversized microphone to spread out materials. Beneath the top surface a shelf held two water bottles, a cup, napkins and a tissue box all neatly arranged. The auditorium was packed beyond its normal 2,500 person capacity. The crowd included news media types, politicians, supporters, consultants, and friends of the debaters and, of course, academics. Dalton and Carolyn sat on the right side of the podiums, loosely assigned to Kosko supporters, with the left side reserved for the President's. Camera crews cluttered the floor directly in front of the raised stage.

Carolyn was seated next to Dalton and Irene Kosko. Ronet was backstage, armed and assisting the Secret Service team headed by Devin McCord. Carolyn turned to Irene and asked, "Is Ed ready?"

"He says he is and I hope that's the case. His strongest asset, I believe, is his ability to analyze issues quickly and then formulate a coherent strategy. Charley Rhodes says he easily adapted to this style of debate—although he'd prefer a cocktail lounge setting."

Carolyn giggled at Irene's comment as she looked at Dalton, who was quiet, ear piece in place and scouring the stage for anything unusual. She felt more relaxed and comfortable now than in the months before. She made note of his earpiece and noticed and nudged him, "Hey JD, are you going to be able to listen to any of this, or just disengage on the discussion and focus on the threat risk?"

The remark was partly a humorous jest and also a serious inquiry. Dalton, Ronet and Ed had minimized speculation that a threat risk would appear here at the university, but he knew not to underestimate Adrestia or Badge Demarche. Ronet was backstage in Ed's waiting room, with two makeup experts charged with making the stocky, short, large-smile man look Presidential. Ten minutes remained before the moderator and the news coverage would begin. Pundits were speculating who would control the stage and move the polls in their favor. Dalton finally addressed Carolyn's tease and said, "I've heard Ed in the practice debates with Charley's people so it will be easy to concentrate on the security, yet it all seems calm so far." A flirty wink following his answer pleased Carolyn.

President Barriman studied himself in the full length mirror. His make-up and dressing team had departed moments earlier. He was pensive, playing with his short receding hair, readjusting his tie and collar, tugging at his cuffs and judging his trim six-foot profile. The staffer knocked on the President's door and announced, "Two minutes to the moderator's opening comments. You must be stage-side at that time."

Badge answered in a firm voice, "Thank you we are ready."

The behavior was familiar; Badge studied his friend with the methods he learned years ago as a research medical psychiatrist. He instinctively knew the President needed a 'boost', a *shot of confidence* to raise him to peak performance during the stressful debate, moments away. Badge waited for the request. He felt certain the earlier offer was percolating in the President's mind.

"Give me a boost Badge. I want to be on top of my game. This is important, right?"

Badge Demarche thought carefully about how to respond. Should he accommodate the President as he had done numerous times over the last three years; or seize a single, unique opportunity now which the Chinese strongly promoted. The circumstances were "ideal" touted Tan Zhang, who shared his brother Lei Zhang's opinion that Badge needed to act decisively for himself and the US-Chinese relations. The President rolled up his right sleeve and waited for Badge to respond. Badge looked the President in the eye and said, "Of course, Mr. President. Good luck in the debate."

The slim needle pierced the swollen vein and 2 cc's of the clear fluid flowed into the President's arm. "You should begin to feel the effect in five to ten minutes, Harold."

"Great. That's just when I'll need it—right? Thanks." Barriman smiled, tried to put his best face on the most formidable challenge to his legacy, and pulled on his sport coat. Badge studied the President as though he was evaluating a patient.

The moderator spent six minutes announcing the first of two debates, agreed to by the parties, and that the President would begin with his defense of the CASP agreement. Every major news network was present, with their most prestigious anchors leading an assembly of their brightest team of analysts. President Barriman began with the standard acknowledgements to the networks, Ed Kosko, the moderator and the audience. He then began a robust affirmative defense of his policies to strengthen America's economy with the generous financial aid of the Chinese, whom he described as a friendly world partner. The subdued crowd failed to stifle a sigh of disgust as he made his comments. Nevertheless, the President was on the top of his game, looking Presidential, focused and in-charge. It was a typical Harold Barriman speech—long on style and presentation, short on real content. Nearly seven minutes later the President finished his remarks, with twenty seconds still remaining in his allotted time. A polite, yet feeble applause came from the viewing audience—albeit mostly from the President's side of the stage.

The moderator then explained, "Mr. Kosko you now have seven minutes to defend the negative position on the subject topic. You may proceed."

Ed Kosko looked directly into the cameras and began his version of acknowledgements before beginning his assault on the President's affirmative defense of the CASP. Kosko proceeded with a smooth tempo and cadence that worked well for him. He strayed from his usual casual, sharp and abrupt style when conversing with Dalton and other close friends. Instead he played to the camera, and looked every bit the accomplished, confident and skilled executive that seemed to resonate with the audience. His tailored dark blue suit, a muted thin pin stripe, played well off the white classic collar protecting a rose colored paisley tie. The lapel pin—a tiny American flag completed the image. His word choice was effective and his delivery evoked a feeling of genuine concern and knowledge of the country's problems. As he neared the end of his remarks, his voice grew stronger; he gestured with his hands to add emphasis, and projected a face of confidence, strength, and bold determination to rescue America.

Ed held the audience interest better than the President, a surprise to Rhodes who watched and listened with a hypersensitive attention. Applause was discouraged during the speeches, but several times when Ed hit a nerve involving over blown government spending, or intrusionist policies stripping Americans of their civil rights through the CASP agreement, the crowd stirred with whispers.

Badge watched with an intense gaze at his man. As Ed neared the end of his first speaking segment, Barriman reached for a small water bottle—it opened easily and he took several long swallows. The moderator then began by announcing a one minute hold for the television networks to show the first of four commercial breaks agreed to during the debate. Ed reached for his small water bottle and took a sip, noticing the heat under the bright stage lights was increasing.

Dalton had said nothing throughout the first twenty minutes of the historical debate when his ear piece broke his concentration. "JD, all is calm back here behind the stage. McCord says all agents reported in. "How's it look four rows away from the stage?"

"Ed looks very good Brad. For a guy who hates politics he's sure sounding like one I could vote for." Carolyn and Irene heard the remark and smiled. The crowd was noisy and abuzz with each side celebrating the performance of their man. Carolyn noticed first, then Irene and finally Dalton. President Barriman began to fidget, undoing his tie and collar, reaching for more water and then looking offstage towards Badge.

"Dalton, look at the President. He's in trouble, something's wrong." Carolyn pointed to the stage. The President collapsed and fell to his knees. The crowd now noticed the President's pallor and released a collective shriek. Badge and two Secret Service agents in his detail rushed out, weapons drawn, and surrounded the President. Badge laid the President down, listened to his chest and yelled, "Tachycardia, get an ambulance crew now." Badge motioned to one of the Secret Service agents, "Get the medical bag in the waiting room!"

The crowd went ballistic, out of control and some people began running for the exits, fearing some form of attack. Seconds later, Badge had a syringe full of a liquid which squirted out the needle just before he injected the President, who remained unconscious and limp. Badge secured the syringe back in his bag, looked up and said, "This should stabilize the President's heart."

The moderator announced a pause as the medical team assembled around the President. Within seconds the television networks, news media and the internet exploded with the news...*President Barriman suffers a blackout and collapses while debating New Libertarian Candidate Ed Kosko. Details coming in now.*

Ninety minutes later at Walter Reed Army Medical Center, several physicians and nurses hovered over the President. He had undergone a rapid and damaging tachycardia, his heart rate running to dangerous levels accompanied with excessive blood pressure spikes.

Badge remained outside the operating room and tried to handle the press. "The President is in good hands and the doctors are trying to stabilize him now. I'll have more to report in half an hour." The press screamed scores of questions to Badge, who left the area and assigned his trusted deputy Chief of Staff, Josh Gaines to placate the news media.

Ed Kosko was tightly surrounded by Dalton, Ronet and Devin McCord. Three other agents formed a second protective ring near the exits and entrances to the auditorium. Dalton feared the chaos and confusion could be a ruse for an attack on Kosko as had been foreshadowed in the cryptic note days earlier. The President's Secret Service detail cordoned off the exits and allowed the audience members to proceed after a security and facial scan. Devin McCord checked in with the other agents guarding the President and reported back to Dalton, "I just learned that one of the President's agents overheard a doctor telling Badge and the Press Secretary that the President has had a stroke and is in a coma, although stable at this time. Badge is notifying the Cabinet and senior Congressional leaders now, with a meeting planned here in thirty minutes. Badge looks to be sworn in as President."

Dalton leaned back and rubbed his neck trying to think through the last hour-and-a-half. He had multiple scenarios developing in his mind: *an unexpected tragic event; the President had a serious heart related issue unknown to the public; or some silent opposition group managed to poison the President.* Moments passed without a word from Dalton as Charley Rhodes scripted a brief, yet compassionate message for Ed Kosko to provide the press in fifteen minutes. Ronet and McCord were preparing a protected location away from the auditorium podiums where a small group of press reporters could ask questions. As Dalton followed Ed's protection team he suddenly recalled Declan's words, from months earlier... *"There will be deaths, some viewed as accidents, suicides, or natural causes, but trust me they will even sacrifice their own, it may seem, to achieve an enduring result. Beneath the surface America is at war with itself. I want to be on the surviving side my brother."*

Dalton's mind raced through the last several weeks: *the attack in Canada, the deaths of Renkin and Garrison, the death of Saul Abboud, the attack on the outer banks, and today the sudden, inexplicable collapse of President Barriman now in a deep coma.* No clear answers came forth, only a sense that a well organized, vast group of power players were trying and succeeding at changing America forever.

Ed stood before a hap-hazard assembly of a dozen microphones, taped and tied together, in a small antechamber near the main stage. He raised his hand and quieted the crowd. Dalton, Carolyn, Irene and Charley Rhodes were off to the side; Ronet and McCord stood security detail directly behind Ed. "I will try to take a few questions about the tragic events of this evening. But before we start I wish to ask all American's to pray for the President's recovery and quick return to health." Ed began.

A loud chorus began yelling their questions. "Mr. Kosko did you notice anything unusual about the President's actions or appearance tonight as the debate began?"

"I thought the President looked fine from my vantage point. He certainly delivered a powerful opening defense of his Chinese policy." Dalton's mind began to stir.

"If the President dies or does not recover fully from his coma, do you think this will help or hurt your candidacy?" Several reporters booed the insensitive question. Ed ignored it and pointed to another flailing reporter.

"We are learning that Vice President Demarche is soon to be sworn in as President. Do you feel he will be up to continuing the President's agenda?"

"I must assume the President had complete confidence in his former Chief of Staff and personal friend when he chose him to fill the VP slot. Let's now take time to see what the President's doctors advise as to the prognosis. Thank you." Dalton's mind stirred again listening to Ed Kosko's heartfelt remarks.

Less than an hour later, the news media were redeployed to the lobby of the Walter Reed Army hospital covering the formal swearing in of Brandon (Badge) Demarche as President of the United States. In the audience standing in support of Badge was another man sometimes called "Flask".

◆ ◆ ◆

Half a world away Tan and Lei Zhang watched the constant worldwide satellite coverage of President Barriman's condition and Badge Demarche's swearing in to the highest office in America. Lei smiled approvingly and directed, "Order the *Varyag II* to position itself near Washington DC on the Atlantic coast and visible from the shore. Order our newest submarine to follow from a safe distance." The room burst into applause from party bosses and military brass. Lei Zhang believed his years of patient support for Badge Demarche resulted in a *dream reality*—an American President beholding and obedient to his leadership.

Tan Zhang replied, "Yes of course, I'll do it now." He rose and joined his military leaders waiting nearby.

CHAPTER SIXTEEN

Washington DC, Pathroads for America Headquarters

The resignation of General Jack Watts was lost on the back pages of most newspapers, and just below the fold on the Washington Times. The President had held onto the short letter without responding for over a week, hoping to meet with the General before his last day and discuss his reasons for leaving. Demarche however wasted no time in selecting Watt's replacement—Chief of Naval Operations, Admiral Harris, a soft man and willing proponent of the sale of the *Enterprise* to China for "scrapping out". Badge could rely on him for a soft stance on China.

The sudden incapacity of President Barriman and the swearing in of Badge Demarche as the acting President dominated the headlines and cable news coverage. It was a polarizing set of events: the progressives knew Demarche was an able politician who many believed authored the Barriman agenda; the libertarian faithful were energized against Demarche whom they saw as too "friendly" with the Chinese leadership and emblematic for out-of-control government.

The first debate had done little to change minds. Those on the progressive left were emboldened by the President's words at the start of the debate and bolstered by Badge Demarche's similar slant. The conservative-libertarians were energized by their new man, Ed Kosko, an affable man with a clear path to restore America. Those left in the middle the as yet uncommitted, were still undecided, awaiting more clarity on the two men's positions. Both men made a vigorous case for their positions. Kosko gained esteem with his supporters when they heard and saw him take on the President's liberal agenda and push back hard on the Barriman policies. He had shown he understood the critical issues for the country and would push for the same issues resolved with the amendments put forth during in the Convention of States—slated to go to the voters in every state the same day as the Presidential election. Badge Demarche on the other hand, was relatively unknown to the average voter, although the far-left establishment knew him to be a clever, forceful progressive committed to continuing the Barriman initiatives.

Charley Rhodes sat back in his oversized high back leather desk chair, tore off his glasses, and smiled at Ed Kosko. "I am very impressed Ed. You handled that surprise situation during the debate with the professionalism of a career politician."

"Aw cut the bull shit Charley, all I did was to try to be respectful and not make a fool of myself. The debate got cut short—that can't help."

"You don't get it my friend. You nailed it. You and the most powerful man in the world debated either side of a major issue for seven minutes and you were convincing. Barriman's performance was excellent, as was yours. Folks expected Barriman to excel, you were an open question. But you performed at his level."

"Yeah but then he collapsed and is now in a coma." Ed felt a twinge of distress. Charley and Dalton noticed.

"Right, he collapsed and for all practical matters is gone. You're still here fresh in the voters' minds. Now Badge Demarche must try to *"inherit"* Barriman's influence. I'm not sure he can. By my metrics you won the first debate even though it ended in a tie, but Barriman isn't here to share the stage. See my point?" Dalton followed every turn in Charley's discourse. Ronet struggled to get the nuances of the message.

Dalton jumped in saying, "Charley's right Ed. You performed very well and then, through no fault on your part, you rose to the winner's role alone when Barriman was replaced by Demarche as President. It's like Barriman's efforts were never scored, yours were."

"Exactly! So now the momentum is on your side and Demarche has yet to be graded by his supporters." added Charley. Ronet smiled as though he had just caught up on the political reasoning.

Ed was serious now; he needed more convincing on his performance. "JD were my words and stage presence really enough to match Barriman's efforts?"

"Yes Ed you held the audience. Your words and message were heartfelt. We all sensed it." Charley Rhodes pushed his glasses back up his nose as he nodded a firm agreement.

"There's a caveat here—Badge is powerful and ruthless. If he determines he can't win a fair and square contest he'll create a *tilt* his way. I still feel he's connected in some way to the death threats against Ed, and now he has a really personal reason to make it happen—you may get his job."

Charley's words caused Dalton and Ronet to flash back to the death threats against Ed and wonder where and when they might be put into play again.

◆ ◆ ◆

Charley Rhodes had Dalton, Kosko and Ronet all sipping coffee and watching an array of screens monitoring all the morning talk shows. The *"talking heads"* were speculating on the impact of the shortened debate and the strange confluence of events which now left two fresh Presidential candidates each without a Vice President to run with them. The introduction of General Watts to become Ed's running mate had been delayed until the media attention on the Barriman and Demarche events diminished. Speculation on whom President Demarche may select as his running mate ran the gamut. Most political pundits felt Badge would choose a true progressive from a solid blue state to please the progressive side of the Liberal wing. Others, including Charley Rhodes, felt Badge would choose a personal friend whom he could trust, and one with a nearly apolitical history.

When Ed Kosko heard the analysis he reacted, "Why would Badge pick someone who doesn't bring in a swing state or some other group, like the extreme environmentalists, or the gay rights crowd?"

"He might, yet I believe he is so self-possessed and narcissistic that he can't convince himself on that type of choice. Remember he was the primary, if not the only, close political advisor to Barriman."

Dalton reacted, "Are we better off announcing Watts as Ed's VP pick before Badge makes his selection?"

"Yes, I think so. Give it another day or two when it won't appear like the 'Kosko-Watts' team is insensitive to Barriman's plight." Ed nodded his agreement with Charley's plan.

Ronet pondered the security concerns, glanced at Dalton and asked, "Adrestia had to have learned by now that both Ed and you are alive and well, having survived the explosion."

Dalton answered, "If, as we suspect, Khamal was Adrestia's contract assassin behind all these threats, you can bet they've seen the press conference earlier. Now we have to be prepared for their next attempt."

CHAPTER SEVENTEEN

Washington DC, the White House Press Room

Press Secretary Jeffery Crandel walked to the podium and addressed the press corps. He had been spending the last forty minutes with President Demarche and Josh Gaines, Badges' Chief of Staff now elevated to the Oval Office duty. The discussion was more of a lecture from Demarche than a Q&A practice session for Crandel. He was instructed to offer no comment on the land development rights provided in CASP, or the Chinese recovery currency intended to make up a large portion of the second tranche of financing. The details of the CASP agreement were slowly leaking out as was expected, but Badge had hoped to reveal it on his own terms after the upcoming election, just fifty-five days away. The news headlines were documenting the first $6Bn installment from the Chinese amidst a swarm of glowing remarks by the progressive faithful that the feared cuts to social programs and green energy policies would be spared. The conservatives pointed out that the defense, agriculture and state revenue sharing budgets were being decimated. The unusually noisy and raucous press corps competed for Crandel's attention after he gave a brief opening status report of *former* President Barriman.

The first reporter, an anchor for a liberal cable network, was allowed to ask the first question. "Have the doctors for President Barriman been able to determine the cause of his collapse and stroke? And as a follow up, what is his prognosis for recovery?"

Crandel had not been Badge's first choice for Press Secretary, but Barriman liked him, and he was clever enough to see that

Badge Demarche should not be challenged or underestimated. The young looking Gaines, was intelligent, articulate, naturally camera ready, and apparently committed to the Barriman, and now subsequently, the Demarche policy initiatives.

Crandel thought about the best answer to the question. "President Barriman suffered an un-controlled tachycardia which apparently created a one or more clots which blocked the blood flow to the President's brain, resulting in the deep coma. Tests are ongoing to further understand the causes behind the sudden heart issue as well as determine whether the President will come out of the coma." A follow-up question was blurted out.

"If the President regains consciousness will his functions like speech, mobility, and vision be restored?"

"The doctors simply don't know at this time. He continues to be monitored constantly in the intensive care unit at the Walter Reed."

A new reporter finally got a break and was allowed to ask a question of Crandel. "Has the President learned of the unusual death, an apparent murder, of Saul Abboud in Dallas near the recent Convention of States site?"

Crandel repeated the scripted talking points perfectly. "The President learned last evening that Mr. Abboud had died. He was a loyal supporter of the Barriman administration and was a personal friend of President Demarche."

A followup came instantly, "Was he working for the Barriman administration or on the campaign?"

Crandel listened attentively to the question and calmly stated, "Mr. Abboud was friend of the President but was not acting on any issue for this or the prior Barriman administration."

President Badge Demarche watched the coverage from the Oval Office. He was pleased with the direct, believable delivery from Crandel. Josh Gaines took notice and asked, "Are you going to keep Crandel on as press secretary?"

"Probably, I have no issue with him so far. Barriman found him to be an effective foil against an inquisitive press, but his test will come as we approach the election and the CASP details leak out. He has to quell the inquiries without fully answering the question." Badge studied Gaines looking for a hint of disapproval—none appeared. Crandel went on to address a few issues concerning the disintegrating jobs report, the increasing trade imbalance and the national polling. Badge felt Crandel was effective, yet untested for the upcoming flood of issues surrounding the Chinese aid deal.

As the press corps moved from issue to issue Badge let his mind wander. He felt smug recalling that his early drug research, perfected by the Chinese, had produced numerous mood- altering treatments, as well as created the original lethal concoction which nearly killed Barriman. The usual "boost" that Barriman had grown to depend upon was substituted with a near-lethal dose, causing tachycardia and the stroke. Numerous tests in Chinese prisons proved the drug to be an effective formulation for lethal injection uses, and when followed up with a "cleansing dose", removed all evidence of the drugs. Badge felt assured the autopsy, when Barriman eventual dies, would not reveal any clue as to the *real* cause of death—thanks to the second syringe he was able to administer to Barriman after his collapse. His efforts had put him in the pivotal role to position America as a Chinese client state. Still he had to stop the New Libertarian Party, and win the upcoming election—with help from the Adrestia unit. As Press Secretary Crandel finished with his reporting Badge was satisfied with the outcome. He looked to Josh Gaines and said, "Let's meet again around five when I've had a chance to consider a VP choice." Josh immediately took the remark to mean the meeting was over and President Badge Demarche needed privacy. As he left the Oval Office, Badge withdrew his personal, special cell phone, read a brief message from Tan Zhang, and then entered a familiar email to a private secure server...Adrestia's headquarters in Budapest.

♦ ♦ ♦

The prominent voices in the New Libertarian Party began to speculate on Badge's choice to fill the open VP slot. The news networks were fascinated at the unique circumstances related to Badge Demarche's ascendency to the Oval Office. The traditional wisdom pointed to a prominent progressive selection which could turn a purple state to the liberals, such as New Jersey or Pennsylvania, yet the cynical voices felt Badge would select a moderate, compliant running mate. The logic being that Badge Demarche, as President, had no interest in sharing any of the spotlight or power, as Barriman had done with him. Josh Gaines was assigned to test a list of possible choices with the progressive liberal leadership. Each potential running mate was nearly indistinguishable from the others: a strong liberal voting history, few if any scandals, and modest political ambitions. One man, former New York governor, Tim Poulton, seemed to stand out in Josh Gaines mind. His confirmation easily carried every Democratic senate vote, with little fanfare.

♦ ♦ ♦

Lars Nevin received a second stern message from Badge Demarche in twenty-four hours. It read...*use whatever resources you feel necessary but complete the primary assignment in the next thirty days or consider the contract revoked.* Lars acknowledged that he'd received and understood the message, then committed it to his memory and deleted the email. He had never seen a warning so specific, yet still he knew the underlying theme—*perform your contract or we will do it—and you may be eliminated.* Lars Nevin knew the Chinese leadership was directing the messaging through Badge. In his dark, secretive world, few assassin groups at Lars' level lived beyond a failed mission. The newer, younger, more lethal upstarts eagerly sought such assignments to build their reputations. Ten years earlier Lars Nevin had done the exact same thing. He knew he had to get personally involved now that the stakes had risen so high.

He pondered the opportunities to target Kosko over the next few weeks based on the limited information available on his schedule. Among the possibilities was a speech to be delivered in ten days at a remote, high-end resort complex, Hemlock Glen Resort, in upstate New York set deep in the forested Adirondack Mountains. The setting was chosen to rally the growing Libertarian presence in the region including the neighboring states of Vermont and New Hampshire. Set on 1,100 acres of low-mountainous terrain, the property included three golf courses, conference centers and an airstrip for small commercial aircraft. Lars personally studied the area maps, rivers, lakes, road systems, satellite coverage, weather and nearby towns. Hours later he emailed instructions to his team in Adrestia the following message... *ready deployment of the three assets used on my last operation, along with four tactical packs. Timing will be forthcoming. Advise earliest departure time.*

◆ ◆ ◆

The *Varyag II* floated nearly motionless for five days as it loaded aircraft, weapons, crew and supplies. The crews were informed and trained in the ship's operation and capabilities. Once authorized for duty at sea, the Chinese military advised President Lei Zhang the warship was ready for service. Hours later Zhang directed the captain to route the carrier on a westerly course that would avoid the major Atlantic shipping routes and arrive a few hundred miles off the Florida coast before turning north to the Chesapeake Bay area. The nuclear submarine along with its ballistic missiles shadowed the *Varyag II* on its journey.

President Badge Demarche read every line of the private intelligence report he ordered concerning the movements of the *Varyag II*. Outside the Oval Office NSA director Al Sanborn sat reviewing the same report. Josh Gaines approached him. "The President is ready for you now sir. I'll take you in."

"Thanks Josh." The NSA director took a deep breath and stood to follow Gaines.

"Good morning director. Take a seat both of you." The President remained seated at his desk, the report lying before him. "What do you think this report tells us Al?"

Sanborn fumbled as he reached for his reading glasses, smiled nervously at the President and began. "Clearly, the Chinese have changed their stated plans to scrap the carrier and have substantially refitted it for service. Yesterday it left the west-African coast and set a course north of Cuba. We don't know their intentions. I'm a little concerned."

Badge looked at Josh and smiled. "Do you think they're planning an attack?"

Sanborn flinched at the suggestion and then recovered to say, "We don't know sir, but I believe there must be another explanation." Josh Gaines looked for a reaction from Badge.

"Relax Al. I spoke with President Zhang last month, and he indicated they felt the vessel was worth more as an active carrier, as opposed to scrap. They are retiring an older carrier which will supply the scrap metal they originally bargained for."

"Well that makes sense, but why move it closer to our shores?" Sanborn was trying to exhibit some degree of critical analysis.

"Right. We talked about that last evening. Zhang suggested some join exercises with our navy to break in their crew. In light of our new cooperative relationship I felt it was a wise move." Badge smiled to Sanborn, projecting calm over the matter. Josh quietly nodded his understanding. "We must keep a lid on this to avoid any detractors to the CASP treaty from coming to a false conclusion."

"Yes, yes of course. I understand, sir."

"Thanks, Al, for coming in. I wanted to make sure we *all* had the latest information in front of us. Keep up the reporting." Sanborn sensed the meeting was over and stood to make his departure.

"Thank you Mr. President. I'll keep you informed." Josh escorted the director to the door and shut it behind him.

Josh Gaines walked back to the President and asked, "Did you really speak with Zhang yesterday?"

"Hell no. But once I saw the latest intelligence, I knew I had to steer Sanborn away from a military posture."

"I believe you've convinced him sir."

"Yeah...maybe. Sanborn was a mid-level, head-down, compliant data geek—not a thinker or leader. Exactly why I urged Barriman to appoint him. The concern now is...what exactly are the Chinese planning. They are feeling very emboldened with my ascendancy to this office, but very concerned about the NLP and their intentions."

"What's next sir?" Gaines awaited instructions.

"Arrange a private conference call between me, you, and Zhang this afternoon."

CHAPTER EIGHTEEN

Seventeen Days before the National Elections

Charley Rhodes had slept very little in the last six days. The polling data was flooding in and he and his team were trying to embolden every move towards Kosko and stunt any moves toward Demarche. Massive electronic wall screens ran a steady stream of news coverage over the two candidates, their spokesmen and the pundits analyzing every shift one way or the other. In the solitude of his own office Rhodes felt the race was too close to call. The average of all polls had Demarche and Kosko in a dead heat at 48.1% to 48.4% respectively. With a three point margin-of-error, it was too close to call. The stakes were enormous: the new Libertarian party had effectively changed the Constitution through its Convention of States efforts, yet a determined Demarche, building on the Barriman's likeability and sympathy for his fate, gave Demarche a four-point boost after his swearing in as President. The compliant liberal media rallied the progressives claiming the NLP would take the country back to the mid-eighteen hundreds, stoking talk of a populist uprising on a sentiment of racism. Demarche's choice of Tim Poulton as VP appeared to have no significant impact on the poll numbers—a good outcome by most political observers. Moreover, Demarche was using the "bully pulpit" often and effectively—calling out the NLP as a political extremist group that would return the country to a reckless social program cuts and hurt the average American. He was comfortable behind the podium with the Presidential seal, and with a backdrop of American flags. Kosko met the challenge and presented a broader view of the situation for Americans: continue on the current political path and risk becoming a client state of China with lost sovereignty and fewer freedoms. The contrasts were enough to spark rude outbursts among members of both sides, causing them to lose control in talk shows and political analysis settings. Still Americans as a group were engaged.

Charley Rhodes reviewed the secret recording Ronet had of then President Barriman, along with Badge Demarche, denying a rescue effort to save the Ranger team attacked in northeast Afghanistan. He struggled to find a way to use it to expose Demarche as weak, or duplicitous and unable to make the hard decisions. Still, he feared that Badge would deflect the charges claiming it was Barriman's decision and that he was in favor of a rescue. That would diminish the charge to a *"he said, he said"* kind of issue, which would likely not change opinions, only harden them. Seconds later, Kosko, Dalton and Ronet strolled towards Rhodes office. He motioned them all in, "Have a seat men. I'll bring you up to speed on the latest polling." Charley leaned back in his over-sized executive chair, pressed the mute button on his multi-screen TV and began.

"We are virtually tied now in the national polls and the electoral college results look almost identical—except that the weather forecasts over the next several days suggest good weather in all the key battleground states and regions meaning the voter participation will be enormous, perhaps a new record for a Presidential election year."

Dalton spoke up, "That means a likely higher turnout among liberals than usual, is that right?"

"Yes, it could mean that. It's happened in the past. But the NLP enthusiasm is very high, four points higher than the liberals. That may make the difference in our favor. Still I would like to use this damning video and audio record of the Nawa Pass disaster. But it's a gamble."

The room went quiet as all pondered the dilemma: release a powerful piece of data which could crush support for Demarche; or risk a denial which plays well with voters and ends up working against the NLP ticket. Dalton had an idea.

"Why can't we publicly make the claim this tragedy happened without releasing the actual DVR. If he doesn't believe it's out there for us to give to the public he may strongly deny it, lay it on Barriman alone and lie to the nation. If he does, release the entire file. It'll spread through the media like wildfire—then let him try to walk it back without looking weak and capable of impeachable acts."

"Damn, JD, I like that idea. What do you think Charley?" Ed was smiling.

"That might work" Charley Rhodes jumped to his feet. "It's a bold approach without much risk of blowback. I have credible sources, which would get this out there in a 'summary-headline' kind of release. Badge would be confronted for a response. If he admits to the events as claimed, he loses the veterans and many folks in states with military facilities. If he denies it he looks even worse, a liar and an incompetent leader." Charley strolled about the room. The group held their attention on him. "From our perspective Ed just deplores the actions as unforgiveable from a Commander-in-Chief, and possible grounds for impeachment— all without making a demand for an explanation. The press will do that, even the liberal rags."

Ed Kosko looked to Dalton and saw that he agreed with the approach to release the Nawa Pass material. "Then it's decided.

The file is released only if Badge denies the events happened or lays it on Barriman. Get it done Charley, I'm headed to the Adirondacks' tomorrow for a three day event." Dalton nodded his approval to Ed's remarks.

Charley Rhodes announced, "I will personally manage the release of the claim and no one on my staff will know where the story originated from. Understood?"

Ronet studied Dalton's face, which seemed to suggest...*game on!*

♦ ♦ ♦

Pathroads for America was a major voice in political analysis, and was respected even by the liberal outlets and news organizations. Scores of independent reporters, photographers and bloggers approached Pathroads every day with either a story to sell or a story to promote under their banner. Rhodes made the claim that, *President Barriman and then Chief of Staff Badge Demarche, made a brazen attempt to cover up a botched covert operation in Afghanistan and abandoned our soldiers, denying a ready rescue team, leaving them to die.*

Rhodes would not disclose his source or that he personally had any evidence, yet he assured his contact the facts were true and verifiable. His anonymity was assured. Thirty minutes later the internet lit up with the news. Questions and comments flowed in and within an hour the major networks, along with talk radio picked up the story. Speculation immediately began on both political sides of the story: it was a hoax to discredit Barriman and Demarche, or, it was true and the administration owed and explanation to the country. By 5:00 p.m. the national news media led their evening broadcasts with a brief summary of the allegations. It had been only eleven days earlier that President Barriman suffered his *"stroke"* leaving him in a deep coma. By the end of the first hour of evening news Josh Gaines had released a statement indicating the President would address the controversy at a 10:00 a.m. press briefing the next morning. Badge ordered the CIA and the Joint Chiefs to remain silent on the claim and that the President's staff would address the issue.

The White House press room was filled earlier than usual and the chatter was vigorous. Josh Gaines entered the room and spoke, "Good morning. I have a few remarks to make before the President comes out. In fact, there was a covert operation against an Al Qaeda leader, Aza Bashir fifty–two days ago in Afghanistan. This was ordered by President Barriman after consulting with the Afghanistan leadership. The President will have more details and will take no questions due to the sensitive matters involving our assets in the region." Josh Gaines left the podium and sat down as the President arrived and began to speak.

"Good morning. Thank you for coming. I will speak to the stories circulating over the internet and now the airwaves concerning recent events in northwest Afghanistan. A few weeks ago we had reliable intelligence that a high value Al Qaeda target was in the Nawa pass region. Our military leaders indicated we could assemble a rapid response team to locate and capture Aza Bashir. After careful deliberation the President decided to approve the mission. I concurred with the President's position. A Ranger team went in during the early morning hours and attempted the capture. Things went wrong and the team was ambushed just outside Bashir's compound. When it was clear that a capture was not possible, the President ordered a drone missile strike and Bashir was targeted and killed. Most if not all of his party were also killed. During the missile assault one of the drones was hit by gunfire and damaged its targeting computer programs. Unfortunately that drone fired an errant missile which ultimately hit our brave soldiers in the Ranger team. It appeared none survived. The Pentagon is now ready to inform the families of these fallen heroes.

As sad as this outcome is, we must remember these men gave their lives in the service of their country, and they eliminated a dangerous Al Qaeda leader set on killing Americans. We should be grateful that President Barriman had the courage and wisdom to order the attack despite the possibility of American military casualties. Thank you very much for your time this morning, and I hope this answers any questions America may have, and that now we can let the families mourn their loved ones." The President left the podium, and Josh Gaines returned. The press corps went into a raucous rant, yelling out questions and accusations of a coverup. Gaines offered no answers to the barrage of questions. Minutes later Josh joined the President in the Oval Office.

"The press is not letting this matter settle, Mr. President. May I tell them you will clarify certain issues in a later briefing?"

"No, we are not going to get into this again—not this close to the election. We stick to the explanation given and run out the news cycle. Hopefully it ends in a few days."

"Alright sir, we'll hunker down and ride it out."

"Exactly!"

Dalton Crusoe, Charley Rhodes and Ed Kosko watched in amazement at the cool, remorseful, and seemingly sincere, unemotional delivery of the message Badge Demarche had for the country.

Ed remarked, "Damn, he actually did it. He lied to the country and smugly thinks he can get away with it." Charley Rhodes was smiling and knew Demarche had no idea a detailed DVR existed on the entire mission which could lead to his impeachment.

Dalton reflected, "I'm not sure he is done with this problem. The press seems to want more answers, and his attempt to lay all this on Barriman is easy when the former President can't respond himself. When do your next polling numbers come in Charley?"

"They come in this evening, around eight o'clock. That should tell us how well Badge did in convincing the country this mission was a great success and we should thank him—and Barriman."

"That should tell us whether we need to actually release the video, right?" Dalton looked for an answer.

"Right. You good with that Ed?" Rhodes wanted to be sure his candidate agreed.

"Absolutely release it. If I didn't do something to expose this lie, I'd never forgive myself."

Charley Rhodes office phone rang. He ignored it and thought through his next steps. Seconds later an assistant banged on Rhodes' office glass and pointed to a live TV broadcast. Charley snatched his controller, pointed it at his office television, and said, "I guess we need to watch this."

The news anchor announced "Breaking News" had just come in from a middle-eastern news network. Seconds passed before the image of Aza Bashir filled the screen with two heavily armed military types covered in black hoods standing in the background. A white sheet served as a backdrop for the three. Bashir began with a statement condemning the "West" for killing innocent civilians, and that his forces would extract their revenge. He then went on to explain in near perfect English that he had foiled a US attack, survived missile strikes and had killed the aggressors. He then held up the dog tags of seven men and called out their names claiming... "my soldiers killed them as they ran away". A photo inserted in the forty-second broadcast revealed a downed Predator drone. He concluded by saying, "I am alive and will continue to lead my fighters until the US and its allies leave our lands."

Charley Rhodes had instinctively recorded the broadcast. He looked around the room and saw faces expressing the same astonishment he felt. Dalton spoke first. "Badge Demarche just got his bet raised. He will have to explain himself—again."

Ronet shifted in his chair like a trapped wolf before saying, "I can personally confirm a drone missile *did not* hit our men. The first one destroyed the house where Bashir was camped out. He had to have been warned of the attack, moved out and set up the ambush. Damnit—Bashir's men killed our guys after Badge abandoned them."

"We'll get the real story out. Besides the video, we have you and Jack Watts to verify what Barriman and Badge did in the situation room." Ed saw that the group's mood had shifted to anger.

CHAPTER NINETEEN

Upstate New York, Adirondack Mountains, Hemlock Glen Resort

Mid October was the perfect time to visit upstate New York. The fall colors were just beginning to show themselves on the aspen and beech trees scattered among the large pine forest areas. Lars Nevin arrived the day before the speaking, fundraising and strategy meetings for Ed Kosko were to start. Adrestia had done a formidable job organizing for the attack plan Lars had outlined. Entering the US was made easier by flying the three members of Lars assassin team into Nova Scotia under the guise of a fishing vacation. From there it was relatively easy to make their way to upstate New York and join Lars outside the Hemlock Glen Resort in a small cabin six miles away.

The three operators, Jake, an Australian, and UK brothers Ned and Jay, arrived at the precise coordinates given them by Lars earlier in the day. Each man was a battle-hardened warrior available for service for a sizable fee, without regard for the political niceties. Lars handpicked the men whom he had worked with years before and directed on several missions. The cabin was basic yet ideal for their mission. It was only one of three identical cabins occupied over a quarter-mile stretch of river. The setting was two-hundred yards off the main highway, obscured by the forest from any traffic. The fast flowing stream in front of the rustic cabin flowed directly into Hemlock Glen forming a small lake before continuing on. Jake jumped out of the Cadillac Escalade packed full of waders and fishing gear which covered four field packs for the team. "Nice place to set up a command post Lars."

"Yes, it is going to be perfect for our work over the next few days." Lars shook the hand of each man and took them inside. One large living room, kitchen and eating area fronted three small bedrooms and a single bath area. A pitcher pump rose conspicuously at the edge of the sink and counter area. In the center of the room a large, wooden table sat with picnic type seat benches on either side. Lars had set up two computers with three screens. The largest screen gave a close up view of the Hemlock Glen site from Google maps; the second screen connected to Adrestia's server through a small satellite antenna perched near the front windows; and the third ran a loop of the rear and river side views of the cabin from small television monitors.

"Looks like you've been here a while getting setup" Jake observed.

"I arrived a day and a half ago, scouted the area, and set up our communications and surveillance equipment." Lars looked at each man. "This mission must be completed successfully at this time or we make the Chinese very upset—and I don't think we want to end up there. Do we all understand?"

"Right boss, we know what we've got to do."

Lars nodded and said, "Let's get into the mission packets, Ok?"

◆ ◆ ◆

Dalton and Ronet arrived in the first vehicle, a GMC Acadia, with Cotter. Ed Kosko was in the second vehicle, a stretch limousine, with two Secret Service agents including McCord, and Wilson. The third vehicle held Charley Rhodes, a staffer, and a third Secret Service agent led by Under McCord's direction, the third vehicle pulled ahead as they approached the stonewall gatehouse. Security confirmed the expected arrival of the Kosko entourage and waved them all through. The long, winding landscaped boulevard drive leading to the main hotel and conference center was a spectacle of flowers and shrubbery. Modest signage directed guests ahead or to a side road to the nearby clubhouse serving three championship courses for the golfer traffic. Dalton noticed the heavy forest had only been trimmed back some twenty yards from the road system and thought about security for Ed Kosko. The remote setting was an advantage yet the surrounding forest covered most of the 600 acres at Hemlock Glen and could provide both concealment and escape cover for attackers. Ronet and Wilson had developed a plan, in conjunction with McCord and the Secret Service team, which made sense, but the warning words of Declan kept returning... *these folks are powerful, ruthless, committed and very dangerous.*

Resort security was not prepared for anything like what Declan had described, and they agreed to cooperate fully with arrangements Dalton and Ronet requested. Hemlock Glen had the capability to house, feed, and provide meeting space for up to 700 guests, including the presenters. The venue had been used several times in prior election cycles to hold fundraisers, rallies, and conferences for political groups. Still the Kosko event was expected to approach the resort capacity, although requests for rooms and conference passes ran twice the estimates from Pathroads for America. Charley Rhodes had experience with the conference center's security protocols for attendee's but no knowledge or experience with protocols for the other resort areas, golf courses, and the surrounding wilderness. Dalton took on the job of coordinating Ronet, McCord and the Secret Service contingent for overall protection.

Wilson walked the long hallway looking for suite 303. He carried his powerful NSA laptop and several files in his briefcase. Arriving at the door to the large business suite, he knocked twice. The door opened slowly, a familiar face appeared and he walked in.

"How long have you been here Declan?" Wilson had not worked directly with Declan Faden Crusoe before, but now they had a common goal to pursue—identify the mysterious source 'Flask'.

"Dalton wanted me here, outta sight, in a kinda remote location, until ya arrived. I'm sure Adrestia is searchin' fer me in the DC area. I've spent the last two days lookin' fer security weaknesses. Ya'll just arrived?"

Wilson began to set up his laptop while he conversed, "Yes. We just got in. JD and Ronet are with Rhodes and Kosko, getting ready for the conference events. You discover anything troublesome?"

"The resort is set up with twenty security cameras, ta catch a breakin' ta a room, a robbery, or car accident—ya know the easy stuff these places deal with everyday." Wilson listened for more. "The problem is the surroundin' forest: no security coverage beyond the developed areas, and three roads, and a river flowin' right through the project. Each offers an entry point to the heart of the resort without any real coverage or security personnel."

"You think an attack might come through the forest?" Wilson tapped away on his laptop keyboard.

"Aye, that's how I'd do it. Get up as high as possible, in cover, and wait fer a shot." Declan shrugged his shoulders.

"A sniper attack. Does Adrestia have those types available?" Wilson looked troubled.

"Ya betcha they do...I knew a few of them. Deadly killers."

"Is Adrestia likely to try a massive attack, like with an armed drone or bomb?"

"Not likely. That takes more planning and preparation. They could try, but I sense they dun't have much time left. I've heard they have ta complete their contract within...days...not weeks or months."

Wilson reflected on Declan's thoughts. "We should connect with Dalton and Ronet shortly—they need to hear your analysis."

"Right."

◆ ◆ ◆

By four o'clock the crowds of New Libertarian Party faithful, news reporters, photographers, lobbyists and contributors had filled the hallways, bars, patios, lounge areas and the golf courses at Hemlock Glen. The resort was nearly full. The fall weather was ideal for outside activity. People were playing golf, tennis, hiking the grounds, running and riding the bike trails. Mixed in among the crowd was a man stretching his calf and thigh muscles, dressed in a running suit, sunglasses and wearing earbuds. Jake had jogged across the resort campus checking out the central hotel building, and its connected conference center containing a large auditorium, shopping area, restaurants, exercise facilities, and several small group meeting rooms. His small video camera clipped neatly and unto his collar broadcast the scenes to Lars Nevin back at the cabin. Jake then picked up his pace, ran into the forest on the golf cart path and quickly vanished into the mature forest. He stopped on a small knoll and looked out from a break in the aspen grove. "Are you seeing this, Lars?"

"Yes, I'm recording it all. Range your distance to the conference center. They call is the grand ballroom. It's the biggest, most likely venue for the Kosko speech."

Jake withdrew a small laser range finder from his running top and reported, "655 yards to the glass windows this side and behind the speaker's podium."

"Can you see the actual speaker podium?" Lars could not see through the reflections off the glass on his computer screen.

Jake adjusted his stand, preventing any excess sunlight from entering the lens. "I've got it—it's about seven yards inside the glass wall. The southern exposure would likely produce a strong glare in the morning, but by mid-afternoon the sun should not be a factor." Jake instinctively checked his watch—3:16 p.m.

"Can you make a shot at that range and place it in a four-inch circle?"

"Yes I can, with a rest and little to no wind. But Ned is better at this than any of us. He can do this at twice the distance."

"Tag the spot on your GPS locator and evaluate at least two fast escape routes. If we are successful, the Secret Service will ID the shooter's position and be all over the area with men and helicopters."

"Right boss. I'll return in an hour."

Lars Nevin replayed the forty minute video and narration from Jake three times, trying to evaluate the best time and place to attempt a sniper shot. Jay returned from his scouting and walked in as Lars made some notes to his file titled: HGR RECONN.

Jay dropped his backpack and explained, "The river widens to thirty meters as it approaches the lake just before the resort. The water is shallow, and manageable except for a couple of sharp turns and a few deep holes. Parts of the golf courses touch the lake edge. We could enter the heart of the resort by water at night and never be seen or heard. It would allow us to get within 100 meters of the clubhouse and maybe 250 meters from the conference center balcony on its west side."

Lars listened with the attention and insight that had marked his fast rise to dominance in the world of espionage and covert operations...*for a fee*. He seldom missed the shortcomings and advantages of one strategy over another. In this case, Lars reasoned the escape plan was more important than the kill scenarios. Depending on the precise movements of the target, and the weather, a number of attractive kill venues would work. He and his team had the skill sets to assure a kill. The concern was the escape: one which left no clues as to the shooter, his accomplices, or their location.

Lars moved to a different computer and ordered, "Jay sit down here and check the internet and the Hemlock Glen website to get an updated schedule for the Kosko event."

"On it boss."

Lars Nevin began to detail a complex plan which would unfold in the next thirty-six hours. He felt confident Badge Demarche and the Chinese leadership would be pleased.

Declan followed Wilson across the grounds to the Conference Center Campus where the Kosko team set up in several adjoining business suites and small meeting rooms. The arrangement was awkward yet functional. Dozens of old metal desks were bunched together leaving a small walkway between them and a large glass enclosed office where Rhodes sat. The four TV's running in his office covered the cable and major outlets. Outside the office in the "bull pen" were a cluster of six screens forming a hexagon around a sturdy steel column holding which held the apparatus along with a massive bundle of coax and power cables. McCord arranged for continuously manned security cameras at the two entrance points. Declan joined Dalton, who waved him and Wilson over while meeting with Ronet. "How long have you been here? What do you think of the security?

"I'm good brother. I got in early yesterday. It was nice ta blend into the crowd while I looked about. I even managed ta do a little fishin' on the rivers yesterday."

Wilson spoke up. "Declan gave me a briefing on his findings and I've just put then in an email to you and Ronet."

Dalton checked his mail and found the report from Wilson. "Got it thanks."

Dalton sat inside Charley Rhodes' massive office, at a small oval conference table holding several laptops up and operating. Devin McCord arrived and joined the group around the table. "We must assume Adrestia will learn of Ed's schedule and deploy an assassin or an assassin unit anywhere they can detect a security weakness. We are maintaining a tight 'close-contact' security with the Secret Service through Devin here. That should be adequate during the two speaking times for Ed, and his movement about the internals of the resort."

Dalton looked to Devin, who remarked, "Yes Dalton is correct. I've coordinated with Colonel Ronet to have four men, plus myself always within 100 feet of Mr. Kosko and two men within fifteen feet. This has been an effective close-protection plan in the past."

Ronet sat listening respectfully, occasionally gazing at McCord, while he read through Declan's analysis as summarized by Wilson. Dalton continued the discussion, "Our biggest challenge will be when Ed is exposed to the outside areas of the resort."

McCord questioned, "Why can't we keep him sequestered within the buildings?"

Ronet spoke up to answer McCord's question. "Good idea, but Ed and Charley Rhodes feel it's politically important for Ed to be seen out in public, waving to cheering supporters, and not timid about being seen in crowds. I'm concerned."

Dalton added more background. "I've talked to Ed directly about any overly exposed situations and while he agrees in principle, he feels he must be seen as approachable and in touch with the crowds. He felt this resort setting would be an excellent and fairly safe setting to create those images and impressions. I couldn't talk him out of it."

Ronet piped up, "On top of that some of the most influential contributors and his close friends want a round of golf with Ed. I half wish it was going to be raining for five days."

The group chuckled at Ronet's' quip, still the danger of being exposed for hours on a forest- bordered golf course was a problem—one the team had to prepare for. Declan sat down without saying a word. Dalton noticed and said, "Declan, what does your knowledge of Adrestia and Lars Nevin suggest in terms of his likely actions? Would he strike here, and how?" Wilson, Ronet, Rhodes and McCord all wanted to hear Declan's assessment.

All knew of Declan's past and his escape to alert Dalton and Ed that they were under a kill contract by a very powerful and dangerous group. Declan took the question seriously and began with some background. "I was bouncin' around doing reconnaissance, security details, and protection when a friend from Northern Ireland asked if I wanted ta work security for a construction conglomerate that did a lot o' work in the Far East and China. Never been ta anywhere near those sites, and was out o' work so I took the assignment." The group settled down and focused on Declan's every word.

"It was a ten month gig, but during that time we were threatened by a drug ring pressuring Adrestia's construction arm ta smuggle drugs throughout the region as we went from job to job. They tried ta sabotage our construction sites and rough up our local crews."

Ronet spoke up, "So Adrestia wasn't involved in the drug trade?"

"Nay, not ta me narrow knowledge. Their construction operations allowed them ta deal with high level officials in various governments—most drug rings were operatin' more in the shadows."

Ronet had a followup. "So what did Adrestia do to stop the interference?"

"Well, we set up a secret security force, heavily armed, and durin' a major night time attack using explosives, we took thum out."

"Were you involved with that action?" Dalton posed the question, hoping to get an answer clearly qualifying Declan for his role now.

"Yeah brother—I led a team o' five men and took out the entire attack force. That's when Lars Nevin really took notice and brought me into his circle of say, twenty men, given the most important contracts."

"You mean like assassinations?" Another question from Dalton.

"I mean like targeting Ed Kosko and...you. That's when I realized I couldna go any further with the man." The group stirred as they heard again the threats to Dalton and Ed Kosko.

"Anyway, I got ta see up close what the man is made of. He's a cold blooded bloke, driven by power and money. He demands strict loyalty, or yer out, then usually dead—dropped in some foundation just before the wet concrete is poured in. He always travels with two armed guards—ex-military, commando types. His deep connections with the current Chinese leaders goes back ten years or more as he did big projects fer them—lotsa projects—hospitals, rail systems, military bases, naval ports and airports" Declan paused and took a sip of his lemonade.

"What *kind* of man is Nevin, really?" Charley Rhodes had to get a deeper impression of the individual in his mind.

Declan's mood grew serious. "Lars is a big man, 6'-2", I think, very fit, muscular, late forties, maybe fifty. No wife er kids...speaks half-dozen languages. He projects an impression o' a calm, clear headed, focused trench warrior—but trained in the world of modern warfare, communications, and the political maneuvering needed ta avoid becoming a casualty. He served in the Australian Special Forces, I'm told, ran a special unit, from where he later recruited his best men. He can be decisive on business and military matters, a strong Generalist who can analyze and strategize his way through about anything. It'd be a grand mistake ta underestimate him...fer sure."

Ronet took it all in, his mind recognizing that Lars Nevin was a formidable opponent.

Declan began again. "This contract on Ed and JD has ta be the creation of yer new President and the Chinese, who now have a tight control on runnin' the US government and your economy. They've got the money to attract Lars—and the motivation to stop, or eliminate the NLP movement. If allowed ta become *new* American law, the Chinese loose all the gains they've made with the Barriman and Demarche administration. With your elections comin' up, they have ta make their moves soon. I'd bet they've looked hard at this place."

Ronet asked, "How do you think he'd devise an attack?"

"Oh, it's hard ta say, fer sure. But I dun't see him doin' a massive attack; ya know big explosions, drones and so on—too much ta run away from once it starts. He's more like ta use a long-range sniper, a deadly toxin, virus, gas... or a close contact assault...if he can penetrate the Secret Service security. It has ta be a covert style plan, so's they can escape without capture and bein' exposed. If really done right, maybe make it look like an accident. We won't even know how it happened fer days or a week, least of all find a trail leadin' to Adrestia. I heard he likes ta get in by stealth, attack in silence, and retreat un-noticed—that's my best guess."

"Would this setting fit that attack scenario?"

"Aye, JD, I think it does. He may have a backup team with armed helicopters ta finish the contract if the stealth design fails—and then escape through the air ta a remote spot where they can disappear again."

"Is this contract critical enough to cause Nevin to personally participate, Declan?"

"If I'm right about the importance of this contract ta the Chinese—they would *insist* Lars lead it. I'd bet he's here...leadin' the assassin team."

Dalton considered his brother's words then studied Ronet and McCord before stating, "We have a lot of work to do in the next twenty-four hours."

Charley Rhodes looked stunned and nervous. He checked his watch. In less than ten hours the states began voting on the slate of amendments arising from the Convention of States. Devin McCord appeared distracted as he read an incoming email on his smart phone, then thought to himself...*I wonder if Dalton knows of this?*

CHAPTER TWENTY

Day Two at the Hemlock Glen Resort

Charley Rhodes had spent many hours and $800,000 buying prime television time on the day state legislatures were voting on approving the amendments to the Constitution which had been debated, refined and selected through the Convention of States effort. He expected that a six-hour slot from 10:00 a.m. till 4:00 p.m. EST would be ideal. Ed Kosko was scheduled to make a twenty minute television address to the nation at three-o'clock, from the Dallas Convention center where he had earlier announced his candidacy for President on the New Libertarian Party ticket. Prior to the speech Pathroads for America planned to run a one hour recap of the Convention highlights, including portions of Ed's impassioned acceptance speech and the summary remarks from six presenters on each of the proposed amendments. The money had been spent on a powerful combination of message, music and imagery full of nationalistic themes, restoring America's status in the world, and reigning in an over bloated and imposing federal government.

It was one exactly week before the Presidential election and many voters were waiting for the outcome of the legislatures' votes on adopting the slate of constitutional amendments. An approval from three-quarters of the state legislatures would energize the conservatives and push the tight polling toward Ed Kosko. A rejection by the legislatures would stymie the NLP and energize the liberal progressives to portray Libertarians as out of touch with what the average American wanted. Ed Kosko stood near the curtain behind his speaking podium talking with Charley Rhodes.

"Are you ready Ed? This is the last chance to not only push for the passage of the slate of amendments through the legislatures but also provide a final contrast between a Kosko presidency and a continuation of Barriman policies through President Demarche."

"I'm ready Charley. I just hope I'm reading the will of the people correctly. They have to be able to see the disastrous path we are on to vote for a major policy change. If they don't we soon reach the point of no return." Rhodes looked at Ed, who seemed concerned, tired and lacking confidence.

"Ed the polls are tight, I readily admit that. Badge was able to use the incapacity of Barriman very skillfully, which gave him a three point bump in the polling. But our base is far more energized and the details of the CASP are creating a drag in Badge's momentum. I foresee a four point spread in our favor after the states approve the new amendments—that should assure a victory for you."

"The trick Charley, as I know you know, is getting past the states' approval of the constitutional changes—right? Without that step, I fear the NLP voters will be discouraged and sit out the election."

"Yes, that is possible, but I don't think we will lose the amendments vote." Charley received a message in his ear piece. "We've just been told—three minutes before you take the podium Ed. Good luck. I'll be just off stage and out of camera view."

Ed nodded, smiled at Charley as he walked away and felt an increasing uneasiness.

Dalton also sat backstage in a small glass-walled room where Wilson and Cotter monitored the security cameras, addressed the Secret Service detail and followed a broadcast of legislatures' voting in a dozen states. Several of the east coast states had completed their vote taking resulting in eight decisions: five approvals and three rejections, on the amendments slate.

"How did the states finish?" Wilson looked back at Dalton for an answer who stood directly over his shoulder.

"The five approvals thus far were expected, Pennsylvania, New Hampshire, Connecticut, Rhode Island and North Carolina. Rhodes really felt New Jersey might vote for approval yet it appears to have joined New York and Massachusetts in rejecting the slate. The final precincts are reporting now."

"Did Rhodes see a last minute change in the polling which turned the momentum for New Jersey's approval?"

"He didn't mention it if he sensed it. He's walking this way...let's ask him." Dalton motioned to Charley, who nodded as he listened to a call through his earphone headset.

Charley Rhodes was decidedly upset. "Damn, Dalton, we may have a problem with New Jersey."

"What are you saying? You mean the voting or the projections?" Wilson left his computer screen and looked at Rhodes for an answer.

"Well, you remember that the slates were approved by the legislatures in some of the states, but the politicians in swing states thought it might be too risky. As a result, some of the legislatures decided to hold referenda to decide the issue of adoption of the Amendments. In those states where the legislatures approved the Amendments, we're sure the results are valid. However, in those states with referenda, including New Jersey, we suspect problems with the legitimacy of the voting results." Rhodes paused to organize his next remark. "My 'watchers' in and around Newark suspect fraud. We have ninety percent of the results in—approvals were running two to four points ahead of defeat—then Newark starts to report and the numbers flip to a five point lead for defeat."

Wilson jumped in, "Charley, how can you be sure of that?" Dalton remained silent thinking and listening.

"We run spot exit polling in large population areas, like Newark. They are very reliable numbers—we've used this method for years. Our exit polling shows no change from the earlier results, yet they are now reporting the final tally has reversed—rejecting approval of the slate of amendments. I just don't believe it." Rhodes was livid, as he touched his earpiece again.

A minute passed as Rhodes concentrated on the message. He looked at Dalton as the call ended. "My Newark team has voters telling them of a *rumor* that all the electronic machines tabulating votes since three o'clock have been set to cast every vote against the slate of amendments. We've filed a complaint with the elections commission. I smell Badge Demarche all over this issue."

Wilson remarked, "That could be bad for Ed in a week if the slate of amendments fail...right Charley?" A new call caused Charley to engage his headphone gear.

"Damn right it could be. Virginia is another state holding a referendum and I just heard Virginia polls are closing and we were tracking a solid four-point lead for approval, and now after polls closed, the trend reversed...we may lose Virginia too...damn that would insure defeat. It could leave us two states short of the three-quarters needed. Without the proposed constitutional amendments in place, a *new* President Kosko would be constrained to undo the mess Barriman and Demarche has put us into. It could also seriously reduce turnout, as most Kosko supporters believe his effectiveness as President depends on getting the amendments incorporated into the Constitution."

Without a hint of indecision Dalton asked, "Wilson, can you navigate your way into the Demarche communications network—computers, servers, faxes, smart phones?"

"Maybe. It's top level encrypted, but I'll dig into it. Remember the work I did to get into the dedicated routing for the *Varyag II* reports? I'll try to get into Demarche's system that way—but we all know this is illegal, right?"

"So is participating in voting fraud. Call it crimes against the Constitution to subvert a right to vote on amendments approved by the States." Dalton looked to Charley Rhodes for his response.

"You're dead on, Dalton. The videos from Declan and Ronet are enough, in my mind, to justify what you propose. If my people can assist Wilson, I can assure their competency and their...confidentiality."

"Thanks Charley. Get moving, Wilson. We need to find out if Demarche or Josh Gaines are directly involved—I'm betting they both are." Dalton glanced at Charley Rhodes and said, "Ill alert Ronet, but both of us should brief Ed and General Watts."

"Absolutely."

General Jack Watts arrived late at the resort. Ronet waited for him in the massive reception lobby. Watts walked in alone, in his full dress uniform, carrying a small bag. Ronet checked his watch—11:16 p.m., as he noticed the General approached.

"Good evening General—good flight?"

"Yes. I grabbed a ride on CIA Director Cavanaugh's private jet, as I left Washington after 8 o'clock."

"Was the director expected to attend here also?"

"No, but we used the flight time and privacy to discuss some troubling matters."

Ronet knew enough to remain quiet and wait to see if he was permitted to learn more. The General sensed Ronet's curiosity but left the subject alone. "What's the schedule for Ed and Dalton Crusoe tomorrow Brad?"

"There is an open breakfast time between 8 and 9 a.m. which Ed will attend and say a few words on his short, but growing campaign. He then speaks to the entire group at 3:30 p.m. for about ninety minutes, followed up by a fundraising pitch from Charley Rhodes, then a cocktail time ahead of dinner at 7:30, when various speakers will rally the troops. Do you need to speak with him?"

"Yes, but it can easily fit into that schedule, maybe near lunch time."

The breakfast crowd was loud and energized to be in the presence of the man who held his own in a nationwide televised debate against the skilled orator President Barriman. The crush of people around Ed Kosko made it difficult for Dalton to stay at Ed's side. Devin McCord was also close at hand and said, "Once Ed is seated and the crowd settles down, we need to talk."

Dalton looked at McCord and realized something was troubling the Secret Service agent. "Fine, let's grab a table near the side and we can have some privacy."

"Good I'll join you in a few minutes."

McCord joined Dalton as planned and after the waitress poured coffee and offered them the grand buffet station, he began to speak. "Months ago I overheard an odd conversation with an agent and Badge Demarche. The agent and Badge argued for a minute or so. Then the agent was quiet, apparently Badge was speaking, until the agent finally said, *'I'll do it, tomorrow after the DC meeting. But I need to hear you promise it's over. I demand proof'.* I made a mental note about it but then basically forgot it."

"Who was the agent?"

"It was Eric Walters, and he's on Ed's detail here."

"Did you ever learn what it was Badge wanted Walters to do?"

"I couldn't figure it out until I was assigned here and heard Ed's story about the death threat he found on his car. The day Ed found the note *was* the very next day after I overheard Walters— Ed discovered the threat warning directly following his DC *meeting* with Pathroads for America, at Rhodes' offices. The threat came from Badge...maybe."

Dalton studied the senior agent and ran several dark scenarios through his mind. "Where is Walters now?"

McCord thought for and instant, and stated, "He's working close security detail now. He's the second tier—at the 100 foot perimeter, not the shadow security near fifteen feet. See he's over there by the south doors."

"Go to talk with him now! Keep him occupied until I call you. I'll have Ronet with me."

"Right. I'll drift over his way, making a normal status check for anything suspicious."

Ronet was sitting alone with General Watts directly in front of the head table where Ed, his wife Irene, Charley Rhodes and a few of his staffers sat. Dalton walked up and calmly greeted the group. "Good morning all. It looks like everyone is rested." He revealed a broad smile, patting Ed on the shoulder as he leaned over and gave Irene a hug.

"Good morning, Dalton. We're ready for some relaxing time before the afternoon talk; can you sit with us for breakfast?"

"Yes, perhaps in a few minutes. I've got some details to check on." He smiled again, conveying a confident mood. Irene smiled back and offered an approving nod. Dalton then circled the head table and approached Ronet and Watts. "General may I borrow this old warrior from you for a few minutes?"

Watts shook Dalton's hand and said, "Go ahead. He keeps jabbering and I'm starving. I'll see you back here after I manage my way to the buffet." The General gave a friendly wave as the two left.

"Brad, we may have a problem." Ronet's face turned serious, as he asked, "What are you talking about JD?"

"I fear we may have a rogue agent in Badge Demarche's pocket."

"Damn, I was worried that character had a plant somewhere. Who are we talking about?"

"Eric Walters may have left the death threat on Ed's windshield under direction from Badge." Ronet stiffened.

"Are you sure about this? I interviewed him and he seems solid. He pulled Demarche from the river a while back right?"

"Yes, he did, but McCord has some compelling information against Walters. My concern is whether he's only a courier—or a low profile assassin—McCord has him occupied for now."

"Hell, either way we can't take a chance. He may be a contract guy for Adrestia." Ronet scanned the room to find Walters.

"Maybe but I doubt it. If he'd had a past or recent connection with Adrestia it should have appeared in his fitness reports. It would have never passed a background investigation even without hard proof of Adrestia's role here. Still Badge Demarche may have protected him. Let's go." Both men looked at each other and knew leaving Walters on the security team was far too much risk to take.

Ronet joined Dalton as they alerted McCord that he should bring Walters to a short briefing ahead of the golf outing. They all met up in a hallway exit from the auditorium. Ronet moved to stand alongside Walters, with McCord behind him and Dalton in front. "Eric we have some things to go over before we head to the golf course. Do you have your weapon on you?"

"Yes, of course, it's right here. Why?" As he reached to his back where his Glock was holstered, Ronet clamped Walters in a neck hold forcing the agent back on his heels as Dalton removed the weapon. McCord grabbed Walters' left arm and along with Ronet pulled him back hard against the wall. McCord swiftly clamped handcuffs on the agent, who looked completely blindsided to the happenings.

Dalton removed the clip from the Glock and ejected a round from the barrel. He looked into Walters' face and said, "Tell me what you agreed to do for Badge Demarche about six weeks ago, and why did you request to be put on this security detail?"

Walters grew angry and despondent. "What the hell are you talking about? Why are you doing this?" Ronet held his hand against Walters' chest while McCord searched him, finding a non-governmental issue smart phone.

McCord stepped around to look the agent in the face and said, "I overheard you arguing and talking to Badge Demarche. As the conservation finished you said '...*I'll do it, tomorrow after the DC meeting.*'...The next day Ed Kosko had a death threat note stuck on his windshield. You put it there on orders from Demarche."

"I did not." Walters struggled to get free of Ronet's grip.

McCord challenged him again, "Yes you did. Badge had something on you...what? Sex, broads, bribes, espionage or something else?"

Dalton considered the situation and spoke, "Eric I have no reason to suspect your loyalty, except for the matter Devin brought up. But you will be discharged from this assignment and the Secret Service unless I'm satisfied you are telling us the truth. What happened?"

McCord scrolled through the menu on Walters' smart phone locating the contacts list and found Badge Demarche name among several calls to Badge around the time of the Ed Kosko death threat note. 'Well looky here Eric, a private number, addressed Badge. This isn't the number I have for him in my service issued phone. Why don't we call him and see if he can sort this all out. What do you think Dalton?"

"Good plan, let's go for it." Dalton stared at Walters leaving no doubt this was not a bluff.

"Alright, alright! Badge did ask me to place an envelope beneath Kosko's wiper when he was in talking to Rhodes. That was all I did. I didn't know it contained a death threat."

'Why did you resist—and what promise did you need to hear?" McCord closed the phone.

Walters abandoned his struggle, looked to McCord then to Dalton and said, 'Ok I'll tell you the whole story." Ronet released his grip, but stood close to the agent, eliminating any attempt at escape. A moment of silence transitioned Walters into a compliant posture.

"Five months ago I fell back into drug use. I had been clean for four years, did my job well and felt great. Then last year I drifted back into some random use, waking up after a *hot* overdose—passed out at my apartment missing a call into Badge. He sent some of his boys to track me down through my smart phone and got me into a private rehab facility. Until then nothing I'd taken had affected my work. Badge quietly took over, got me discharged, squelched the media and helped me, so I really owed him my life and career."

McCord quipped, "Had the bad luck of a medical professional seeing your tracks, eh?"

Walters shot a glare at McCord then continued, "He interviewed me, took notes, a video and voice record on my drug history, mostly booze but then cocaine—I couldn't leave it alone. He was going to help me I thought. He threatened to expose me and have me removed from the Service when I resisted his requests. He is a doctor, medically trained. Instead he started using me for 'dark assignments'."

Dalton noticed the odd expression on Ronet's face, a facial confirmation he held about Badge Demarche's corruption. Dalton spoke up, "Did Badge personally order the death threat against Ed?"

"I don't know. I doubt it—he always had dedicated operatives to do much of the dirty work. I was just a compromised agent he used as a handy delivery boy, and knew I'd have to keep quiet."

"Who were the operatives he used?"

"I only heard of two, Saul Abboud, and a lesser character named Max...that's all I know."

McCord looked to Dalton who was thinking, preparing a response. "Eric why are you here on this assignment?

"I want to keep this job. I've been clean and sober for six weeks now. The promise I wanted from Demarche was to give me the entire medical file he'd created and no more dark assignments. He agreed—if I completed *one* more assignment for him—provide daily reports on the Kosko schedule."

"Have you been doing that for...President Demarche?"

"Yes, for the last three days I've been on assignment." Walters looked humble and beaten down. Dalton noticed.

"Eric, do you want to go to prison for treason?" Dalton was convincingly serious.

"No, No. I want to do my job. I'll go back into rehab, if needed. I can beat this. Really, I mean it this time." Walters appeared to be sincerely penitent over his actions.

"I'll recommend you be released without shame, but you have to do exactly as I demand."

"Ok, what do you mean?" Walters began to shiver.

"You will do exactly as I or Agent McCord request. If you disobey you will be charged and imprisoned, after Colonel Ronet interrogates you. Do you understand?" Ronet grinned at the veiled threat.

Walters remained motionless and silent for several seconds before saying, "I'll do what you want, what is it?"

Dalton answered, "You will help us trap President Demarche in a lie."

CHAPTER TWENTY-ONE

Afternoon Day Two at the Hemlock Glen Resort

The partly cloudy sky revealed some bright orange colors on the horizon even at 9 a.m. The forecast indicated a fifty percent chance of thunderstorms by early afternoon. Still the temperature held at a comfortable 70 degrees as the golfers took to the tee. The course was in magnificent shape with the last morning dew rising slowly off the fairways and greens as the sun made its way to the ground.

Ed Kosko was part of a foursome, including Dalton Crusoe, Jack Watts, and major donor Jeffery Terrance, CEO of Enertek, Industries. On every third hole the foursome behind exchanged one of its players with the fourth man in Ed's group. This rotation allowed six major contributors to enjoy three holes with their NLP champion of the right—Ed Kosko. Each invitational golfer had donated $100,000 to the campaign to elect Ed Kosko and swat balls with him for three holes. Three Secret Service agents followed Kosko's movements anywhere on the course. The sprawling resort had its two eighteen-hole courses intertwined with each other over approximately 425 acres of dense hardwoods, aspen and ash. Six of the golf holes had areas roped off where conference attendees could view the players. Heavy security checks were in place to screen hundreds of eager supporters of the NLP and their candidate Ed Kosko.

Jack Watts rode with Dalton in the second cart behind Ed and Jeffery Terrance. The chatter was excessive for most serious golfers but this was as much interaction and photo ops as a golf match. The first hole was a long par four of 390 yards, with a mild dogleg left. Dalton took the tee and made a smooth swing catching the ball near the toe, which produced a soft draw, landing 245 yards out near a fairway trap.

"Watts stood behind Dalton and remarked, "Nice shot, Dalton. Looks like you play a bit, right?"

"I played in college a bit, but since those days it's not often I can get away for a fun round. Today I'm pretty much into Ed's security more than my club selection."

The General smiled, took the tee and delivered a powerful straight drive ten yards past Dalton's. "Nice drive General—you obviously get in some regular golf play."

"Yeah, I do get out a bit, but never under these circumstances—Secret Service, reporters, business types and politicians." The General sat back down in the cart as Dalton drove down the fairway.

"You've been a friend of Ed's for some time I understand." The General knew Dalton's background but few details of how Ed came to be such a strong friend.

"Yes, he's truly my best friend, and a mentor of sorts. He and my dad were friends and I met Ed through their relationship. When dad died suddenly Ed was there, along with my mother for sure, to keep me in college and working hard. I owe them both a lot." Dalton sensed the General's curiosity growing.

"He calls you JD...initials?" Watts inquired.

"Yes, Jameson Dalton Crusoe, can be a mouthful sometimes...so it gets taken down to JD among friends...like you General." Dalton gave an approving nod to Watts.

"Nice story JD." A pause followed as the cart halted waiting for Ed and Terrance to quiet down and take their second shots. "Ed Kosko and I became friends shortly after he joined the NSA as its head—before he recruited you by several years. Former President Conner really trusted Ed, and you I'm told on several missions—some damn critical to the country."

"Yes you might say that. I view it as being put into common assignments that quickly grew to be serious national issues. I was lucky to survive many times."

The next two holes went by as most golf play does, good shots, poor shots, lots of laughter and joking, still through it all, Dalton listened in his ear piece to the reports from the security team and Ronet. All seemed normal.

As the golf entourage prepared to leave the twelfth green, Jason Dickson, CEO of Freedom Life Insurance Group, hopped into the cart with Ed Kosko, before moving on to the thirteenth hole a par five. All four men hit their second shots well, with Dalton and Jack Watts inside the 150-yard marker by thirty yards. Ed lay twenty yards short of the marker but Jason landed a yard off the monument. The standard sized cement block painted white had been modified seven hours earlier by Lars' men, Jake and Ned, with a two-kilo brick of C4 holding an electronic detonator, covered by the top surface of the original block. A tiny antenna protruded up a half-inch where the grass edge met the block surface.

Lars' man Jake lay on the ground 140 yards away, and twenty feet above the fairway, in a dense stand of yellow pine bordered with patches of pampas grass, standing four foot high. His camouflage clothing, face paint, and web netting cover rendered him invisible except in an extremely close encounter. The thirteenth hole had no spectator areas near the green, as the hole was configured to end near a bend in one of the streams meandering through the course. He watched the twin carts of players, closely followed by two more carrying security men. Ed pulled his cart up for his shot. Ahead lay Jason's second shot, just at the 150-yard monument.

"The pin looks back, right Ed?" Jason walked toward the 150 yard white painted block and stood over it. Jake watched through his forty-power spotting scope. He moved the sight line back eleven yards to see Ed Kosko step out of the cart and take a step towards Jason at the 150-yard marker. Jake extended the antenna on his remote detonator, as he watched Ed to see if he would walk near Jason. Lars Nevin watched on his laptop as the fairway view of the action came streaming in from Jake's transmitter connected to the ranging scope.

"Yes the pin is back. I'll laser it to the pin." Ed stepped back, retrieved his laser and captured the reflective crystal midway up the flagstick. "It's 159 yards from here to the hole Jason."

Lars Nevin spoke to Jake. "Hold for a moment. We need Kosko inside a five-yard radius to assure a kill. He may move up to make another yardage check."

Ed thought a moment and offered, "Let me come to your ball and get a fresh distance Ok?"

Ed started to walk towards Jason; Lars ordered, "Stand ready Jake."

Jason, spoke up, "No worry Ed, I'll step it off back to you. It'll be close enough for my game."

Jake held his vision on the two golfers. Ed had moved only three yards closer to the *lethal* monument. "Do I detonate? Both are close."

Lars studied the image before him. "Hold, Kosko is not in the kill radius. Stand down."

Jake asked again, "Are you sure? He's only eight yards away."

"No hold off. Stand down. Let's wait and see if Crusoe gets near the block." Lars did not want to risk exposure and fail a kill opportunity.

Ed Kosko hit his third shot which went left of the green and away from the planted personal bomb. Dalton and Watts remained behind until Jason made his approach shot, hitting the green in regulation. Watts said, "Let's go look for Ed's ball...he's way too busy chatting with Jason Dickson."

Dalton grinned at his friend's weak shot and thought he could use some help searching. As they drove off to the left side of the fairway, moving further away from the 150-yard marker, Jake held the detonator ready to activate when he reported, "Our targets are too far away. What are your orders, sir?"

Lars was a patient man, and was willing to forgo this first opportunity, to complete his assassination contracts for Badge Demarche and his Chinese masters. Other kill scenarios had been developed and were waiting for the proper moment. "Do not detonate. Shutdown detonator, stow your gear and return here to the cabin here. Understood?"

"Yes sir, understood. On my way."

Dalton and Watts strolled to the green as Ed found his ball and chipped it on. Waiting to putt last Dalton observed a Secret Service agent walking along the fairway edge when a flicker of light, deep in the fairway woods, caught Dalton's attention. He reflected for a moment: heavy cloud cover, little direct sunlight, dense woods, isolated golf hole and a fast flowing river. After putting out, Dalton touched his mic and ordered the agent, "Check out the woods to your right, I may have seen movement."

A reply came, "Roger that, sir."

The next five holes proceeded smoothly, with healthy applause every time Ed Kosko made a good shot. The outdoor casual sporting event cast Kosko as a normal guy, capable of relaxing, kicking back, and unafraid to reveal his golfing challenges. The crowd reaction was positive. As the eighteenth hole was played out, the large gallery of visitors watched a dozen security- screened reporters surround Ed and his group. They were allowed to capture hundreds of photos with the donors, Dalton, Watts and others. Dalton saw Charley Rhodes waving just as his phone rang. "JD, its Charley. Official totals just came in, the slate of amendments failed...we were short two states...New Jersey and Virginia. Several recount challenges have been filed, but we won't have a resolution until after the election."

Dalton reflected on the news and said, "Let's meet at your office here after Ed speaks. I have a plan to consider."

CHAPTER TWENTY-TWO

Fifty Miles East of Chesapeake Bay

The *Varyag II* arrived on the eastern US Atlantic seaboard at 2:20 a.m. The refurbished aircraft carrier was now fully functional and battle ready. As daylight revealed the presence of the giant ship, the news reports came in from nearby commercial shipping traffic, sailors, cruise lines and TV helicopter crews anxious to get coverage of the Chinese warship in US waters. President Demarche issued a press release and a subsequent news conference by Jeff Crandel that the *Varyag II* came at the invitation of the US to participate in joint naval exercises. Still, the talk radio pundits were skeptical and warned of a dangerous intrusion of a foreign power into the sovereign waters of the US. The loyal progressives took the talking points Badge Demarche, Josh Gaines, and Jeff Crandel had prepared for them to use during the morning talk shows. It all had a similar theme: we are living in a different time now, when nations must join together to strengthen their common threads and resolve their areas of disagreement. At the local level the lofty explanations still left Americans unsettled and fearful the USA had abandoned its core principles.

Cities across the nation held town hall meetings where the tensions concerning the Chinese actions were discussed. Some feared an invasion, others were relieved the Chinese currency, the new twenty-five dollar note, had arrived as promised into local coffers and individual checking accounts. The sense that the weak economy was receiving a stimulus-improved confidence, yet others feared the CASP agreement would eventually undermine American sovereignty. Sixteen conservative "red states" formally organized militias just as the Convention of States finished its work to define a slate of amendments to halt the executive government overreach.

♦ ♦ ♦

Tan Zhang stood on the open deck platform of the *Varyag II* Combat Information Center adjoining the Bridge observing military exercises. Shenyang J-11Fighter aircraft were practicing touch-and-go landings. On the flight deck were two J-20 stealth fighters, making a debut in the Atlantic Ocean. Four Z-20 helicopters, each a clone of the US Sikorsky Blackhawk, circled the carrier and stood watch for any sea rescues. Badge Demarche specifically ordered the US military to keep all aircraft grounded within a fifty-mile radius of the *Varyag II*. Despite the order two F/A-18's were launched when four Chinese J-11fighters appeared on Norfolk radar. Rear Admiral Chad Dempsey called his friend and confidant, Jack Watts, to explain the situation.

"Jack, the radar officer was not aware of the President's directive. Your replacement General Harris is a joke, and before we could get our hands around the issue we had two F/A-18's airborne and closing fast on the *Varyag II* J-11's fighters. They got too close and one got tangled in a jet wash, went into a flat spin, and couldn't regain control and the pilot had to bail — lost the aircraft."

"Was there any armament fired?"

"No, it simply appears as though the 18's approached so fast as to overrun the Chinese fighters and damn near collided with them as they turned."

"Did we recover the pilot?"

"Yes, he's fine but the boys down here are pretty alarmed, wondering why we are letting the Chinese undertake training exercises fifty miles off our capitol. Do you know what's really going on?"

"I'll have to get back to you Chad—right now I have no damn clue. In the meantime, alert me to any and all directives from Harris—Ok?"

"You got it Jack."

The reports were coming in from all along the eastern seaboard. The Chinese aircraft were flying low enough over the coastline to prompt hundreds of citizens to capture photos and videos and alert the nation through social media. By 4:00 p.m. the White House was forced to send Jeff Crandel out to address the issue. The press room was raucous with anxious reporters trying to get their stories filed. Jeff Crandel arrived and attempted to hush the throng of reporters all calling out questions. Finally the crowd quieted down and Crandel began with an announcement:

"Today, at approximately 1:40 p.m. two United States F/A-18 aircraft mistakenly launched to investigate a presumed intrusion into US airspace near Norfolk Virginia. Sadly one of the twin aircraft was caught in a jet-wash and spun out of control, resulting in loss of the aircraft. The pilot was able to successfully eject and was unharmed. The F/A-18's were in close contact with Chinese aircraft in the vicinity and the respective maneuvers to avoid a collision led the F/A-18 to lose control and crash. The pilot was recovered by Chinese helicopter crews supporting the mutual training exercises the US had planned with the Chinese military this month."

Crandel pointed to a front row reporter, generally favorable to the administration, in his questioning. "Good Afternoon. Is it true that a Chinese aircraft carrier named the *Varyag II* recently moved to our eastern shore for its military exercises? And if true, why is this exercise done so close to our populated east coast?"

The press secretary had rehearsed responses to several likely questions and began, "As you know the Chinese government and this administration have been working closely over the last year to achieve the CASP agreement which now is helping the US economy. That close relationship has led to discussions and agreements regarding America's military structure which as we all know are a major component of our nation's budget. These exercises were planned to develop areas where US and Chinese cooperation on military matters can achieve a more effective force response and of course reduce the costs. That is why they have come to our shore; it was our invitation. "

Few in the press corps we satisfied with the answer and shouts came from every side asking if the Chinese were now controlling our military. Crandel attempted to handle the barrage of questions but lost control of the session and promptly ended the Q&A, returning to the Oval Office. Within minutes the social media were wild with claims of treason, selling out, and a conspiracy on Demarche's part, and that the CASP agreement had far more negatives than positive points for the average American. Liberal pundits downplayed the significance of the *Varyag II* off our shores and instead highlighted their rescue of the downed American pilot. Conservatives viewed used the incident and the Chinese fighter aircraft intrusion of our airspace as a violation of our sovereignty, and stability, making it clear it would be a rallying cry for the oncoming election.

Back in the Oval Office Badge sat with Josh Gaines watching the botched news conference. As Crandel arrived Badge said, "You lost control Jeff. I thought you had planted a few softball questions to take the fire out of the crowd?"

"They were not about to be redirected Mr. President. I tried to put the incident in the best light, but they were so focused on tying the administration to the lost aircraft I felt it best to adjourn."

Badge Demarche thought for a moment before turning to Josh Gaines. "Prepare a full statement as to what we are trying to do with this new arrangement with the Chinese. Emphasize the benefits to Americans; downplay the fears of losing sovereignty or our military control to the Chinese. Focus on the pilot and his family, his fortunate rescue by the *Varyag II* crew. I want to see something in thirty minutes. We'll issue it for the evening news lead."

"Yes Mr. President." Gaines went off, taking Crandel with him.

◆ ◆ ◆

The Hemlock Glen Resort golf outing staged for photo ops and "gripping and grinning" by Ed Kosko with the able and willing conservative donors concluded near 2 p.m. Jack Watts sat in his room and watched the news coverage of the aircraft incident with the Chinese off Norfolk Virginia. Rear Admiral Chad Dempsey had also watched the news coverage and called Watts. "You seeing this news conference, Jack?"

"Yeah, it looks like Demarche is going to downplay the incursion into our airspace, probably with strict guidance from Lei Zhang or his brother."

"Have you had an update from Flask in the last few days?"

Watts reacted cautiously. "No, but I expect one soon. I fear the reports of the Chinese ordering troops to surround the Capitol may be true. It may be timed with the close of voting on the amendment slate from the COS. Pathroads for America believes votes in New Jersey and Virginia may have been altered to result in a defeat of the amendments."

"Good God man, can Badge Demarche really project his corruption that deeply into the states' voting apparatuses?"

"He can and may have done just that. After all, persuade a few willing operatives with the technical capabilities a knowledge and access to the voting machines and you can create every vote you need."

"The people will go nuts if that can be proved. They'll hit the streets and riot 'till they get satisfaction."

Exactly, which is why I think martial law may be coming in the next few days, just before the Presidential election. Badge might cancel or delay the election until civil unrest subsides. Now I have to focus on getting intelligence on Badge's plans, support Kosko and try to win this damn election in a few days."

CHAPTER TWENTY-THREE

Seven Days before the General Election

The nation erupted on news the COS amendment slate had failed. Progressive liberals hailed the victory as proof the country truly wanted more big government even if it meant partnering with China for a time. Conservatives pushed the argument that corruption at several state voting commissions caused the amendment slate to fail, when in reality it should have passed handily. Expedited court rulings were largely stalled and misdirected by the Demarche administration. Hundreds of nighttime marches and protests began to form across the nation. The anger swelled among conservatives as rumors spread that Demarche's progressive operatives had corrupted the voting process to turn New Jersey and Virginia against the amendment slate. Blog sites flooded with calls for armed disobedience; President Demarche and his aides took notice.

Ed Kosko was coached by Charley Rhodes to deliver a few calming ideas to keep the COS initiative alive at the beginning of his speech. The grand ballroom was an impressive venue for Ed Kosko to deliver his conservative message to his followers and donors. The sprawling speaker platform positioned the podium seven feet above the main floor seating creating a dominant, powerful portrait of the speaker. Large windows tinted to reduce the sun's glare from the southern exposure offered an impressive view of the golf course carved out of the dense forest.

Dalton studied the device from every angle and could not find a single clue as to its origin, design or contents. Rhodes, Wilson, Cotter and Ronet finally arrived at the Hemlock Glen Resort grounds keeper's maintenance crib. "My fairway superintendant found this shortly after you all finishing playing today. It's not our equipment. Do you have any idea what this is?"

Dalton's mind first ran towards a set up for GPS communications, and golf cart monitoring. A second later he warned, "Take a close look at this boys, but do not touch."

Ronet took off his sport coat and walked full circle around the package which lay alone on a table. "Where did this come from?"

"The golf course staff found this thirty minutes after we finished play, beneath the 150 yard marker on hole thirteen."

"What the hell is it? Any clues guys?" Wilson asked.

Ronet moved to within six inches of the item. "Looks to be ten inches, by two by three—wrapped in oiled canvas and burlap, with a micro receiving antenna one inch high protruding off the long side. It looks heavy."

"Well I doubt it's a geocache find, or a control for the course yardage measurement system, or a GPS signal tied to the carts." Cotter guessed.

Ronet gave a stare then remarked, "I'd back off a bit. This could be trouble."

Just then the maintenance crib door opened and it was Declan. "Take a look at this, Declan. Does this tell you anything?"

"Aye, sorry I'm late. What ya got?" Declan walked through the cluster of folks examining the parcel and said, "Clear the room! It's a C4 bomb with a remote signal detonator core."

Ronet said, "Are you sure? It doesn't look like a C4 bomb."

"Yeah, I've built them exactly like this? That's the idea—cover them in burlap to appear harmless, like a stash of coins or bills. Open the overhead door, now."

Dalton lifted the door open as Declan gently unscrewed the small silver antenna from its connector, carried the device outside and laid it in a large concrete flower box.

Once back inside, Declan said, "Lars is here, planning an attack. He likely hoped to get one or both of you this morning on the golf course."

"Ok, if he's here why didn't it trigger when we were playing?" Dalton questioned.

"It's not a lethal blast beyond maybe twenty yards. He needed the targets within that radius, even closer to assure a kill. The trigger is manually armed and remotely detonated."

Ronet speculated, "So someone, watching the activity, had to first arm and then detonate this damn thing right?"

"Oh yeah, fer sure. Someone was there watchin' and waitin'..."

Dalton reacted, "So it's still capable of being blown now?"

"Nay, unless the detonating man is nearby, watchin', and has the detonator armed. No worries now, I removed its antenna." The group stood silent.

"This thin' needs to go back brother." Declan studied Dalton's face.

"What?" Dalton reacted.

"I'm sorry. I mean we must make it *look like* it's back in place."

"Of course, Lars will not leave a bomb for later discovery. Right Declan."

"I can quickly remove the C4, replace with sand and glue, and re-wrap it in the burlap. JD, get me out on a maintenance golf cart, and I'll replace it. Lars may try ta grab it after dark, fer sure."

Wilson was thinking. "We could plant a GPS tag inside this 'burlap bomb'—maybe track it to Lars location."

"Wise plan men. Lars will not leave it here. Cotter, work out the details and get it done soon, Ok."

Charley Rhodes was sweating and looked pale. Wilson and Cotter were astonished having never seen such a bomb disguise. Ronet was angry and forming a defensive reaction to the fact Lars Nevin was nearby. Dalton felt he and Ed had been lucky on the golf course. Declan lit a cigarette.

Dalton regained his composure and said to Ronet, "We need to meet with Ed and Watts now, before Ed's speech in two hours. Wilson, find McCord, brief him and have him put his men on high alert, an attack may come anytime."

CHAPTER TWENTY-FOUR

Hemlock Glen Resort, Upstate New York

Fifty minutes ahead of Ed's speech Dalton set a new defensive plan in motion. McCord met with Eric Walters and had him call Badge Demarche's private phone and leave a voice mail detailing the remainder of the day's activities. Dalton, Rhodes and Ronet crafted the message, and Declan reviewed it and felt it was too tempting for Lars Nevin to ignore, considering all the pressure the Chinese were putting on Adrestia and President Badge Demarche.

McCord stood next to Walters and heard the entire message Walters was ordered to deliver. "It's Eric, nothing special to report today except they announced the location for Kosko's 4 p.m. speech to his contributors. It will be in the grand ballroom. Crusoe and General Watts will be in attendance sitting near Kosko. Sounds like early tomorrow they wind down and head out of town." The call ended.

"Well done, Eric. That may help us if Badge uses the information to alert Adrestia to a fresh opportunity. Let's hope Badge acts on your information—if so it may help your case. Maybe Lars will try again at the resort. If he does, we'll be ready for him. Meanwhile you remain under arrest and confined to your room."

"Devin, I could help. I really don't have a problem with my job—it's just that damn Badge Demarche had me over a barrel. I never had an issue with Kosko."

"That may be true, but *you* delivered the death threat to Kosko. I can't set that aside. You'd best now wear the tether and the door to your room will be locked with an officer outside. We'll talk again later." Eric Walters resigned himself to the fact he'd broken faith with the Secret Service's calling, even if at the command of a corrupt administration official. The prospect of going to prison for treason was haunting.

◆ ◆ ◆

Lars Nevin organized his final option to kill Kosko based on the information forwarded by encrypted email from Demarche. Time and opportunity were slipping away. He needed to act, and act quickly. Two days of monitoring the effects of a slowly setting sun on the glass wall left few occasions for a clear kill shot over the 660 yards distance. Jay had gathered some materials which explained the layout and features of the resort, along with a program guide prepared by the New Libertarian Party. Ed Kosko would be introduced by Charley Rhodes, prior to his walking down the wide center aisle and taking the stage. Ed's remarks were scheduled to take about seventy-five minutes, and followed afterward by a Q&A period of twenty minutes. His speech including some visual aids would be simultaneously displayed broadcast over two massive projection screens angled to offer views to the left and right sides of the auditorium. Lars felt that around fifty-five minutes into the speech the sun angle along with the benefit of expected partial cloud cover would be the most opportune time for a clear kill shot.

Ned reviewed the plan Lars created. "It looks like close to five o'clock the auditorium glass should begin to darken, depending on how much cloud cover blocks the horizon. Kosko should still be speaking then and standing at the podium. All I need is a few seconds when the glass clears to find him in my scope. I can get him."

Lars checked his watch. "Get into position. Call in when you are setup. Take Jake as your spotter; you stay on the rifle; you may only have a second or two."

"Right." Jake left to ready his gear and CSASS sniper rifle, three clips of .308 ammo and a spotting scope.

Dalton met with the entire team before Ed's speech; Kosko, Watts, Rhodes, McCord, Ronet, Declan, Wilson, Cotter and nine assigned Secret Service and six state police officers, mainly handling traffic security and perimeter checks. The briefing began with a summary of the findings on the golf course. "The C4 device, while small, would have been lethal if we had gotten close enough to assure a kill. I suspect that Ed or I never got close enough to guarantee a kill, so they passed on the opportunity. The point being--we know Lars and or his team is here."

Dalton paused as he handed out a marked up map of the resort. "Their next best chance has to be at this afternoon's speech by Ed. Police with bomb sniffing dogs are checking the entire resort...nothing found yet. It may come as a sniper attack and we are taking *special* precautions to avert that possibility. While unlikely, according to Declan it also could come as a suicide attacker. Between me, Ronet and McCord, Ed will never be less than fifteen feet from one of us. The other agents will make a twenty-five foot ring of protection and the remaining agents and state police will constitute the outer protective barrier...around 100 feet away. The handout shows the rough positions we all maintain while Ed speaks and our travel route back to our suite of rooms."

The room was filled beyond capacity. Security was tight. Extra seating was provided near the back wall. The same campaign music used in Dallas was being blasted through the speaker system as Ed Kosko walked from the rear to the podium. Charley Rhodes had given a brief yet rousing introduction to the man all in the room hoped would become the next President of the United States. He removed part of the immediate pain at hearing the COS amendment initiative was defeated—at least for the moment, but buoyed the attendees' hopes that a new President could move it along. The applause continued for over a minute once Ed took the stage; Dalton checked his watch, 4:09 p.m., and then scanned the audience, looking for anything unusual. Watts, Dalton, Ronet and McCord all sat in chairs either side of and behind the podium. All but Watts were armed. Mounted cameras captured the scene from several directions, some capturing the crowd others zooming in for closeups of Ed as he enthusiastically made his points. The crowd was energized. Dalton touched his earpiece saying, "Wilson, how is the video recording coming along?" Ronet also heard the comment.

"Recording going fine. All looks good here."

Ronet observed, "The clouds are increasing, it will darken the sky soon."

"Noted. Cotter, are you in place?" Dalton checked with his man outside the resort directing the state police.

"All is fine here also. State police in place including the air support we called for."

"Good. Stand by." Dalton checked his watch...4:55 p.m.

◆ ◆ ◆

Over a quarter mile away and seventy yards into the autumn woods, stretched out, lying down, hidden under a camo mesh cover strapped between trees and the ground behind them, Jake and Ned watched through their scopes at the glass windows of the grand ballroom. Jake looked through his spotting scope and reported, "Ranging now. Target is in view, 661 yards to impact, temperature 66 degrees, wind mild right to left, gusts to six miles per hour, visibility...improving." Ned made the fine adjustments to the scope.

Lars Nevin followed the activity through a remote camera built into the CSASS rifle's scope snug against Ned's right shoulder. "How is the image through the scopes?"

Ned answered, "Brief moments of darkened sky allowing us to see the target. Still, sun glare most of the time."

Lars listened in and gave the order, "You are authorized to *GO*. I am shutting down here at the cabin; heading to departure point 'River One'. Jay is standing guard at the zodiac. Call me when target is down, get here within ten. Helicopter will depart at 5:40 p.m. at the latest. If conflicts arise, head to 'River Two' departure site ASAP—departure after sunset. Are we clear on schedules?"

"Jake answered, "We are clear sir."

Ned held his scope on the massive glass wall without moving for four minutes, when Jake announced, "Good cloud cover now entering our field of view, sun is almost low enough to miss the glass. Are you ready?"

Ned took a slow, deep breath as he replied, "Shooter is ready, target in view now, glare gone." Jake watched through the ranging scope and clearly saw Ed from a rear left angle speaking from the podium. Ned touched the trigger, found Ed's neck and aimed just above at the point where the white collar of Ed's dress shirt lit up in the scope, held the position and gently squeezed off a shot.

"Target hit." Ned instinctively jerked the bolt slide, loading a fresh round in the chamber if needed. "Target down. Moving out to River One now."

Lars Nevin had arrived at the dense cover near the river bend only a minute earlier. He sat next to the inflatable raft, assault rifle in hand, and began to pull off the camo netting covering the four man craft. He heard the report from Jake and responded, "Waiting at R1 now. Any resistance encountered?"

"None, not any movement nearby. On our way." Ned took a quick look back, and caught a last glimpse of the shattered glass wall fronting the grand ballroom.

Wilson watched from inside the communications room serving the grand ballroom. He witnessed the shot and alerted the team, "Dalton, a shot fired into glass wall, it shattered, video show stopped. I'll join Cotter outside."

"Roger that. McCord will stay here on the stage with the Secret Service team. Ronet and I will leave now and join Cotter and Declan."

Dalton and Ronet stood during an applause moment as Ed was concluded his remarks and slowly walked off the stage in the

Convention Hall—the alternative location Dalton had arranged for Ed's speech at the opposite end of the resort's main facility. Ed looked and waved confidently to him as he knew Dalton's plan had worked—so far. Unaware of the shot at the far end of the resort, the audience proceeded directly into a Q&A. McCord and his team were close and watchful.

Wilson had just left the Hemlock's main entrance and ran into Ronet and Dalton rushing to join Cotter in a large Cadillac Escalade. "Well, Dalton, you were right. They did plan on a sniper attack. Shot the hell out of the glass wall and hit the image of Ed on top of the neck—left a nice big hole in the drop-down screen. I immediately stopped the video showing on the screen so they'd figure they hit him. Worked good!"

Declan and Cotter were already in the running Caddy. Cotter began an update, "We have a New York State Police chopper flying in now to help with surveillance. Declan did some calculations and put the likely shooter stand in any of three spots.

"Right. The closest spot is across the golf course, not far from the river, and up into the dense pine areas—about 600 maybe 700 hundred yards to the glass wall. Adrestia folks have made lotsa kills at that distance. Everything Ok with Kosko?"

"Ed's cool, still talking and being closely guarded by McCord and his agents. By the way Declan, great analysis on how Adrestia operates. It helped craft the plan we used. " Dalton opened the compact tactical pack, retrieved the Glock 40 and slammed in a full clip, as he looked at Declan.

"No problem JD, my butt is in a sling with 'em ya know, so's gettin' ahead of Lars is important—real important." Declan gave a sloppy crafted salute to his half-brother.

Dalton smiled, "Let's find those bastards."

Wilson continued to tap away on his laptop. "I'm getting a sporadic, weak signal from the GPS tag in the 'burlap bomb'."

"Where exactly?"

"Southeast of here...I'm trying to pin down the location."

Lars heard rustlings in the brush and pine straw surrounding his position. He dropped his profile low and shouldered his rifle. Jay followed suit. "Don't shoot boss, we made good time getting here. No real reaction from the resort as yet." Jake announced.

Ned followed up, "Yeah, Kosko went down with the crashing glass. The 308 found its mark. Hard to believe we haven't heard more commotion—they never knew we were here."

"Maybe—let's hope so. Get in the raft, we are moving upstream. Hide you weapons, remove your tactical vests and suit up like fisherman...we still may encounter opposition."

Lars started the small, quiet outboard motor and gently steered the Zodiac inflatable upstream and away from the Hemlock Glen Resort. Jay, Ned and Jake sat motionless as they motored past the cabin where they had set up their communications and "base camp" for the mission. They were beyond the actual property edge of the Hemlock Glen Resort just as they heard a familiar sound—the low rumble of a nearby idling helicopter flying towards them. Lars reacted quickly and pulled the zodiac under the sprawling branches of a willow tree covering a narrow bend in the river. Moments later, the darkening sky lit up when the state police helicopter flew overhead towards the resort.

Jake looked up as the treeline obscured the distant chopper and remarked, "Well, they called for help now. How much farther 'til we get to our helo?"

Lars was contemplative, and said, "Fifteen minutes if I can keep our speed up."

◆ ◆ ◆

Cotter sped the Escalade down the paved road servicing the resort, then onto a gravel county road, and the last quarter-mile over a two track which led to the location considered most logical for Lars Nevin's sniper assault. Wilson kept the com link active with McCord and his team who were at the resort maintaining a close protective security around Ed Kosko and Jack Watts. "All is quiet around Kosko. McCord says he and Watts are through with the official speech and now involved in small group chats with donors."

Declan studied the surrounding forest as they arrived at where the two track ended. "I can see glimpses of the resort to the northeast. This could be near Lars' setup spot."

Ronet agreed that the location provided excellent cover, and access for a skilled sniper. Cotter stopped the Caddy as Ronet devised an approach plan. "Let's be smart about this search— Declan and I can walk to the ridgeline in a flanking fashion and take a look. Back in a flash if nothing shows...Ok?" Declan checked the assault rifle handed him by Wilson.

Dalton nodded his approval, adding "We'll set up a perimeter around the Escalade, and connect with the police helicopter coursing the area. Brad, remember Canada—watch out for a hidden trip wire."

"Right, JD, so right."

Moving at a slow walk, forty yards apart, Declan and Ronet reached the ridgeline. Declan froze, and spoke softly, "This is the shooter's perch, right here."

"You sure?" asked Ronet.

"Oh yeah, ground is flattened, stake marks, probably for a camo screen, and a sightline through to the resort." Declan stood still and kept looking.

"Anything else to confirm they were here?"

"Yes, this little beauty." Declan scraped away pine needles near his boot... "A spent 308 casing."

Dalton heard the news on his headset and cautioned, "Be careful guys." Dalton and Cotter shouldered their weapons and scanned the area. "All clear from my position." reported Cotter.

Wilson rolled down his car window, Dalton took notice. "Just got a strong response from the GPS—two miles southeast from right here."

"Pass the location onto the state chopper. Tell them we are on the way." Dalton called his team back to the Escalade.

Jake, Ned and Jay pulled the netting and branches off the hidden Sikorsky helicopter. Lars jumped inside and began preparing for liftoff. The men loaded three heavy cargo boxes which held computers, satellite links, weapons and gear used in the mission. "Get in. We're up in one." Lars fired up the engine, the dash sprung to life and gages lit up. Jake and Ned strapped in and kept the side cargo doors open ready to repel any interference. The sky had darkened to the point where a few stars were showing. Lars revved the chopper and it lifted up just when the State Police helo came at them at tree top level. The intense floodlight blinded Jake momentarily as he heard, "State Police. Drop your weapons and land your craft. Land your craft."

"Take them out, now." Lars held his position, twenty feet above the ground. A rapid burst from Jake's rifle disintegrated the floodlight, the chopper turned quickly and began to climb and circle away. Jake continued firing until a smoke plum confirmed he had hit the engine's hydraulics. Still the state helicopter turned back towards Lars' team and began a massive assault.

Ned fell to the deck, "I'm hit, I'm hit..."

Lars reported, "Fuel tank hit and computer are damaged. Switching to total manual control."

"Damnit Jake...take them out" Lars righted the Sikorsky to give Jake a direct shot. He held constant fire until his forty-shot clip emptied. The state helicopter spun and slowly fell, landing hard on the ground with the blades ripping through the pine branches. Fire erupted in the cabin, and two men jumped to safety just as the craft exploded sending a massive fireball skyward.

Cotter was driving southeast at seventy miles per hour when he yelled, "Look at that! I hope that's not the state chopper."

"It is...I can't get a response on the radio...they're down." Wilson reported.

Dalton noted, "We are what, a minute away?" Wilson confirmed the ETA guess.

"Everyone arm up; get us there as soon as possible Cotter."

Lars Nevin fought to get lift, but between the dead load and the four-man team, the helo struggled to stay airborne. He hovered around the landing site trying to avoid the flames rising from the downed state chopper. Seconds later gunfire erupted and bullets ripped through the cabin and cargo bay. Lars lost control and the engine began to sputter. "We're going down—Jake and Jay lay down some protective fire, I'll help Ned. Head to deep cover."

Dalton and his team arrived to see the crippled, burning remains of the state police helicopter following the explosion. Sixty yards away sat Nevin's Sikorsky, shut down, with the blades still slowly spinning. No one appeared to be on the ground as the Escalade came to a stop the lights still on. Dalton ordered his team to move out. "Get out quickly. Stay close to the vehicle until we see where any fire is coming from." To his surprise, no gunfire came from the dense woods surrounding the men. Then a call from the forest, "State Police SWAT team over here—left side of your vehicle. We're coming out."

Ronet remained cautious, swung around, aiming at the woods, "Stand firm until we have visual confirmation."

Seconds later, two men, dressed in police SWAT garb came out, holding their weapons up. "Officers Williams and Hendricks here. Is agent Wilson with you?"

"Yes, I'm Wilson. What happened men?" Wilson first lowered his weapon followed by the rest of the team.

"As we approached low and saw them preparing to lift off, they fired on us after ordering them to drop their weapons. Then they really opened up on us and we went down—lost our pilot and another agent—and the aircraft."

"Did you see where they went?" Dalton asked.

"They ducked into the woods over there—four of them." The senior SWAT officer pointed to the south.

Dalton looked at Ronet and began assessing the situation. "Wilson, how far to the first highway or paved road?"

Wilson knew the area from his research and answered, "Three miles to the east is a two lane state road. This river winds that way and crosses the road. The forest goes for miles in every direction with hilly patches of pines, hardwoods, meadows, pothole lakes and a few small farms—pretty isolated."

"Can you call in for road barricades two miles either side of where the river passes through the road?" Dalton feared Lars Nevin and his men might try to hijack a car using the river to escape.

Three hundred yards away, hidden under the darkness, Lars and his men were in the zodiac again, silently paddling toward the highway. Ned was triaged by Jay, in stable condition having stopped the bleeding from his thigh. Lars kept a watchful eye at the glow of the crash site over the treeline and remarked, "Keep paddling boys, soon we can start the motor—we're not dying in upstate New York,"

Fifty-five minutes later Wilson's efforts with the two SWAT officers arranged a blockade on State Highway 26. Four cars and eight officers barricaded both sides of the river crossing approximately a half mile back. A pair of officers with "sniffer" dogs walked the road between the barricades. The sky was completely dark, there was little wind and the temperature had dropped to around 58 degrees. Lars Nevin and his three man team of battle tested mercenaries dragged their zodiac onto the river bank and smothered the craft under a bed of pine needles. Each man stripped down their combat shoulder rucksacks to ammo, satellite communication gear, radios, first aid packets, and combat-hardened computer tablets. They began a slow stealth approach to cross the highway and escape the police barricade and Secret Service agents. The flashing lights of the police cruisers were visible above the treeline on either side of the river crossing. Lars assembled his satellite antenna and called into his North American project communications center, based outside Montreal. The operations manager answered the call. "Yes sir. I did receive your earlier message. The cargo transport helicopter, ACH-3, has been equipped, staffed, and armed, as requested and left twenty-seven minutes ago. They are led by Sergeant Grant and should arrive at your position in six minutes."

"Patch me through to Grant." Lars scanned the tight perimeter established by his men and asked, "Any problems boys? Our ride out is six minutes away. Stay alert."

"No problems so far, sir." Jake offered.

The earpiece crackled as the call connected. "Sir this is Grant. We are coming in from the northeast, low and hot, but in silent mode twenty feet above the trees. What are our orders?"

"What armament did you manage to gather on such short notice?"

"Sir, we have two M203 grenade launchers, a .300-caliber Barrett MRAD, along with night-scoped assault LEO rifles for each man. We are ready for extraction. Can we land or will we extract with lift harnesses?" Grant had the construction cargo chopper stripped down for speed and set up for a standard kidnap and rescue mission.

"I fear the resistance may be significant—state police SWAT officers and Secret Service agents—maybe fifteen total—others pursuing us on foot. Come in low but fast, stay off the highway until ready to fire grenades. First engage the eastern barricade, then proceed to the bridge, hover and drop two lift harnesses. We'll go up two men to a harness."

"Roger that sir. Expect arrival in three. Good luck sir."

Dalton and his men moved quickly through the woods avoiding several sharp bends and turns in the river. Wilson charted a land course to gain time over the river trip to the bridge. The GPS routing cut a mile-and-a-half off the river route. Ronet ran point for the five-man team. He stopped, and motioned the group to halt and whispered into his mic, "The bridge is only about three hundred yards ahead. Unless Nevin surprises us with a novel escape plan, he should be close."

Dalton knelt down to address his men. "Lars is either here or he escaped some other way. If he's here we must flush him out soon, or he will use the cover of night to escape. Wilson confirmed with McCord that all is secure at the resort. Let's alert the state police we are going to drive them to the road. Brad, you good with this approach?"

"Yeah, we can't wait. We can control the conflict here with all the firepower—if he's here. But if he escapes, or is already gone, he may never surface again." Declan exchanged a glance with Dalton confirming Ronet's assessment.

Cotter was the first to notice. He raised his hand to quiet the group. "Listen."

All five men immediately recognized the faint sound—the low-level hum of an approaching helicopter. "Wilson, have the State Police sent another chopper?" Dalton asked.

"No, not yet. Not that I've been told."

Declan stood and said, "Lars has called in his K&R unit ta extract himself and his men." A silence followed when he added, "Believe it—he called in his extraction team."

Ronet led the team toward the bridge when a massive explosion erupted from the eastern barricade location. Dalton remarked, "He just took out the road blockade. They're preparing to extract. Get to the bridge now."

Ronet charged through the 150 yards of forest leading to the bridge with the others in close pursuit. Over the bridge, Grant held the chopper thirty feet off the pavement, and lowered two lift harnesses. Lars and Jay strapped in first and signaled to begin the lift when Jake noticed Ronet, Declan and Dalton stepping onto the road. Ronet fired several rounds at Lars but missed. Jake swung around and fired a burst hitting Dalton in the right calf muscle.

Declan yelled, "Dalton's down, get him off the road." Cotter grabbed Dalton by the rucksack and began to drag him off the road.

Wilson paused to load another clip, when Declan noticed another sniper in the helo fixing his laser dot on Dalton's chest. Declan moved to shield Dalton when the sniper fired and hit Declan in the left shoulder. Dalton screamed, "Declan."

Wilson scoured the chopper with rounds hitting Grant in the head. The chopper spun and drifted off towards the river dragging Lars and Jay into the water. Wilson steadied his rifle scope on the open cargo door and peppered the shooters with a dozen rounds. Ronet and Declan jumped the guardrail and ran to the river. The chopper nosedived into the bridge and broke apart hanging over the guardrail; the propeller blades continued to spin churning up the water as they broke apart. Cotter arrived and aimed a powerful flashlight into the water. Ronet stood rigid in a firing position and asked, "Do you see them Declan?"

Declan scanned the river and the far shore only twenty yards away when he saw Lars helping Jay to stand. "They're on the right—at the river's edge." A fireball flashed over the river as the fuel tank blew.

The entire scene lit up for several seconds when Lars saw his missing operative as he steadied his assault pistol. "So you thought you could defeat me, eh?"

A four-second flash of light sent a half dozen rounds at Declan, hitting him in the head, chest and stomach. He fell to the ground—lifeless. Dalton watched from the bridge as Wilson futilely triaged him. Cotter unleashed massive return fire dropping both Lars and Jay, killing both. Dalton began to lose focus, the pain was increasing, he thought of Carolyn, his mother and Declan before passing out.

CHAPTER TWENTY-FIVE

One Day before the National Elections

President Badge Demarche did not like the latest polling numbers. The slim advantage certain pollsters felt was there as a carryover from Barriman's early first term win had dissolved. Ed Kosko had come on the scene only a few months before, yet never had to endure the self-destructive primary process. Ed Kosko's performance during the ill-fated Presidential Lincoln style debate boosted his numbers to a dead heat with Demarche. The Chinese were furious that Adrestia had failed to eliminate the New Libertarian Party's momentum. They were determined to turn America towards the client state model through their advocate—President Badge Demarche.

The previous week had been a disaster for the administration: the press failed to ignore the claims of voter fraud during the COS amendments approval; Charley Rhodes successfully leaked details and got strong coverage over the death of Wren Cove and the two videos showing the Barriman-Demarche team as corrupt; and now the involvement of Adrestia's "unit" in assassinations aimed at administration opponents. The Chinese had lost patience and commanded Badge to exercise Executive Authority to declare a national emergency and institute military control of the country.

Badge Demarche secretly welcomed the message from Chinese President Zhang as US cities were mobilizing for vigilante action against the Federal government. Josh Gaines set the stage for President Demarche to announce his plans to quell the mood in the country.

The President entered the press briefing room and began his remarks. "Good morning. I want to announce several steps I am taking today to secure the homeland from riots and disruption of our election process. As we can all readily see, the country is struggling to adjust to the troublesome economic times, the absence of President Barriman's leadership, and the vitriol surrounding the Convention of States loss at the polls after Americans voted their will. As a result I am ordering a military intervention to protect the Capitol and the offices and agencies around Washington DC. Therefore, effective immediately, the I95 beltway surrounding the larger Capitol area will be managed by the military, providing security checks and overseeing all traffic in and about the area. I've instructed General Harris to engage our troops with the assistance of the Chinese military which as you've heard are presently participating in joint exercises on our east coast. I anticipate that the duration of these steps will be short and I look to lifting these security measures sometime after the election and before the Christmas holiday. Thank you for your time today."

The President quickly left the podium as Josh Gaines took over and tried to calm the raucous press corps. General Jack Watts sat at his temporary office at Pathroads for America along with Ed Kosko, watching the television coverage of the President's announcements. "Badge Demarche just crossed the line to treason in my mind," declared Watts.

Ed Kosko blew out the heavy smoke coming from his Habana cigar and offered, "If Chinese troops surround the Capitol, the country will explode. We could lose the democracy."

Charley Rhodes tapped on the office door as he opened it."You two see this crap from Demarche?"

Kosko answered, "Yeah we saw it. What does this tell us Charley?" The General drifted off into deep thought.

Rhodes sat down and said, "He's losing the voters, and I'd bet the Chinese doubt his effectiveness to deliver their agenda. They are about to control the administration's every decision."

"Do you think we'll win tomorrow?" Kosko asked with concern in his voice.

"Yes, we should, I hope so. We are getting lotsa coverage on the videos—TV, radio and social media. But his support is immovable, regardless of what we expose. Fact is Demarche still has operatives out there to mess with the election outcomes." Jack Watts remained focused in thought without saying a word.

◆ ◆ ◆

Election Day

The weather was generally dry and comfortable throughout the continental US. Voter turnout began early and appeared to be robust. Never before had the sovereignty of America been such an open question. Late in the day many eastern cities including Philadelphia, Atlanta, Miami and even Boston, drew huge pro-change crowds, shouting chants supporting Kosko, the New Libertarian Party and the Convention of States initiative. Charley Rhodes sat slumped in his oversized leather chair watching his array of television screens. He looked weary, sweaty and nervous but remained steadfastly focused on the exit polling numbers and incoming election returns.

Dalton Crusoe arrived and slowly walked into Charley's office with the help of Carolyn. "Dalton, you're released. Great news. What's the prognosis?"

Carolyn moved a comfortable chair away from the small conference table and assisted Dalton to sit down. "Well, I was hit pretty badly in the takedown of Lars Nevin. It took two surgeries to patch me up, and I lost a lot of blood. Wilson saved my life with some effective triage at the river."

Carolyn stood aside as Charley came over to shake Dalton's hand. He impulsively hugged Carolyn and offered, "Thanks for caring for this guy...he saved the country by keeping Kosko, and he alive against the assassination attacks."

"You'd think a smart guy like JD could avoid trouble—yet he always seems to attract it. I may have to take over his travel schedule." Carolyn gave a sly glance at her man, as Charley chuckled. Dalton quietly nodded his head.

"I heard Declan is still in an induced coma, is that right?"

Dalton revealed a somber look as he answered, "Yes. He's in trouble. The head shot came close to killing him. The bullet is still in his brain—when the swelling recedes docs will operate. Then we'll know if he'll survive." Carolyn had spent hours with Declan, and Dalton over the last three days praying and comforting both men as best she could. She saw the anguish Dalton was enduring knowing he may well lose his half-brother.

"Any clues as to how the voting is going Charley?"

"It's still early and polls yesterday still show it as a dead heat. This latest stunt to order military control of the Capitol is starting to concern the average voter—it's damn scary. I should get a strong signal by mid-afternoon on how well Kosko is doing."

"Keep me updated Charley. I'll be meeting with Ed and Jack at noon about some thoughts they both have on President Demarche's role with the Chinese." Carolyn looked curious about Dalton's comment.

◆ ◆ ◆

General Jack Watts arrived last and shut the door to the small conference room at Pathroads for America headquarters. "You look good JD, how are you feeling?"

"Well I'm getting back to normal, mainly sore. Luckily I was easily patched up without major organ damage—Declan however faces a real tough battle going forward."

"Yeah, damn shame—I heard he and Ronet were at the front of the gunfire exchange."

Ed jumped in adding, "You had the right plan to outsmart Lars Nevin, JD. Even with all his resources he went down. Nice job."

General Watts sat down with Dalton and Ed and leaned in to make a point. "I have to reveal something to you men. This is absolutely confidential: my life and others could be in jeopardy if revealed."

Dalton and Ed were totally attentive. Watts continued, "For almost three years I've run a shadow intelligence group inside the administration. There are a dozen men and women in the NSA, CIA and even cabinet members who do not trust Badge Demarche, or before that, Harold Barriman, to honor their oath to

America. One is actually a Supreme Court justice. They have kept me informed through a moniker, 'Flask'—to protect my identity. The militarization of the Capitol with the involvement of Chinese forces is the latest example of his treasonous actions."

"Really? Declan was told to research a leaker in the Barriman administration labeled Flask...that's you?"

"Yes, JD I am. I walked a delicate line as Chief of Staff, advising the administration, and learning hidden facts about the underlying corruption. In reality I was more of an intelligence spy than a leaker. Today's election may give us the opportunity to halt the entire agenda under Demarche."

"How is that Jack?"

"First Ed Kosko has to become the President-elect...to legitimize my recommendation."

Ed responded, "Jack, what is your objective—impeachment of Demarche?"

"No, we've seen that fail with the hardcore liberals supporting the administration's agenda. We are inclined to take a different tack, assuming certain events."

"I know, from my contacts, that Demarche's operatives have blackmailed or bought off, with Chinese funds, election officials in seven key states to change Kosko votes into Demarche votes. They did the same thing on the voting for the COS amendments—turning 'Yes' votes into 'No' votes. Critical voting machines in numerous selected districts have been set to record another bogus Demarche vote simultaneously alongside each Kosko vote. You'd never win with that structure."

"How were you able to find this out," Dalton queried.

The General replied, "We managed to intercept emails to Demarche's operatives and changed their instructions slightly", Watts said with a sly grin.

Dalton followed the logic and asked, "What were you able to do?"

"We recalled and altered the emails before they ever hit the recipients' inboxes. The new instructions looked genuine but deleted any directions to alter how votes were cast or tallied. Taking the real pulse of the American voter, along with the weak defense Demarche gave against the two damming videos Ronet and Declan obtained, Demarche should lose—big time." Ed Kosko stared at his friend Jack Watts astonished at his revelations.

"Ok, so we should end up tomorrow with a Kosko/Watts win. What happens next?"

"Let's order lunch in and I'll lay it all out. I think Brad Ronet should be here too."

Dalton's mind was spinning at hearing Watts admit he was 'Flask' and said, "I'll call him now."

CHAPTER TWENTY-SIX

The Day after the National Elections

The liberals were seething; the conservatives were ecstatic. The early polls had closed with exit polling showing a solid trend for an Ed Kosko presidency. By midnight it was clear the Kosko/Watts team had won 282 Electoral College votes, thus claiming a victory. By 8:30 a.m. the next morning the final total was approaching 322 votes, a powerful mandate. The streets of major cities were flooded with joyous crowds, frequently confronted by liberal groups that refused to accept the tidal wave of change. Police were overrun trying to separate and control the opposing throngs of supporters. Local news agencies reported violence, beatings, and rioting. Several cities reported shots being fired and police barricades being overrun. Liberals called for National Guard protection from the conservative crowds, who, for the most part, were merely rallying to celebrate and support the New Libertarian Party success. Nevertheless, society was disrupted and business was stalled following the election. The core thirty-six states that had initiated the COS effort organized armed militia, to sequester and protect the voting equipment in their states. Constant news coverage ran segments showing the groundswell of opposition to the CASP agreement.

President Badge Demarche was up early and dressed for the day when his private phone rang—an unmistakable alert that either the Chinese or Adrestia contacts were on the call. Josh Gaines entered the Oval Office and began to recite the latest Electoral College vote totals when a phone ring interrupted.

Gaines knew this was a personal private phone carried by the President. He began to exit the office. "Wait, Josh. It's Ok, stay here a moment."

Badge took the call. "Mr. President, it appears we have a situation." Chinese President Lei Zhang made very few direct calls to his friend and partner in bringing structural change to America, but today was different.

"Yes, Lei, we had a rough day at the polls. We lost by a wide margin despite all our efforts to push our agenda for the country forward. I'm working on a plan to minimize the election outcome."

"Mr. President I fear you have very few options left. You failed at the best option which was to break up the NLP and eliminate the man they rallied around Mr. Kosko. I've also heard our friends at Adrestia failed and were killed in a final effort to fulfill their assignments."

"That's also true. Lars Nevin and his top men were killed as they attempted an escape. The location was remote and the conflict was at night; briefly reported as a medical helicopter crash. We were able to misdirect the press. We feared Kosko's supporters would use the actual facts as a rallying call for more votes and try to draw a connection between Adrestia and the administration."

President Lei Zhang took charge, saying, "We have a plan to halt the President-Elect from taking office. You will declare martial law using your military under the control of *our* forces starting around the Capitol. You can declare the demonstrations in your cities as a national emergency. I am sending Tan to be my representative as you both formulate *new* American policy."

"I'm not sure I can make that happen, Mr. President. Chinese forces might incite more resistance at this time."

"Then sir, we will send more forces to assist in the effort. You must now order your military leaders to *stand down* and follow orders from my commanders. Frame it as part of the new alliance between our two countries. You are the Commander–in-Chief. My brother Tan will arrive in Washington late tomorrow; please listen to his advice. He will have a *certain* plan to eliminate Mr. Kosko." The call ended. Badge felt the trap the Chinese placed him in years ago tightening, realizing that their goal was to eventually render him powerless.

Badge looked to Gaines and instructed, "Prepare a press release indicating I have invoked martial law to control the mob activity in the ten largest cities. Indicate the directive is immediately in effect and I will address the nation this evening."

"Yes, Mr. President, I'll get right to it."

By 1:00 p.m. the news media was totally focused on the events in the major metropolitan cities. From Atlanta to Winston-Salem crowds overwhelmed the city centers, screaming their particular viewpoints and frequently attacking their foes. Josh Gaines made a believable case that national civil order was out of control and that the President had ordered the National Guard to be dispatched to nine cities, mostly on the east coast to secure the areas.

As the National Guard rolled out the presence of Chinese troops was subtle and largely unreported. By 9:00 p.m. President Badge Demarche addressed the nation. He began as follows:

"The nation has gone to the polls and voted on matters before the nation. First the Convention of States initiative to amend the constitution has failed and then we had our national elections. I have called President-Elect Kosko and offered to assist him in the transition period. Meanwhile many of our cities have seen some disturbing events in the last few days. We are at a critical point in our recovery and our citizens and businesses do not need riots, killings, destruction and interference in our daily lives. I urge all Americans to work toward a better future for the nation through the stimulus funding under CASP, and other assistance coming from our Chinese friends. To protect the nation's security during this important time I am today, instituting martial law within the 495 Beltway including the Capitol and Washington DC. Access will be provided through new identity cards to officials and citizens with legitimate business in the secure areas. Individuals and vehicles with be subject to search and screened for entrance to the protected areas. Similar security procedures will be established in the New York financial district. Other areas in the nation may be added if circumstances fail to improve."

The President exited the Press Briefing Room quickly and Jeff Crandel took the podium and tried to handle a barrage of questions. Josh Gaines who had attended the briefing followed the President back to the Oval Office. Gaines checked a text on his smart phone. "Tan Zhang just landed at Dulles. Secret Service agents are escorting him here. Is that the plan?"

"Yes, I indicated I'd meet with him after my press announcement. I'd like to discuss a joint press conference where we can highlight the CASP benefits for America, and try to diminish the distress caused by images of Chinese warships occupying our harbors."

"The social media are swamped with images of the beltway barricades and now the *Varyag II* entering the bay. There's a lot of anger brewing out there now," Gaines offered.

As the President was making his pronouncements, four-thousand US National Guard soldiers, took to the 495 Beltway exit and entrance locations. Notably the forces were led by three hundred uniformed Chinese officers, alongside one-hundred US officers. The entire news media was drawn to the scenes where tanks and armored personnel vehicles jammed the beltway, setting up barricades, checkpoints, and camo painted communication trailers. Beach property owners flooded social media with videos of the giant Chinese carrier, *Varyag II*, entering Chesapeake Bay as take-off and landing drills continued. Overhead a Chinese helicopter slowly traveled the Beltway route, capturing images and following the deployment of troops. At 5,000 feet, a pair of Chinese fighter aircraft flew a reconnaissance route from New York to Hilton Head and back again.

♦ ♦ ♦

General Watts welcomed Ronet into the meeting with Kosko and Dalton. "Have some lunch Brad. You need to hear what I've got to say."

Ronet sat down, snatched a turkey and ham sub sandwich and remarked, "You guys follow what's going on the internet? This damn CASP deal is going to change this country forever—unless we stop it now."

"Exactly my thoughts, Brad. With the election results confirming, despite corruption, a Kosko/Watts win, we can try a plan to remove Badge Demarche as President immediately. It rests on the proposed COS changes to the Constitution, specifically Section 4 of the 25th Amendment."

"How does that help, they were defeated right?" Ronet struggled to follow the General's logic.

Dalton's mind raced through the points General Watts made and remarked, "Damn Jack, I think I follow your point. Rhodes believes the election inspectors can prove the tampered voting machines stole a COS victory in several key states."

"They are examining the machines now—right?" asked Ronet.

"Yes, yes...and if the Election Commission confirms the amendments passed, then we have an option. One of the COS amendments expanded Section 4 of the 25th Amendment to provide a mechanism whereby an existing President and his VP can be removed from office for incompetence or impeachable offenses. If, during a 'lame duck' session, a *new* President-Elect has been determined, the existing President can be removed immediately."

"Who determines his competency?" Kosko questioned.

"Five Supreme Court Justices, selected by the Chief Justice who manages the determinations. They can be empowered by a two-thirds vote of the Senate or a legal petition, signed by thirty senators to review factual claims of malfeasance or incompetence. And their ruling is instantly law." Dalton was energized at the plan.

Jack Watts reacted, "That's it Dalton—that's the exact plan."

Dalton looked to the General and asked, "When did this plan come about Jack?"

"Well, I didn't really get it until one of my contacts called me with the details." Watts looked pleased at the group response.

Dalton pressed on, "One of your 'Flask' operatives?"

"Yes...the Chief Justice to be clear. He assures me he and two other solid justices will examine the details of the two videos, the election fraud, and several clues to Demarche's ties with Adrestia, and the Chinese. Other contacts confirm at least thirty senators will sign the petition."

Ed Kosko, stood walked over to Jack Watts and said, "Damn Jack, you make a helluva great VP." The group laughed and listened to Daltons next words.

"I'll check with Charley Rhodes and see where we are on the voting fraud findings. In the meantime, you better start filling your cabinet appointments."

"There's one more issue you should know, Ed. The military commanders are committed to following their Commander-in-Chief, until his leadership is shown to be treasonous. With one call I can have all the Joint Chiefs announce their allegiance to you Ed."

Ed Kosko grew very serious, "Are you certain of that Jack?"

"Dead serious Ed. Dead serious. We can push the Chinese out of our territory. All I need is authorization once you're President."

CHAPTER TWENTY-SEVEN

Ten Days following the National Elections

Thirty five senators, six of whom were now "lame ducks' voted out of office in the election, all signed the legal petition addressing crimes against the Constitution by President Badge Demarche, and by extension, former President Harold Barriman. Two days earlier the Election Commission officials completed the review of voting irregularities, confirming the COS amendments had actually been approved by voters, thus immediately bringing the amendments into the legal framework of the Constitution.

Chief Justice Simpson quickly announced the formation of the Special Justice Committee to review and pass judgment on the claims against the administration. They expected to have an expedited decision within ten days, in light of the severity of the petition claims and the tension in the country. President Badge Demarche was panicked, and the Chinese leadership felt they had limited time to secure the changes they wanted though the CASP agreement. The public mood was still fractured, with liberals and conservatives arguing about the best way forward for the country. Once the details of the assignment of 240 million acres of prime wilderness land to the Chinese for oil, gas, and mineral development were made public, the nation became focused on the emerging details of the flawed agreement. The restrictions on firearm ownership, government takeover of ammunition production, and its distribution only through a lottery system finally turned the majority of the country against the crippling CASP deal. Chinese political interference and incursions into

American air space further rallied calls for regaining American sovereignty.

Vice President-Elect Jack Watts operated as a de facto Chairman of the Joint Chiefs and kept the military at a battle ready status but not engaged with the increasing number of Chinese troops landing on American shores from a growing armada of war ships maneuvering off the east coast. American allies quietly began to send messages and emissaries to announce support for Ed Kosko and his initiatives. The Chinese kept Tan Zhang in Washington as outgoing President Badge Demarche tried to restore his support base, amid daily denunciation of his plans for the country. A prime time television broadcast by Tan Zhang failed to change the country's mood. The massive rejection of the new Chinese recovery currency pegged at $25, issued and backed by them, disillusioned the Chinese government. Banks failed to accept or carry the $25 bill, and consumers waged nightly community burnings of the new currency.

Exactly fifteen days after the historic approval of the Convention of States amendments, and the election of Ed Kosko as the new American President, the country watched the swearing in ceremonies. Two days earlier Badge Demarche had resigned effective on the swearing in date for President Elect Kosko. The resignation of Demarche was forthcoming when the five justice committee voted unanimously to allow removal of the President on crimes against the Constitution. In sworn testimony before the Justice panel, Eric Walters provided the complete details of his orders from Demarche essentially dooming Demarche in exchange for immediate discharge from the Secret Service and loss of pension. Ed Kosko pledged to rescind the CASP agreement and to try to scale back China's influence and interference in the US political arena. In a strange irony former

President Barriman died during Kosko's inauguration while still in a coma, freeing Badge Demarche from further questioning.

Lei and Tan Zhang were not easily dissuaded by Demarche's demise and insisted the CASP deal was still intact and America could not survive without it. President Ed Kosko promptly filled his cabinet and asked Colonel Brad Ronet to become Secretary of Defense, a move warmly welcomed by the military. Dalton Crusoe was asked and accepted the role of Special Consultant and Advisor to the Office of the President.

Vice President Jack Watts stood shoulder-to-shoulder with the new Secretary of Defense Brad Ronet to announce actions to secure the country from any and all threats to American sovereignty. Hours before the Watts and Ronet remarks, various pundits for the news networks heightened speculation that a military conflict could ignite between US and Chinese forces.

Vice President Watts began, "The defense secretary and I have spoken with each of the Joint Chiefs and ordered a raising of our defensive posture to Def Con 3 from Def Con 5. Moreover, we have activated naval and air power assets to maintain a perimeter around the Chinese forces in the Capitol area as well as their warships in Chesapeake Bay. We have formally asked the Chinese military to remove all combat personnel and assets and return to international waters immediately. We expect their full compliance. Thank you. We will take a few questions."

Hands flew into the air and a senior reporter stood. "Gentlemen—would you describe the present situation as one step from combat actions?"

Ronet took to the microphone. "We do not believe that is the case. However, Americans have clearly demonstrated their will— restore sovereignty. We've made it clear to President Lei Zhang and his surrogates that the Kosko administration will not tolerate an armed foreign power within our borders. A deadline now starts, ending in fifteen days, which requires all Chinese troops to depart our shores. Negotiations are underway to restructure the controversial CASP agreement. We expect the Chinese leadership to heed the will of Americans."

The press briefing ended shortly thereafter with the nation anxiously awaiting the Chinese response.

CHAPTER TWENTY-EIGHT

The Wedding of Jameson Dalton Crusoe and Carolyn McCabe

The several hundred wedding guests had no problem with the travel to the Turks and Caicos Islands, as the weather on the east coast had turned decidedly cold and windy. Rather the weather at the Beaches Turks & Caicos Resort Villages & Spa was ideal; seventy-nine degrees, mild wind, full sun, crystal clear blue water, and silky sandy beaches for miles.

Dalton sat on his room's balcony and looked out to the ocean, along with Ed Kosko and Brad Ronet having a scotch. "This is a real nice single malt JD, have you tasted it before?"

"No, it's brand new to me—Jura, from the Isle of Jura. I like it too, recommended by Declan from his time in Ireland and Scotland. I wish he could be here."

Ronet asked, "He's still in an induced coma right?"

"Yes, I last saw him four days ago and the doctors were waiting for him to stabilize a bit more from removing the bullet from his head." Dalton feared he might lose his half-brother after just learning of him a few months ago.

"Declan was a great asset to deal with Adrestia. Lars may have killed us all if Declan, and you, hadn't figured out how he would react and then how to outsmart him." Kosko raised his glass to applaud both brothers. "By the way men, Watts just called me and the final Chinese troops are leaving DC and boarding a transport to the *Varyag II*."

"That's great news Mr. President," remarked Dalton, teasing Ed with his official title.

Ed shot a look at Dalton and Ronet. "Come on JD—I'm not gonna let you keep that up while we're sharing a drink."

The men all enjoyed their Jura, neat, while they stared out to the beautiful sea. The soft rolling waves breaking at the shore relaxed Dalton. It was four o'clock and in one hour Dalton would take Carolyn McCabe to be his wife. It had been a long time coming, almost six years since they met in graduate school at Wharton. They had remained a couple through the years, even though they both had expanding careers which frequently interfered with their "getaway" time. Painful memories of attacks on Carolyn while accompanying Dalton on assignments flashed through his mind. More than once he felt he had lost her to a crazy man or assassin. Dalton relived his most recent fight with the premier assassin Khamal, until his death at Dalton's hands, in the North Carolina woods.

The Wedding Ceremony

Dalton stood, dressed in a white tuxedo with an open collar on his linen shirt, on the wide beach near Providenciales. The sun had dropped low enough to allow no need for sunglasses. Next to him stood Ed Kosko as his best man, and Brad Ronet as a groomsman. Wilson and Cotter sat in the front row on the groom's side. Over two-hundred special wooden chairs were lined up in rows in the sand. A satin cloth over a temporary plywood deck held down on the sides by bright flowers in white-laced covered pots provided the bride's walkway to the covered gazebo. The wedding song began and Dalton stood tall and smiled as he got his first look of the day at his beautiful bride. Carolyn had a shoulderless gown, with a seven foot long lacy train. Her flawless skin had some tan to suggest she had not been in the Caribbean long. She smiled at Dalton as she walked slowly towards her man. Her uncle, and only living family member, Sergey Kreftkova, the senior, dignified ex-Soviet officer with US asylum, held her arm lightly. As Carolyn approached Dalton she had a broad smile and a hint of a tear in her eyes. Just as the ceremony was to begin Dalton looked back and there was his mother Elizabeth, glowing with joy while pushing a wheelchair with a man seated. They approached and Dalton kissed his mother. Declan looked up, extended his hand and said, "Hello brother, I love ya." Carolyn winked at Elizabeth and Declan, pleased she managed to get Declan and Elizabeth Crusoe united.

The ceremony was brief but traditional, and after exchanging vows the pastor said, "Dalton you may kiss your bride." Dalton delivered a long passionate kiss and embrace. The audience rose to honor the handsome couple. Before turning to acknowledge the applause of the crowd, he asked, "How did you get Declan and mom here together without me knowing?"

"Tell me you love me and I'll reveal my secrets."

"I love you Carolyn McCabe Crusoe. How does that sound Mrs. Crusoe?"

"It sounds wonderful JD. I love you so much and I've never been happier."

Declan and Elizabeth shared a joint hug with JD and Carolyn.

ACKNOWLEDGEMENTS

I sometimes hear other authors speak of writer's block and the strain to break through it. Often authors put so much of their thought and time into their manuscripts that one feels like a shackled scribe tapping his way to the story's end. At times, I feel positioned to write but a bit disconnected from the story, slowing me down—writer's block. For me, a quiet period as I sit down to write helps. Then, when I'm least expecting it, the next moments can be captivating particularly when the words and ideas flow faster than I can type. When the final scenes burst forth the rush of typing to reach the end is very satisfying. Then the next phase begins—the copyediting.

I've learned authors are poor copyeditors of their own work, so I have surrounded myself with capable individuals from within and without my publisher's team to undertake the editing. The results can be very humbling when content flaws or weaknesses, formatting, spelling, and grammar are all revealed to you. And then you have to go back and *think* about the story you've just written rather than merely *reading* the story you've just written. This is when the team supports my writing.

My team begins with my wife, Vicki, and my first reader. She focuses on the story content and flow frequently catching subtle inconsistencies typically overlooked by the author who subconsciously assumes the reader knows as much as he does. She also provides a critical insight, read as *"reality check"*, on the love relationship Dalton and Carolyn maintain throughout all their turmoil.

Another *near* first reader is James L. Yates, at Quad Services, an avid reader and skilled proof-reader as well as a valued critique source. Jim is one of my most valued reviewer's. As in my earlier novels, an added bonus is Jim's wife, Barb Yates, an English Literature instructor, provides further insights to the overall story structure.

A personal friend, and our *"travel concierge",* Linda Freeman, had conspired with Vicki, to promote exciting travel vacations which have become integral elements in my novels. Linda provided the concept of an unknown half brother, Declan, who enters Dalton's life and adventures. Vicki added the notion that he should be raised in Ireland, which fell nicely into the story development. The newest member of my team, Jim Skipper, participated in the final copyediting/review before the publisher efforts on the manuscript. Jim's efforts were as expected— thorough, detailed beyond expectations as he polished the "edges" of the novel to make it a stronger read. Jim knows I encourage him to make recommendations to adjust the story flow where he felt it added to reader impact. His inputs were poignant and he was careful to not over-write my voice in his recommendations. I am very grateful for his help. Numerous reference sources aided in my research, in particular, Mark R. Levin's work, "The Liberty Amendments, *Restoring the American Republic*", (New York, Thresholds Editions, a division of Simon & Schuster, Inc., 2013).

Jonathan Jay Womack, Editor–in-Chief at Charles River Press, my original publisher, and a friend, deserves an acknowledgement for his support of my first two Dalton Crusoe novels. His assistance, writing advice, patience and encouragement, even on this newest novel, have been much appreciated.

The team at Winter Goose Publishing continues to market my third Dalton Crusoe novel, "The Secret Templar Alliance". I appreciate their support as I took a different path with this fourth Dalton Crusoe novel. In particular Jessica Kristie, a valuable resource, has been supportive as I worked through the novel.

Finally a special thanks to my extended family, friends and business associates who have expressed their joy in my writing journey.

ABOUT THE AUTHOR

Richard Trevae

Richard Trevae offers readers a moving adventure through his current action/political thriller featuring Dalton Crusoe as the highly skilled NSA operative.

His earlier novels include *The TARASOV SOLUTION, The ISRAELI BETRAYAL and The SECRET TEMPLAR ALLIANCE* and present a suspenseful world of espionage and intrigue.

Formally trained as an engineer-businessman, Trevae has been successful in Finance and Management. His journeys have provided a rich backdrop for the exotic locales featured in his books. He lives with his wife along the sand dune bounded shores of Lake Michigan where he is writing his next novel.

Follow Richard

www.richardtrevae.net   richard@trevae.com

Amazon: amazon.com/author/richardtrevae

Facebook: https://www.facebook.com/pages/The-Dalton-Crusoe-Novels-by-Richard-Trevae/105285249540053

Twitter: twitter.com/trevae